HAPPY PLACES

CLAY SAVAGE

Ocean Park Press

Happy Places. Copyright © 2021 by Clay Savage

www.theclaysavage.com

Published by Ocean Park Press, Los Angeles, California

ISBN 978-1-7338806-4-0 (paperback)
ISBN 978-1-7338806-5-7 (ebook)

ALSO BY CLAY SAVAGE

The Last Getaway

The Identical Opposite

For Kate in her Happy Place

CHAPTER ONE

FLYNN BARNES HAD no idea that by merely offering the scrap of paper with his phone number scrawled on it, he sent the probability of his death skyrocketing to seventy-one percent. His parole had just come through, which ordinarily would portend better times ahead. But when his cellmate, Thomas Thacker, accepted the scrap of paper, the probability of his demise jumped up another five percentage points, and if Thacker, upon his own parole, were to actually call him, the probability of Flynn's demise would reach ninety percent—an inordinately high number for a thirty-year-old man in general good health whose workplace doesn't include a sign reading *Employees don't have combination to safe.*

"First drink's on me," Flynn said.

Thacker smiled, exposing his yellowing teeth. "We see each other, that's a parole violation, mate."

"A couple beers," Flynn shrugged. "What's the worst that can happen?"

"Our asses end up back in here," Thacker said, his thick Manchester accent adding a certain melancholy to the words.

"Don't be so negative. What is it with you Limey bastards?"

"The weather, mostly."

Flynn's green eyes narrowed. "Just stay out of trouble and don't piss off the parole board at your hearing."

"Unfortunately, I lack your ability to ingratiate myself to fucking idiots."

"Don't sell yourself short. You fit right in."

Thacker's smile widened and he tucked Flynn's number into his pocket.

Offering the phone number did not mean Flynn's potential demise was worth noting by anyone, of course. Not yet, anyway. Those responsible for computing such things would not so blithely assume such an irrevocable course as mortal death, even at seventy-six percent. After all, a truly immeasurable combination of events would alter the Probability Index, rendering moot any preparation for one particular outcome.

The two men stood at the edge of the common room, near the metal gate separating Flynn from freedom. This particular California state prison was the second government-funded shithole he had resided in over the past eleven years, the first being Avenal State Prison, where he'd spent eleven months at age nineteen for grand theft auto. This stretch was two years for grand larceny, with the added wrinkle of identity theft. "You're so displeased with who you are," the judge had said upon sentencing, "you thought you'd try being someone else. In the future, if you're going to screw up someone's life, stick to your own."

An old-timer sat at a table behind Flynn and Thacker, teaching three newbies in orange jumpsuits how to play spades. Ten or so other men sat in metal chairs watching *When Harry Met Sally* on an elevated television, while a few others wandered around the cement-floored space like they had someplace important to be.

Today, it was only Flynn who was going anywhere. He

watched the grey-haired con deal the cards and bit down hard on his back teeth.

"I'll see ya in six months," he said turning back to Thacker, with an outstretched hand.

Thacker nodded once. "Maybe so."

Flynn wasn't entirely sure how old Thacker was. Maybe four or five years older than he was. A few times, in bad lighting, he thought maybe Thacker was pushing forty. His hairline was intact but thinning at the edges, and the lines on his forehead dug deep. Thacker was one of those guys who had been fighting since he was a kid—didn't matter with whom. It wasn't that he had anything to prove—he was too easygoing to peacock through life—but he sure as hell wasn't going to allow anyone to beat up on him to prove what they needed to. There was a long train of guys who had misjudged Thomas Thacker and paid the price. He was a few inches shorter than Flynn at five-ten (if he kept his shoes on) and wasn't particularly muscular; but he was thick, with very little fat to slow him down when the need arose. In Flynn's judgment, Thacker was as solid as a man could be and as solid a friend as he'd ever had.

Flynn told him, "I would've been in bad shape in here without—"

"Forget it," Thacker said, finally taking hold of his hand.

"I just wanna say that I appreciate—"

"I got it. I'll be seeing you, Flynn." Thacker let go. "First Guinness is on me."

"I'll stick with Budweiser. A nice cold one."

"Bloody hell," Thacker chortled, "why don't you just have 'em piss in a bottle for ya?"

Flynn picked up his duffle bag and smiled. "I said a cold one."

A lanky guard with baggy eyes stepped to the bars behind them. The gate buzzer sounded, the lock released, and the heavy gate slid open. "Let's move it, Barnes," the guard said. "We still gotta get you processed out."

Flynn looked at the men milling around the cell block behind Thacker, heard a cracking bit of dialogue from Billy Crystal through the busted speaker on the television, then turned to the guard and grinned in a manner that—if not analyzed too closely—could be mistaken for charm. "I'm gonna miss you most of all, Scarecrow."

"Let's not get too emotional," the guard said, stepping aside for Flynn before slamming the gate closed. "We both know you'll be back."

Flynn turned toward Thacker, the cell bars now between them. "You call me, and I'll help you any way I can."

Thacker said nothing. He stuck the tip of his tongue into the space between his two lower front teeth and nodded a final goodbye.

Running the afterlife is a tricky business; thus, the Probability Index was instituted as the industry standard once mankind had evolved into something responsible enough to harbor a soul (exactly seventy thousand, five hundred and eleven years following the advent of the brain stem). Since that momentous occasion, the Probability Index had been employed with great success, the only drawback being the unnecessary work it can cause the Facilitators, who operate on a very tight schedule. After all, the moment a person dies (or *graduates* as it's known postmortem), they need to be fully prepared to usher them into the next stage of life. And it can be somewhat thorny knowing when to start the preparations, as two people *graduate* every second. Shuffling them through to their designated destinations is quite a daunting task when dealing with such immense numbers. And free will is a bitch on scheduling.

If John F. Kennedy, for instance, had noticed the chewing gum stuck to the heel of his left shoe as his car passed through Dealey Plaza and had chosen that very moment to duck down and pick it off, his probability of graduating would have plummeted from ninety-nine percent to twenty-four as soon as the first bullet whizzed past and the motorcade sped up Elm Street to safety. And his Post-Graduate Facilitator would have had to scrap all the preparations for his arrival. This is why many Facilitators won't even *begin* preparations until an undergrad reaches at least a ninety-five percent probability of graduating.

As Flynn walked out of the lonely prison complex dug from the hard dirt a few miles southwest of Death Valley, he clutched the strap of the duffle bag containing everything he owned, oblivious to the fact that, because his brother had followed through on his offer of a lift home, his Probability Index was now at eighty-two percent and climbing.

Andy Barnes leaned heavily against the trunk of his grey BMW, unsmiling, as he watched Flynn's slow approach across the parking lot. Most everything Andy knew of life on the inside came from watching movies, and over the long months, despite his repeated efforts to push his worries away, he'd envisioned all manner of abuse happening to his reckless little brother. Whatever dire scenario he played out in his mind's eye, it inevitably ended with Flynn bleeding on the floor of the communal shower or wearing a shockingly bright shade of lipstick. But it seemed, as Flynn drew near, that other than a swollen cut slicing his forehead, he had remained physically intact. He still moved with the same athletic fluidity that had inspired Andy's secret jealousy when they were kids. Andy gave no sign of relief at seeing his brother in such fine shape, however, because Flynn would most assuredly take it as a compliment, a tacit acknowledgment that he could take care of himself, which Andy knew full well he could not.

Andy knew this because for as long as he could remember—from back when they were children and he had lied in order to protect Flynn's alibi when school was ditched or curfew was ignored, to covering his gambling losses when he bet more than he had in the bank, to telling the police that he had not seen him for days when he was, in fact, hiding in the bathtub—it was he who had always taken care of his brother.

He remained still now, arms crossed, sizing Flynn up to determine if some switch had finally been thrown, turning him at last toward the light of adulthood. Experience insisted that it was a stupid, *useless* hope, but he clung to it like a life preserver, the only thing keeping him afloat in the choppy waters of their relationship. Silently, they considered each other for a long moment before either spoke.

"Where's Dad?" Flynn finally asked.

Andy's gaze remained fixed. "Still asleep, I'm sure."

"You think he knows where I've been the past twenty-two months? Because he was asleep when I left too."

Andy shook his head without effectively masking his disdain and lifted himself off the car. He popped the trunk and waited while Flynn tossed his duffle bag inside. Flynn was slow about doing it, however, never once taking his eyes off his brother as they engaged in an impromptu staring contest. With the bag at last in place, Andy slammed the trunk and they continued to lock eyes. Even with the miserably hot Mojave

Desert sun bearing down on their heads like a drooping roof, Flynn would not lower his eyes from his brother's condescending gaze.

"Have you had enough yet?" Andy asked.

"Have you?"

Andy nodded toward the prison. "I was referring to *that*. This bullshit of yours has to end. I'm not gonna keep helping you if you're not interested in helping yourself."

It was such a familiar threat that Flynn figured his brother hardly believed it himself. "You didn't have to pick me up if you didn't want to."

"Are you purposely being obtuse? I'm not talking about me picking you up—I'm talking about your whole goddamn life."

"My whole goddamn life?" Flynn asked, chuckling. "You actually plan this conversation ahead of time? Figured this was the best way to break the ice?"

"The ice was already broken, Flynn. You fell through it, remember? What I'm saying is I'm tired of pulling you out."

Flynn shuffled his feet and reached for the car. "Then why don't you open the trunk so I can get my bag back and look for the next bus."

Andy leaned in, blocking him.

They'd spoken only once in the last seven months, when Flynn's parole had come through and Andy had made arrangements for his return to the world. Despite the lost time, it seemed they had nothing to say to each other, other than yet another rehashing of all the same, exhausting arguments. Andy, who was two years older, was also two inches taller, which he used to his advantage. He leaned closer, until their perspiring faces were only inches apart. "What's it gonna be?" he asked.

Flynn didn't know what it was going to be. He only knew

what had been. And what had been for the past two years was a slow oozing of time that had only grown heavier as the months piled up on his back. Every tick of the clock had been a tiny weight dropped into his pocket as he worked the line in food services for fifty-five cents an hour, cleaned and recleaned his cell, and played and replayed the same, boring board games with too many missing pieces. He turned and studied the cement of the prison rising like a tomb behind the tumbleweed of barbed wire gates. Sweat trickled under his shirt. He thought of the skinhead with the White Power tattoo on his chest and spidery blue veins running down his forearms who had slapped him across the head after taking his dinner roll, leaving the cut just below his hairline as a thank you. Flynn pictured the nail-hard skinhead choking down a stew of bread, blood, and teeth while Thacker generously used the heel of his shoe to help him swallow his food. Then he flashed on Thacker, having risked his own parole to defend him, now sitting alone in his seven-by-eleven-foot cell.

"I've had enough," he said.

And then he climbed into the car.

The BMW roared down the highway toward Los Angeles, Flynn's head outside the window like a dog's, letting the hot wind slap at his face as he released a primal whoop. When he sat back in his seat, Andy cranked the air conditioner and rolled up the window. For a long while, neither brother spoke. The air conditioner blew a forgotten pleasure on Flynn as he played with the radio, flipping from station to station until Andy reached over to shut it off.

"You know what I could go for?" asked Flynn.

"After two years, I have a pretty good guess."

"No, not that. Well, actually, yes, that. But I mean right now. Before we get home."

"What?"

"A Big Mac, or maybe a Filet-O-Fish."

Andy glanced at the clock. "Sounds good."

Flynn turned and watched the world whiz by, a world he knew had not noticed his absence.

Another mile passed in silence. From the corner of his eye, Andy caught Flynn again looking at him as if deep in thought. He had the fleeting consideration that, despite the rancor and loss of time, maybe his little brother appreciated all that he'd done for him. But then Flynn said, "Make that a bucket of KFC extra crispy."

Andy glanced at the speedometer—seventy-five miles an hour. He accelerated to eighty. "I have to get back to work for a big delivery," he said. "You can get something at Dad's."

"Dad's? I don't need to see him today. I'll talk to him later, once I get settled."

Andy shifted his weight. "You're gonna be getting settled at his place."

"What the hell're you talking about? I'm staying with you, aren't I?"

"I never said that."

"I know, but I assumed."

"That's on you."

"C'mon, man. Don't stick me with Dad."

"That's your only option. Erin and I moved in together."

"No shit? When?"

"Almost a year."

"Damn! So you know what prison is like, too."

Andy laughed. "Nice. Maybe don't try that joke with her."

Flynn again looked out the window. "Fuckin' Dad's," he said, almost to himself. They rode again in silence until Flynn said, "I had no idea you two were that serious."

"That's because you don't pay attention."

Flynn suppressed the instinct to be a smart-ass. He knew that after four years of dating, his brother truly loved Erin Bannon, or at least believed he did. Flynn, however, didn't believe in such a thing as *true love*. Such a concept required purity and nothing in life was pure; everyone and everything came with an agenda.

Despite his efforts, Flynn could not contain himself for long and the thought swirling in his mind flew out of his mouth. "Working all the angles, huh?"

"What does that mean?"

"It means this thing with Erin is good business all the way around."

"My relationship with Erin isn't a fucking *business* decision."

"Fine, relax."

"Saying *relax* after you piss people off is annoying, you know that?"

"So's having to live with Dad."

Andy sighed.

"I didn't mean to piss you off," Flynn said, after a moment. "Hell, if you were only after her old man's money, you wouldn't be messing around with living together, right? You'd be getting that ring on her finger as fast as possible."

Andy readjusted the position of his back against the seat. Coiling his hand around the cool leather of the gearshift, he informed Flynn that he and Erin would be married in five months' time.

Flynn stared out his window. He considered it an early wedding present to not say anything more than, "Congratulations."

A few hours later, the BMW idled in front of a weary-looking apartment building in Sun Valley, the asphalt-rich neighborhood half an hour outside downtown LA that their father, Harry Barnes, had called home for the past fourteen years. It was one of many low-slung buildings along the narrow street, just a few hundred feet from an auto repair shop and a metal polishing warehouse. The paint along the sides of the slumping apartment building was faded to a burnt yellow, and what stucco remained on the front was badly chipped. Some industrious tagger had spray-painted over an "Apartment For Rent" sign, changing it to "Yo Momma For Rent." Flynn absently rubbed the stubble on his cheek. "There's no place like home," he said. "I sure as hell don't understand why he hasn't moved out of this dump."

Andy popped open the trunk. "Because he's too lazy to get off the couch."

Flynn opened his door, a warning *ding-ding-ding* chiming from the dashboard until he climbed out and slammed the door closed. Andy remained in the car with the engine running as Flynn retrieved his duffle bag from the trunk, but he watched his little brother through the sideview mirror. Flynn moved quickly, intending to end their strained time together without any more added fuss, hello and goodbye, see ya when I see ya. But his quick getaway was foiled when Andy lowered the passenger side window.

"I talked to Ernie Casillas last week," he said.

Flynn wasn't surprised; it was common for parole officers to reach out to families to make sure there was a plan in place for a "successful reentry into the community," as they say. But he sure as hell didn't want to wade into the weeds about it with his brother—it was obvious that he was anxious about what life would be like with him once again lingering at its edges, so as far as Flynn was concerned, the less involvement Andy had, the better.

"It's all under control," Flynn said. "I'll go over everything with him tomorrow at my supervision review."

"Yeah, I know," Andy said. "But he was curious about your work prospects."

Flynn rested his arms on the door frame and let out a sigh. "He's not my pimp. I'll be fine. I'll be spinning Mattress Sale signs on the corner before you know it."

"Aiming high, that's good."

Truth was, Flynn wasn't aiming anywhere. How could he? There was no target. He had no savings, and the two hundred dollars of gate money the state supplied upon parole would be long gone soon enough. He could pretend he had more viable career options than spinning signs, but the reality was that not many people would ever take a chance on a freshly released ex-con with lingering authority issues. That didn't mean his deep reservoir of pride would allow him to ask his brother for help. Not that it mattered. Deep down he knew he wouldn't have to.

"What did you tell him?" he asked.

Andy's own pool of pride, while certainly not as wide as Flynn's, was at least as deep, and his answer came with a certain shame. All of the bravado about no longer being interested in pulling his little brother to safety, all his macho challenges to his character, had been a show. It was his own brand of weakness that he couldn't let Flynn drown, even if it meant being dragged down with him. "I told him I'd get you a job at the warehouse," he said.

And there it was. Just as his subconscious had already

divined, Flynn might be free, but the leash was still attached, and the state of California wouldn't be the only hand pulling it taught. "New ice forming under my feet, huh?" he said.

"I've already discussed it with Erin's father. He's on board."

"I guess he'd have to be, considering we're gonna be family in a few months."

"He doesn't *have* to do anything," Andy corrected him. "But he's willing to do what he can. You'll have a couple days to get settled, then we'll put you to work."

Flynn glanced toward the dump he was to call home and ran his hand over the back of his neck. Fuck it, he could always quit if the leash got pulled too tight. "We're not talking anything that requires getting up early, are we?" he asked, looking back at Andy. "I'm not much of a morning person."

Andy's jaw clenched. Nothing had changed with Flynn. The good folks at the California Department of Corrections and Rehabilitation had clearly failed on that second part of their mission.

Flynn, staring back with the dead-eyed gaze of a porcelain doll, basked in the heat coming off of his brother's hardened face as a lifetime of resentments burned and crackled in the stagnant air between them. It was only when Andy's lips parted with a sharp intake of breath that Flynn finally relented. "I'm just screwing with you," he said. "I appreciate the offer. Sounds good."

"You're such an asshole," Andy said, shaking his head.

"Yeah," Flynn conceded.

Andy managed a small chuckle as he handed him a set of keys. "The top lock's been sticking. You might have to try it a few times."

Flynn stuffed the keys into his pocket and patted the car's

doorframe. "Thanks for the lift. For everything." He started toward the tired building and the tired old man waiting for him inside.

"Hey…" Andy called out.

Flynn turned and waited.

"I'm glad you're—" Andy tried. "I mean it's good that, well, you know."

Flynn flashed his wicked grin, the one that could get him out of or into all sorts of trouble, and said, "You stole that from a Hallmark card, didn't you?"

It took three tries before the key worked. Flynn picked up his duffle and used his foot to push open the door, taking a moment to embrace the grandeur. The place was heavily lived in, with badly worn furniture crammed tightly together, the light brown carpet doing its best to hide a constellation of stains. Weeks' worth of unread newspapers were employed as a makeshift side table next to the tattered cloth couch, a stained yellow ashtray with twelve or so cigarette butts resting atop the pile. A disposable plastic tray with the crusty remnants of a microwaved meal sat on the coffee table next to the television remote. The whole place—his father's entire world—smelled like stale beer.

Flynn dropped his bag, setting the keys on a side table next to a framed family photo taken twenty-three years earlier. In it, Harry Barnes was flanked by nine-year-old Andy and seven-year-old Flynn. Their mother was there, too, but her face was taped over with a picture of a warthog cut from an old *National Geographic*.

Harry Barnes shuffled in from the back bedroom like a tired dog with shot hips. He wore a terry-cloth robe that looked like it could have been sewn together from the frayed carpet. His tanned face was spotted unevenly with grey stubble, and his chest sagged inward as if eroding from the hillside of his rickety shoulders. In all, he looked like the building in human form.

After a moment of self-conscious silence, Flynn realized he was going to have to be the first one to speak. "Hey, Dad," he said.

"I heard you come in," the older man answered. "You have any trouble with the door?"

Flynn's eyes held steady on his father. "I've been living with the 'let's make knives out of toothbrushes and stab people in the neck' club for goin' on two years without so much as a peep from you. And the first thing you want to know is if I had trouble with the fucking door?"

Harry scraped an orange-tinted speck of crust from the corner of one eye. "Andy didn't want to come in?"

Clearly, his old man wasn't interested in combat and Flynn was too tired to work any harder to pick a fight, so he relented. "He had to get back to work."

"Mm-hmm," Harry said. "Looks like you took care of yourself. You look good."

"So do you," Flynn lied.

"Nah," Harry insisted. "I gained some weight."

Flynn eyed the loose skin hanging from his father's cheeks. He seemed to have aged ten years since they were last together. "It doesn't show," Flynn said. Harry opened his robe to reveal a rounded belly protruding like a watermelon over his boxer shorts. Flynn nodded. "I stand corrected."

Harry swallowed hard and with considerable effort. "Sorry I didn't get down there to see you," he mumbled.

"Forget it. I understand," Flynn said, even though he didn't.

Harry's mouth opened, but no words came out. There were a thousand things he wanted to say to his youngest son, things he had even *rehearsed*. But with the moment upon him, he appeared to have forgotten all of his lines. He asked Flynn if he wanted a beer. Flynn did. "Get me one too, would ya?" Harry said.

Flynn shuffled past him with an awkward pat of his arm. Harry didn't react, his eyes on the photo of his fractured family on the side table. It'd been close to twenty-five years since they'd been in one piece. Back then, Harry Barnes spent his days up a pole as an electrical power-line installer making sixty thousand a year with a bird's-eye view of life. "Many different types of people in this world," he used to say, "but we keep 'em connected." Despite his philosophical assertion of being a conduit for the magical power of interconnectivity, the electrical lines running through his own family were severed when his beloved Karen-Marie unexpectedly made it clear she'd had enough. With the force of a lightning bolt striking a transformer, the lights went out, leaving the Barnes men alone in the dark. What private desperation she'd been living with, she didn't explain. One day she was there, the next day she wasn't.

Flynn returned with two bottles of Bud and Harry turned into him and wrapped his arms around his torso. The move was so sudden, so unexpected, that for a moment Flynn thought his old man had tripped. "You okay?" he asked. Harry grunted a half breath of air but said nothing. Feeling his father's weight against his body, not falling, but holding on with purpose, Flynn finally comprehended what was happening.

"Good to have you home, son," Harry said.

By the time Flynn thought to bring his arms up, his father was already letting go.

"Game's on if you wanna watch," Harry said, taking one of the beers and crossing to the couch. He turned on the television and took a swig. "Lakers and Houston," he added, settling his ass into the flaccid center of the sofa cushion. "Should be a good one."

Here was a quandary. Flynn intended to spend his first night of freedom with the stripper of his choosing, not watching a collection of muscular men in matching tank tops run back and forth dribbling a ball. He considered his options, gauging how much energy each choice required, then gave a tired shrug. Sitting on the couch beside his father, he kicked off his shoes. "We're gonna have to get a few more beers in here."

Harry nodded. "I've been thinking about putting a cooler next to the couch."

"That'd be good," Flynn agreed. "You know if there's a KFC around here?"

"No idea."

"Then you think we could order a couple pizzas?"

"Sounds good."

Flynn settled into the couch, his body giving in to gravity. "And some garlic bread."

"Sure."

"And maybe some pasta."

The ancient television hummed to life and they waited in shared silence as the sound slowly caught up to the picture. After almost two years without any communication, all they had between them was small talk, hunger, and pity. But for the time being, Flynn figured, that would be enough. His decision to stay with his father that night lowered the probability of his death to seventy-three percent.

But it was not to last.

CHAPTER TWO

UNDERGRADS **THINK OF** life as a sort of lottery, with humans relegated to the status of tiny bouncing balls waiting for the day when their number comes up and they are sucked into the vacuum of the great beyond. While some undergrads see this event as *winning* the lottery (the chance to be with their perception of a Supreme Being or perhaps have sexual intercourse with Marilyn Monroe), others see it as *losing* the lottery. Especially when the sucking sound of the eternal vacuum is preceded by someone asking, "Is that thing loaded?"

But the truth is, while undergrads do spend a considerable amount of their lives bouncing into each other, their lives are less like a lottery and more like an extended blind date. Put simply, how each undergrad *responds* to all that slamming around with everyone else determines the sorts of relationships they will have once they graduate. The true meaning of life, in other words, can be found by swiping through any number of dating apps.

During this blind date portion of life, undergrads are in a constant state of flux. In any given moment, they are moving both *toward* graduation and *away* from graduation, all without giving much thought to the amount of attention they command as eternity prepares for their arrival. If they do give it any thought, they arrogantly assume they have it all under control. Ironically, while they go about their business as if the entire world revolves around them, they don't realize that, unfortunately for them, it actually does.

Undergrads assume they have all the time in the world to figure everything out, trusting that when they are old and close to (what they see as) death, the wisdom they managed to avoid their entire lives will suddenly come to them. To put it bluntly, they're complete idiots.

Undergrads believe they have all the time in the world because they mark time by seconds, minutes, days, months, and years—as if these measurements actually mean something in the grand scheme of things. They say things like "It feels like an eternity" when their patience wears thin. Boy, do they have a nice chuckle at that one after graduating.

For Flynn, the first morning he awoke in his father's apartment, time was still measured as a burden he had to carry. There was no future he could imagine, he had no interest in reflecting upon his past, and his present weighed on him like a millstone. He was stuck like one of those wooly mammoth statues he'd marveled at as a kid down at the La Brea Tar Pits, forever struggling to break free of its dark, unforgiving hold.

Opening his eyes and regaining his bearings, he felt like he'd been asleep for a week. Incarceration had taken a heavy toll on his system. The night before, listening to his father's snores through the thin walls, it had struck him—even with that freight train chugging through Harry Barnes's nostrils—how quiet it was. In prison, the noise never stopped. A radio was always on or someone was always talking, or rapping, or arguing, or flushing a toilet; some guard was always rattling keys, or slamming a gate, or shouting orders. Living between concrete walls was like living in a steel drum. But now the world had gone mute.

He lay on his back, the first time in two years off a thin prison mattress, without a stiff blanket scratching his skin or a bed frame that creaked with every movement. Reveling in the decadence of having two pillows at his disposal, his mind unspooled the simmering, subconscious alert for danger he'd lived with for those two horrible years in the joint. He registered the smell of the coffee pot his father had kept warm.

First day of the rest of my life, he thought.

Flynn still had a year on his license, so he borrowed his father's beat-to-shit Ford Taurus and drove to Van Nuys for his meeting with his parole officer, Ernie Casillas. Sitting opposite each other, a precisely organized desk between them, Flynn absently tapped his foot against the leg of his chair.

Casillas looked up from his computer, his reading glasses resting on the center of his flat nose. "You always this nervous?"

"Only one chance to make a first impression," Flynn said, stopping his foot, even though it had been boredom sending it aflutter, not nerves.

Casillas used one of his sausage fingers to push his glasses back up his nose. "It's not first impressions that matter," he said. "It's last."

Ernie Casillas was six-three and weighed a good two hundred and forty pounds. Every parolee made the same crack about how well he'd do in prison, and Ernie always chuckled like it was the first time he'd heard it. He finished up on the computer and printed out a few forms for Flynn to look over and sign.

"I'm not looking to trip you up, Mr. Barnes," he said. "I'm not gonna be your best friend or nothing, but I do want you to succeed. You always be straight with me, don't fuck around, don't miss any meetings, return my calls and emails, do your community service, and we'll have a good relationship. Understand?"

"If you mean this is gonna suck, then yes."

"Eighteen months of probation ain't no walk in the park, but it's a hell of a lot better than prison."

"You ever been? You look like you'd do okay in the joint."

Casillas chuckled. "You in a relationship? Got a girl?"

"Yeah. She's a stripper over at 4Play."

"What's her name?"

"I don't know, I haven't met her yet."

"Good luck with that," Casillas said. "But tipping dancers well isn't gonna satisfy the judge's orders." He reached for a stack of papers on a low shelf by the desk, pulled a page and placed it in front of Flynn. "Here's a list of organizations you can contact for your community service requirements. I suggest the starred ones first. They're the most open to working with ex-cons. Call a few of them by tomorrow and let me know where you end up. I'm gonna need a contact name. You got access to a car?"

"My dad's."

"When do you start work?"

"Few days, I guess."

"This ain't a quiz show, I don't need you guessing. Find out the exact date, then email me your schedule when you get one."

Flynn kept his eyes down and read his conditions of parole. It was all the shit they'd already gone over. Obey all laws. Notify the parole agent if you get a ticket or are arrested. Report to the agent in person upon request or a warrant will be issued.

No travel over fifty miles without notification. Agree to home searches without notification or warrant. No contact with known criminals. No drugs. No weapons. No this, no that. Flynn lost focus halfway through. "You want me to call when I make a poo-poo in the potty?" he asked.

Casillas dropped his glasses on the desk and rested his elbows on either side of them. His forearms were bigger than Flynn's calves. He stared across the desk with eyes that did not blink. "You have a problem following rules?"

"Just trying to figure out how close you and I are gonna get."

"I'm gonna be up your asshole if that's what it takes."

Flynn grinned. "Then I'm guessing you do wanna be notified if I have to use the bathroom."

Despite himself, Casillas smiled. "Son, you better fly right or you're gonna land someplace you don't want to be."

"Wait until you come for a home check," Flynn said. "I've already landed."

"Follow the rules, Mr. Barnes," Casillas said, picking up his glasses and scribbling another note in Flynn's file. "I guarantee you; things can always get worse."

The work schedule Flynn ended up emailing his parole officer showed he was on the clock four days a week down at Bannon Imports. Two morning shifts, two afternoons, depending on when shipments came in. Stocking, sweeping, restocking, resweeping. Not much different than his routine in the joint. Except in the joint he didn't have to fill his free time with court-ordered community service. Two days a week, every week, for two hundred lousy hours, at the New Hope Community Center, which turned out to be the only place within an hour's drive open to taking on an ex-con.

Flynn was beginning to question if parole was a blessing or a curse. Every week was the same. Email Casillas his schedule on Monday, volunteer at New Hope on Tuesday, go to a strip club on Wednesday (hump day, as Flynn referred to it), call to update Casillas on Thursday, complain to Andy about everything on Friday, volunteer again at New Hope on Saturday, and rest on Sunday (just like Jesus, Flynn explained to his father).

Seven weeks passed. Somehow.

Flynn remained in a dark place, refusing the warmth of day, wearing his misery like a coat. Like every other Friday since climbing aboard this hellish merry-go-round, he was in a full sweat, his hands aching and his back knotted like a shoelace from loading reams of Chilean wool onto the high metal shelving units at the far end of Bannon Imports's massive warehouse.

Andy stepped up behind him, just like one of those fucking prison guards, reeking of condescending authority. He made a show of counting the reams, then made a mark on one of the invoices on his clipboard. "Looks like you're almost finished," he said, clicking his pen shut before sliding it into the pocket of his shirt.

"Yeah," Flynn wheezed. "Thanks to the helpful way your minions keep poking me with their pitchforks." He readjusted his Levis around his waist. Even with the fast-food free-for-all at his father's, he had actually *lost* five pounds since leaving prison.

Andy looked out to the loading dock, at the seventeen newly delivered reams of fabric lying on the pallet like beached whales. "I'll get Manny to help with those."

"Forget it, it's fine."

"I thought misery loves company."

"I guess you'd know," Flynn said. "This is your company after all."

"I might be further up the food chain," Andy corrected him, "but I only work here, just like you."

Flynn wiped the sweat from his forehead. "Not *exactly* like me."

"You can't start at the top, Flynn."

"I guess not. Owner of the place only has one daughter, right?"

Andy looked around to make sure nobody overheard the crack. Seemed he was always doing that when he talked with his brother. "I started here doing exactly what you're doing," he said. "Minus all the whining."

"You don't think I can handle more responsibility, do you?"

"First of all, this is how Hoyt wants it done. Everyone pays their dues, learns the ropes from the ground up. Secondly, you can't even handle getting out of bed on time. Don't think I didn't notice you cruising in here late this morning. Eight o'clock means eight o'clock."

"I explained that," Flynn said, blowing out a sharp breath. "I was up until two last night."

Andy flipped another invoice on his clipboard. "Yeah, I know. I talked to Dad. He said you were watching *Caddyshack*." Uninterested in further debate, Andy started off toward the front of the warehouse. Looking back at the wilting mass of flesh that was his brother, he said, "I'll send Manny over."

An hour later, Flynn sat on a low cement wall in the rear parking lot, hidden behind a row of idle delivery trucks, eating a burger and beer lunch when Andy came out to see him. "You have a problem with the lunchroom too?" he asked. Flynn held up his bottle of Bud as if it were a picket sign.

"Perfect. Just keep it to one, all right?" Andy glanced around again. "The policy's in place for a reason."

"I'm not looking to start a revolution here."

"And it wouldn't hurt to eat with the others. They should get to know you. Lot of rumors floating around that we could knock out if you'd open up a little."

"I prefer to remain an enigma," Flynn said, taking a swig of beer.

"How's your back?"

"Fine. Hurts. But what the hell, I had a few inches to lose anyway."

Andy considered him the way a jackrabbit considers the ebb and flow of traffic before crossing a highway. "Listen," he said, "I just had a conversation with Hoyt about your job here."

"Is that right?" Flynn said, taking another swallow of Bud.

"Yeah, it is right, Flynn," Andy said. "So, you really want to sit there drinking your stupid beer like you don't have any clue where this conversation is heading? I thought you lacked judgment, not intelligence."

Flynn was impressed by the fortitude on display and chose to behave himself. He put down his beer and gave Andy his full attention. "What exactly was discussed?"

"We've got inventory coming up. Prep starts tomorrow morning."

Flynn considered the implication behind the information but didn't want to appear too eager. He took a bite of cheeseburger and nodded, a small tear of mustard catching on the corner of his lower lip.

"It's a big job, somewhat tedious," Andy went on. "But it's better than loading pallets. You got some mustard there by the way."

Flynn used his thumb to clean his mouth. "What exactly does all that have to do with me?"

Andy laid out the plan he'd discussed with Hoyt—if Flynn could successfully help Jimmy Bannon, Hoyt's twenty-two-year-old son and Andy's future brother-in-law, with inventory prep, starting the next day, a promotion from the loading dock would be considered.

"Just *considered*, huh?" Flynn said, sucking on his teeth.

"We've got plenty of guys working here a lot longer without getting that sort of consideration. Having an attitude about the offer is not the way to play this."

Flynn nodded. "Yeah, I got you."

"Hoyt likes you for some reason," Andy continued. "He thinks you're a pain in the ass, but he likes having you around. He said you remind him of Cool Hand Luke."

"Fuck yeah," Flynn grinned.

"Let's not get too cocky. Paul Newman was acting, remember? When the cameras stopped rolling, he went home to his movie-star wife and counted his money. You go home and jerk off in your father's spare bedroom."

"Point taken."

"Hoyt agreed that a little more responsibility might do you some good."

"Extra pay wouldn't hurt either."

Andy studied him, as if gauging Flynn's every response against the ledger of past missteps he kept stored in his memory. "It's not about the money," he said.

"Only people with money say that."

"It's not *only* about the money."

"Fair enough."

"This is a family business, Flynn. And Hoyt already thinks of you as family. That makes this the best opportunity you're gonna get."

"I appreciate what's being offered. I won't half-ass it."

"I hope not. Inventory prep starts at seven tomorrow morning."

"Seven? Fuck that."

This time Andy didn't fall for it, though he did once again look to make sure nobody was close enough to take his brother's complaint seriously. He then reset his prison guard stare. "Don't blow this."

Flynn raised his half-empty beer bottle in a salute to his big brother's loyalty and poured the rest of it into the alleyway. And then, with every fiber of sincerity in his aching body, he assured Andy that he wouldn't.

But that night, *John Wick 3* was on Showtime and Flynn's Probability Index inched up to eighty-seven percent.

The next morning at exactly 8:45, Flynn stepped inside the warehouse through the back loading bay. Using a shelving unit as cover, he glanced like a nervous squirrel up the wide, metal stairs leading to the loft office for any sign of his brother. Once convinced the course was clear, he waded into the small army of workers already in full sweat.

As casually as he could, he crossed the sprawling room to the rear wall, where the clock was mounted next to a cascade of yellow timecards. Taking two paperclips from his back pocket, he unwound one end of each and placed the thin steel wires into the lock directly under the plastic casing covering the face of the clock. It took a few moments, but Flynn's deft fingers found their groove and with two simple flicks and a half turn of the wires, the lock popped, and the casing jarred open. Flynn rolled the clock back to straight-up seven, punched in, and then reset the time.

He was heading for the coffee table when Jimmy Bannon sidled up next to him, intently matching his stride step for step. "Hey Jimmy," Flynn said, patting him on the back. "If I'm walking too fast for ya, just let me know."

Jimmy was not only short, he was skinny by any standard not set in sub-Saharan Africa, and he had the misfortune of being in his second year of wearing braces, due to something about soft gums and curiously shifting bicuspids. "Where have you been?" Jimmy protested without raising his voice above an anxious whisper.

"Lots of places," Flynn whispered back. "How 'bout you?"

Jimmy shook his head, which for him was a shocking display of aggression. Jimmy Bannon always avoided direct confrontation. Otherwise, he might have warned Flynn that he was, *in fact*, the owner's only son and would, someday, *in fact*, own the place, and therefore could, *in fact*, fire him. *Someday.* For now, all he could do was swallow what limited pride he'd managed to hold onto and ask a question to which he already knew the answer. "Weren't you supposed to help me start the inventory prep this morning?"

Flynn stopped at the coffee table and poured a cup. "Coffee?" he asked.

"No."

He took a sip and winced. "Good call. It's disgusting." He dumped a packet of sugar into his paper cup and took another sip.

"I'm serious," Jimmy said. "You were supposed to be here."

"I know," Flynn said, placing the full cup back onto the table. He felt sorry for Jimmy, the way he seemed to truly believe that *inventory prep* was the axis on which the world turned. "And I really am sorry, but have you ever seen the John Wick movies?"

"Of course."

"Well, then."

"I don't understand what you're saying."

"What I'm saying is, when the actual counting gets started, you can count on me. In the meantime, can we keep this between the two of us?"

"Sure," Jimmy relented, as though afraid to cross him. "It's just, this is the first time my dad's put me in charge of anything. I don't want to mess it up."

Flynn looked intently at him. "Jimmy, your father believes you can count really, really high. And I'm fairly certain he's right. Don't doubt yourself."

Jimmy sighed through his braces. "Thanks," he said.

"Oh, shit," Flynn said.

"What?"

Flynn didn't answer him, as Andy bounding down the stairs from the loft office was enough to fill in the blanks.

"I'll tell him you were here," Jimmy said under his breath.

"Forget it."

By the time Andy arrived within striking distance, Flynn had his hands up. "I can explain," he said. "I was gonna be here, but Dad needed me to help him with his—"

"Shut up," Andy said, stepping close. He turned his ever-present clipboard around and jabbed his finger at the top page. "Tell me what that is."

Flynn was self-aware enough to know that his brother's anger was not designed merely to make a point about personal responsibility in front of the boss's son. He also knew he could not easily talk his way out of the problem, whatever it was, the way he had with Jimmy. But whenever cornered, Flynn's self-awareness always failed him, replaced by a stubborn instinct to stand his ground and preserve his inflated sense of self-worth at all cost. "I'm pretty sure it's an invoice," he said.

"Look closer," Andy snapped. "You see that little dot? That's called a decimal point. Which means the number I'm pointing at is nine fifty, not nine *hundred* and fifty."

The warehouse fell quiet, all eyes turning to the confrontation. A radio perched on the intake desk playing oldies rock continued to blare until someone shut it off, and then there was absolute silence. The truth was, Flynn was not well-liked by most of the fifty or so employees of Bannon Imports—Hoyt Bannon's opinion of his alleged charms notwithstanding. It was an almost universal opinion that Flynn was not to be trusted, that he was—as politely as it could be said—*shady*.

"Do you have any idea how screwed up this shipment is?" Andy asked.

Flynn took in the human mural of faces focused on him, knowing that behind the worried expressions, there was a tingling of pleasure over his mounting troubles. "I'd have to go with somewhere between very and extremely."

Andy tossed the clipboard onto the coffee table, spilling Flynn's coffee cup. "This isn't a fucking joke!" he yelled. "Dammit Flynn, what the hell's wrong with you?"

Flynn retrieved the thrown clipboard and eyed the mistake made the day before when he had signed off on the delivery for Peruvian cotton slacks. There was little use in arguing and he considered taking the blame like an adult. But, after another quick glance at the faces staring back at him, including those of the three short-haired secretaries perched high up in the windows of the loft office like disapproving owls, he said, "Manny was supposed to sign for it, but I couldn't find him."

"Then find someone else!"

"I would have, but the delivery driver was in a rush."

"You're seriously gonna blame this on the guy driving the truck?"

"Well, don't put it all on me. I'm not the one who screwed up the invoice in the first place."

"That's why we always check them against our paperwork!"

"Nobody told me that!"

"That's because it's not your job to sign off on deliveries!"

Hoyt Bannon's voice stopped the argument in its tracks. "Everything all right, Andy?"

Andy stiffened and turned toward the last person he wanted to see. Hoyt stood there in his black polo shirt and pressed slacks, his shock of white hair perfectly in place. He had a pinched look on his narrow face, as if daring the world to confront him with a problem he couldn't lick.

"Everything's fine," Andy said. His eyes flicked to Erin Bannon, who had stepped up beside her father.

Erin brushed her straight black hair off of her shoulder and set her chin the way she did whenever she was on edge, her left brow arching slightly. She might not know the particulars, but over the four and half years they'd been together, the litany of complaints and concerns Andy had about his wayward little brother had been a recurring topic of conversation. It was apparent from the looks of things that Flynn had disappointed him yet again.

"Doesn't sound like everything's fine," Hoyt said. "What's the problem?"

Hoyt wasn't quick to anger, but he wasn't a push-over either. The sign out front had his name on it, and he took that responsibility seriously.

"We had a mix-up with an invoice," Andy said, "but we'll get it straightened out."

Erin's eyes darted between the two brothers. She knew that, once again, Andy was covering for Flynn. She had silently feared that Andy was only setting himself up for more stress and disappointment by taking Flynn on at the warehouse, and now that inkling had gone from abstract to concrete.

For reasons she could not fully grasp, Andy could never manage to allow his little brother to stand or fall on his own. She was her father's daughter, after all, a true believer in self-determination. Even her own little brother hadn't earned a place upstairs at the company yet—and wouldn't until he proved himself capable. Growing up wealthy could have blunted the Bannon kids edges, the safety net of their parents' money stretching over a black hole that swallowed their drive. But both worked hard, got good grades in school (Erin's good enough for acceptance into Brown University, Jimmy's to San Jose State). They had learned from childhood not to take anything or anyone for granted. The way Flynn took Andy for granted. On the one hand, it was commendable—inspiring even—that Andy would not close off his heart to his little brother; on the other hand, as far as Erin could tell, the wasted goodwill had become an exhausting exercise in self-flagellation.

"Let's everyone get back to work," Hoyt said, in an almost conversational tone.

Though it was mostly an act of willful ease, the tension in the warehouse slowly dissipated and oldies rock once again rang out, Elvis Presley lamenting a letter that had been stamped "return to sender."

Flynn, eyes hovering somewhere in the vicinity of Andy's chin, limply handed the clipboard back to his brother.

"Can I take a look at that?" Hoyt asked.

Andy handed over the evidence of Flynn's incompetence.

Flynn ripped off a clutch of paper towels and started cleaning up the spilled coffee. Damned if he was going to stand there like an idiot waiting to be told, again, how stupid he was. As far as he was concerned, they could shove their opinions of his work up their asses. And while they were at it, all those other shit kickers in the warehouse pretending they weren't still watching him out the corners of their eyes, hoping to see him get fired, could stick it up there too.

Hoyt scanned the invoices and Andy waited. The mistake would no doubt be seen immediately, the numbers incoming and outgoing were so far off it would be impossible to miss. But Hoyt's expression never wavered as he flipped through the papers. "How's that inventory prep coming along, son?"

"It's okay," Jimmy said.

"It's going a lot better than okay," Flynn said, dropping the now soggy paper towel into the trash can under the table. "He's doing a great job." While most people in his position would find continued silence a wiser course of action, Flynn never played defense, only offense. Silence was a form of retreat, only making it easier to get shot in the back. "In fact," he added, "before I knew it had even started, the job was almost finished." He grinned at Andy, daring him to set the record straight about his absence that morning. He had to know; probably got there early, just to prove a point. But Andy remained silent—didn't even look at him.

Hoyt nodded at Flynn without comment, then raised the clipboard. "You called on this already?" he asked Andy.

"Yeah. They're checking with the manufacturer in Vietnam now. They'll send an updated invoice this afternoon. Once we get it squared away with accounting, we'll reconcile with the distributor."

"Excellent," Hoyt said. "We'd like to borrow you for a couple hours if you can get away."

"What do you have in mind?" Andy asked.

Erin stepped close to place her hand on the small of Andy's back. Her reliable touch worked as ballast to his raging emotions. "This was the only time I could get away from the gallery," she explained. "We're going to the club for a late breakfast and to talk entrée options for the reception."

"Her mother's already there driving everyone nuts about it, I'm sure," Hoyt said.

Though he'd already eaten, Andy liked the idea of getting away from Flynn for a while. He looked at Jimmy. "You two finish the inventory prep. I want it done before I get back. And Jimmy, make sure he gets it done right."

"Okay," Jimmy said.

"You need clarification, Flynn?" asked Hoyt.

"Clarification?"

Hoyt hesitated, as though allowing Flynn a moment to absorb his meaning, the way a teacher might ask a third grader who had challenged his authority. "Do you understand what's expected of you?"

Flynn could have said any number of things. Could have continued to defend himself or shift blame elsewhere, could have barked at the old buzzard that he didn't appreciate the condescending tone he struck. He even had a few choice responses for that last option locked and loaded. But all he said was, "I do, yes."

"Very good." Hoyt handed the clipboard back to him.

Watching the three of them leave, that soon-to-be-oh-so-fucking-happy family unit, Flynn roughly tossed the clipboard on the coffee table. Jimmy flinched and looked warily at him. "You okay?"

"Of course I'm okay."

"It could have been worse," Jimmy said, his narrow shoulders shrugging slightly. "I thought you were gonna get fired."

Flynn stared hard at him. "You think that would've been worse?"

Jimmy hesitated, as if not sure if he was supposed to laugh or not. "Don't you want this job?"

"Want and need are two different things," Flynn said, walking away.

The phone in Flynn's pocket vibrated. His first thought was that it was Ernie Casillas, checking up on him. Casillas was *always* checking up on him. Hell, Andy had probably already texted him to complain, telling him to tighten that leash. Flynn considered ignoring it, but if it was his PO, he might call the warehouse to track him down, and one of those old lady owls would assuredly rat him out. He dug out the phone and hit the answer button.

At that exact moment, his Probability Index clicked up to ninety percent and his Post-Graduate Facilitator penciled him in at the bottom of his to-do list.

CHAPTER THREE

THE KING'S DRAGON Pub regulars were an odd mixture of homesick Brits and local Yanks too old, too broke, or too ugly for the hipper LA bars. It attracted a discordant array of tourists and college students, along with bikers, businessmen, and soccer dads. It was also the perfect spot for the unexpectedly quick reunion of two former cellmates looking to get drunk.

Thacker raised his freshly refilled pint glass for another toast to his early release. "To prison overcrowding," he said to the bartender, the words slurring slightly (though he was not yet drunk by his lofty standards).

The bartender, a sixty-ish lifer who looked like he might have tried to be an actor in his younger days, gave him a thumbs up. "And for the fourth time," he said, "congratulations. Just take it easy, got it?"

"No problems here, mate. Non-violent offender. And if they hadn't seen it that way, I would've beat the crap out of them right there in the hearing room." Thacker laughed the laugh of a free man.

The bartender arched his brow. "Pace yourself."

Thacker waved him off, then turned to watch Flynn concentrating hard on throwing a dart. "Steady now," he called out over the din of conversation and The Kinks's "Destroyer" pounding from the bar speakers. He needed to lean sideways on his bar stool to get a better angle on things. There were about fifty people inside the King's Dragon, crammed around tables and standing in tight circles beneath a collection of televisions soundlessly playing music videos and reruns of Premier League football games.

Flynn gave a slight test of his wrist by moving it forward and back; then, with one quick jerk of his elbow, he let the dart fly. The dart stuck with a dull thud into the wall to the left of the board.

"Don't throw so hard," Thacker instructed. "Just toss it."

Ignoring Thacker's advice, Flynn sent another dart cutting through the air. With a stinging ping of rejection, the dart bounced off the metal outline of the board and flew back toward him. "I think these darts have actually grown to hate me," he said, squinting at the spent projectile now lying at his feet.

Thacker used the side of his black leather boot to kick out the seat next to him. "Come sit down before you hurt yourself."

Flynn grabbed his beer and squeezed through a group of college-aged frat types to slump forward on a bar stool. "And can I tell you another thing?" he asked, returning to a conversation they'd already picked up and dropped a handful of times.

"I figured you would."

"He wouldn't be such a fucking big shot over there if he wasn't marrying the owner's daughter."

Thacker chuckled into his glass. "And you'd be out on your ass too, from the sounds of it."

Flynn's voice raised an octave. "I wasn't the one who screwed up the invoice!"

"All I'm saying is your brother isn't the only one benefiting from a family connection."

"Oh! And that's *another* thing," Flynn said, his face flushed with booze and complaint. "I'm not so sure about that gene pool he's jumping into. Her little brother looks like he should be sitting on a porch-swing playing a banjo."

"I have no idea what you mean by that," Thacker said, making his way through the top third of his fourth Guinness.

"You've never seen *Deliverance*?" asked Flynn.

"Is that a movie?"

"Yes, it's a fucking movie. Squeal like a pig? The hillbilly kid with the banjo? Burt Reynolds?"

Thacker nodded. "I've heard of Burt Reynolds."

"My dad ranks him number one, all-time best movie star. I'm not so sure."

"Yeah, that's bullshit. Sean Connery is number one."

"Or Adam Sandler."

"Fuck you."

They spent another ten minutes debating who belonged on the Mount Rushmore of movie stars, but eventually, like an exhausted salmon finding its way home after an arduous trip to nowhere in particular, the conversation found its way back to the situation at hand. Which was this: Flynn was miserable. Work was too much, well, *work*, and the prospect of a life under the demanding thumb of his big brother was proving to be intolerably cruel.

Thacker waded deeper into his Guinness haze and slowly thought the circumstances through, weighing all options with a surgeon's care before at last declaring the best course of action to remedy Flynn's pitiful state of affairs. "You need to get laid," he announced, as if he'd received the wisdom from a burning bush. Like Moses looking down on his people from high up on Mount Horeb, Thacker surveyed the room, finding several candidates suitable to lead his unsteady friend to the land of milk and honeys.

"Those two in the corner would do fine," he said, nodding at two pretty young women laughing like they hadn't a care in the world. "We just have to hope they're blind."

"Forget it," Flynn said, spinning around on his stool to rest his arms on the bar. "I've been there, done that. It's a nice momentary escape—I don't mean to say *momentary*—but it's fleeting, you know? I need something that'll last. Something to get me *out*, not off."

Thacker's tongue found its customary resting spot in the gap between his two front lower teeth. "You need to keep your priorities in order."

Flynn's tone grew short. "You've been out what, a week?"

"Give or take."

"You're still high from the fresh air. Pretty soon you'll be choking on it just like me."

"Then I'll drink more. That's the answer to everything."

"I thought money was the answer to everything."

"Sure, but only if you use it to buy booze."

"Says the man without a job."

Thacker took a moment and rearranged his napkin on the bar. "I've got a few things lined up."

"Bullshit. Like what?"

Thacker drained another third of his drink. "Maybe I'll drive a truck. My PO seems to think I shouldn't aim much higher than that. What a fucker that guy is. Maybe he should've aimed a little higher or he wouldn't be babysitting the likes of us."

"Well if you want it, you can have my job. I'll lay odds on how long you'll last."

"I suppose it depends," Thacker said, smacking his lips after another deep sip of his beer. "Does it come with dental insurance?"

"Please. You wouldn't last a month before you got the itch for some scam to put a little easy money into your pocket, and you know it."

Thacker paused. "I guess an honest day's work is only for honest men."

Like a junkie feeling the rush of that first hit out of rehab, Flynn felt the flow of adrenaline he'd been addicted to since the sixth grade, when he stole a box of Twinkies from Miller's Market on his way home from school. The feeling brought out by the pilfered Twinkies was, as Flynn would later explain, "Like heroin, only with a rich, creamy filling."

Flynn looked seriously at Thacker. "So where does that leave us?"

Thacker smiled. "Finally."

"Finally, what?"

"You finally got around to asking the only question you truly have."

"Which is?"

"Cut the bullshit, mate. Back in the joint, you didn't give me your phone number so you could help me. You gave me that phone number so *I* could help *you*."

Flynn's lips were wet with beer, his eyes glistened as his sly smile returned. "You've been doing some thinking, haven't you?"

"I've been doin' a lot more than that." Thacker leaned close, whispering now. "I've been in touch with Covington."

Hearing Covington's name warmed Flynn's blood. All of the stories he'd heard from Thacker tumbled from his memory like a landslide, each one loosening more rocks of inspiration. Billy Covington was a local legend in Manchester, an almost mythical hero to small-town dreamers like Thacker who were too lazy to work an honest day for a measly living. "He talked big about taking on the world," Thacker had said. "And damn if he didn't deliver." As Covington's influence grew over the years, he became not only exorbitantly rich, but so well-connected he could pull a string in London and move a mountain in Brazil.

He had started out a typical thug in Moss Side, dealing drugs out of his dingy flat and beating up Afro-Caribbean immigrants out in the streets. But he was smart enough to know that if he stayed in Moss Side he would soon enough die in Moss Side, just another pasty Englishman drained of blood in some alleyway. "So he went to school under Albert Donovan," Thacker had told Flynn as they sat in their cell, imagining a life that might someday amount to something other than the petty scams that landed them there. Albert "Hats" Donovan, Flynn learned, was the third-ranking member of the Chessington Crime Syndicate—an organization aligned with the Irish mob—and he taught Covington the finer points of racketeering, money laundering, and arms dealing. "But Covington was never one to take orders for long," Thacker explained, relaying the manner in which Covington managed to have sex with both Donovan's wife and his girlfriend before breaking free to find his way to America, the land of opportunity.

Thacker had looked up to Billy Covington with a reverence customarily reserved for Popes and football players, and he had followed him to America when he was seventeen years old. "He was a hard ass," Thacker admitted. "Treated me a bit like a pet, teaching me a few tricks for his own amusement. But it paid off." Thacker learned all the basics of criminal life: how to work a scam, how to intimidate your way clear of a confrontation, how to slip a hand into a coat pocket or purse and be on your way home with dinner money long before the mark frantically tried to remember where they'd left their wallet.

Nowadays, Covington could not be bothered with such inconsequential, small-time efforts. He was strictly a big game hunter now. While money laundering for large syndicates in Chicago and Ponzi schemes aimed at rich widows in New York still held their charms, Covington had turned his attention to more refined tastes. Art theft mainly. Over the years it had become a passion of conceit for the uneducated street-thug-turned-crime-boss.

"It's time we left the small-time shit behind, too," Thacker said now, as the two friends sat at the bar inside the King's Dragon.

"Did you tell him our idea?" Flynn asked, his pulse beginning to trot.

"I did."

"You didn't commit to anything, did you?"

"Of course not. Not before talking to you. Hell, I wasn't sure you could actually get a job from your brother if we decided to try this."

Flynn brought the beer bottle to his mouth but didn't drink. "He offered my first day out."

Thacker had heard all about the dynamic between the two Barnes brothers. "Of course he did."

"I almost turned him down."

"But you didn't."

"No."

"So here we are," said Thacker.

Flynn turned the bottle in his hand. "Covington's interested?" he asked after a moment.

"More than interested."

Flynn again flashed on those countless nights he and Thacker had sat in prison, detailing an idea neither was convinced would actually amount to anything. The notion had first been contemplated as a way to relieve the boredom of having nothing else to do but watch a ticking clock. What began as a game eventually took a turn. They had gone over every detail of the phantom plan so often, had played every role so adroitly, had premeditated every turn so precisely, that it almost seemed as if the imagined hustle had already happened. They knew every question that could be asked and had at least two answers for each and every one of them.

"There'd be a lot of groundwork at Bannon's that I'd have to take care of," Flynn said. "At the moment, I'm not the most popular person in the warehouse."

"You'd have time."

"How long?"

"It'd take at least a month or two for Covington to set something up with his contact."

They went over everything just as they had when sitting in their cell, every detail laid out end to end. "And then he'd have to convince someone down there to go along with it," Flynn said. "To ship everything, I mean."

"There's plenty of people down there looking to make money. And if not, Covington can be very persuasive."

Flynn glanced around the bar with a prisoner's paranoia, making sure nobody was paying attention to their conversation. "Andy's loyalty to me only goes so far," he pointed out.

"If he finds out, he won't hesitate to have my ass kicked right back into the joint."

"No one's gonna find out," Thacker said. "Bannon Imports is the perfect setup. It'll be a piece of piss."

Flynn didn't need to be reassured. If he played his part, acted his ass off to convince Andy and Hoyt he was ready for more responsibility, it would all fall into place. They couldn't lose. Fate had thrown the two of them in the same cell, and it was as if God himself had delivered them to this very moment, an opportunity dropped from the universe, the score of a life-time. Nobody would ever find out. Nobody would get hurt. Nobody's life would change—except for theirs. Flynn's stomach lifted, buoyant with the feeling of possibility. No more punching the clock. No more back-breaking pallets to be loaded. No more judgmental stares. True freedom.

"We're gonna do this, aren't we?" he asked, grinning.

"Why the fuck not?" Thacker asked, his grin matching Flynn's.

Flynn couldn't think of a reason. The two men raised their glasses.

Thacker said, "To the fools of—"

He got no further before a drunken moose of a man wearing a faded Oakland Raiders t-shirt drunkenly bumped against him, sending his glass to the bar in a wet explosion of barley and hops. "Bloody hell!" Thacker yelped, jumping to his feet, his chin and shirt spotted wet.

The moose brushed him off with a snort. "Watch yourself next time."

"Kiss my ass, ya wanker," Thacker retorted.

The moose's two equally drunk buddies laughed and goaded a response. The moose moved in, his enormous forehead towering a good four inches above Thacker's. "What did you say?" he demanded, as if his daring it to be repeated would compel the stocky Brit in the stupid leather boots to cower and apologize.

Flynn knew for a fact, though, that the stocky Brit in the stupid leather boots would do no such thing, so he squeezed between them, stopping the moose's forward momentum. "Take it easy," he said. "It's nothing personal, you just remind him of his mother."

The moose considered Flynn, then evidently decided neither of them were worth the effort. He headed back into the surrounding forest of drunkards with his still laughing compatriots.

"What the hell you do that for?" Thacker snapped at Flynn, his Manchester blood piqued for action.

Flynn tasted the creamy filling of his heroin-like high as he held up a wallet. "Next round's on the wanker."

Thacker's fever broke at once and he laughed. "Nice fuckin' pull!"

Flynn tucked the wallet away as the bartender stepped up with a towel.

"I'm cutting you guys off," the bartender said, wiping up the spill.

"Oh, don't be a cunt," Thacker snapped at him.

The bartender's eyes widened. "What did you call me?"

"He's English," Flynn explained.

"Yeah, I picked up on that. You two are done here."

"Fine," Flynn said, grabbing his almost empty bottle of Bud before it was taken away. "We just have one last toast to complete." He raised the bottle to Thacker. "To the fools of the world," he said.

"Without them," Thacker finished the toast, "the rest of us could not succeed."

As the two friends headed out into the cool night air, drunk with the possibility of renewed life, Flynn's Probability Index reached ninety-five percent, and preparation for his arrival to the afterlife began in earnest.

CHAPTER FOUR

A QUICK CHRONOLOGY: In 1493, Emperor Pachacuti leaves Cuzco, Peru, to establish the Incan Empire. One hundred years later, Spanish Conquistadores, led by General Francisco Pizarro, energized by greed for Incan gold, bring the empire to ruin. Two hundred and ninety years later, the National Museum of Archeology, Anthropology, and History is founded in Lima. Another hundred years pass and the National Museum is endowed with a collection of golden artifacts discovered near the temple fortress of Sacsayhuamán—where the Incas worshiped the sun god, Inti. Sixty-three years later, Hector Quinones moves to Cuzco with his wife and teenage son Manco to get started in the Alpaca raising business. Eleven years after that, young Flynn Barnes steals a box of Twinkies from Miller's Market in Los Angeles, California. Four years pass, and Hoyt Bannon signs a contract with Hector Quinones to import Alpaca cardigan sweaters for Banana Republic and Target. Four additional years lapse and Hector's son Manco discovers he can make more money selling cocaine than sweaters and his reputation rapidly grows. Seven more years pass and Andy Barnes begins working for Bannon Imports, where he falls in love with Hoyt's daughter Erin. Another three years pass, and Flynn gets out of prison for the second time, gets a job working for his brother and, along with his ex cellmate Thomas Thacker, plans on using Bannon Imports as a cover to smuggle into the country some of the very gold artifacts that the Incas revered, General Francisco's Conquistadores had been chasing, and the English gangster Billy Covington was intent on stealing.

Thacker was excited. "Found out Covington sent one of his men to Peru to meet with this Manco Quinones guy."

"Damn, this is moving fast," Flynn said, speaking softly into the phone pressed tightly to his ear as he cut through the warehouse. "Does he already have the merchandise?"

"He was kind of cagey about it," Thacker said. "Told me to worry about our end of things, not his."

Flynn walked past Manny and some other dude whose name he couldn't remember and jumped down from the loading dock into the alley behind Bannon Imports.

"Yo, Flynn," Manny called out to him. "You goin' on break?"

"No, I'll be right back. I gotta help my dad with something real quick." When he was out of earshot he said to Thacker, "If he can't get them out of that fucking museum, this is all for nothing."

Thacker's tone shortened. "Would he waste his time sending his guy all the way down there if he wasn't sure he could do it?"

Flynn paced in the alley. "I guess not."

"He likes to keep control, that's all. So how 'bout you do the same? Last estimate I heard, the shit he's looking to steal is worth four million, minimum. That means if we pull this off, our cut will be five hundred thousand each. I'm no math genius, but that's definitely a hell of a lot more than nothing. Just keep doing what you're doing."

What Flynn had been doing was demonstrating to Andy that he'd turned a corner, that indeed the switch had finally been thrown. For four weeks, he'd been in early, out late, and in between there was no whining, no slacking, and no mistakes. He was slowly and steadily building trust—the one commodity he needed most and could not buy or steal.

His parole officer received only good reports from Hoyt, and Andy wondered what the hell had gotten into his brother, but kept quiet, offering only praise and encouragement. Even the other workers in the warehouse noticed the change, but kept their distance. There were no overtures of friendship, and that was fine by Flynn. He had no need for connections and viewed his time at Bannon Imports as a sort of extended magic trick. Show them only what you want them to see, and then disappear in a cloud of smoke. Until the day came when he could quit, he would keep his head down and his hopes up.

Another month of studied perfection passed before the worm finally turned. Flynn finished unloading the final pallet of the day and used his shirt to wipe the sweat from his face. He walked toward the open warehouse door to allow the evening breeze an easier target and stretched the muscles in his back, pretending not to notice Andy and Hoyt watching his every move from the giant window of the loft office. And then, with the groundwork finished, his brother walked directly down the center of the path Flynn had laid out for him.

"Flynn," Andy called out from the office door. "Can we see you a second?"

Flynn looked up and offered a weary wave, then headed

for the stairs leading to the loft office. His con had worked to perfection.

Harry Barnes placed a six-pack of Coors on the frosted glass table between the two beach chairs on his balcony and sat with his youngest son. The sound of speeding cars from the nearby 5 freeway hummed in the stagnant air, and the amber glow of the departing sun illuminated the decaying world around them in such a way that it almost seemed worth fighting for. Flynn was not fooled by the illusion. He drank half his beer in one swallow and stared off. He was already long gone, already living another life.

"Shipment manager," Harry said with a quick intake of air through his hairy nostrils. "Not bad."

"Title sounds better than what the actual job entails," Flynn said. "But it gets me out of the warehouse every once in a while."

"Better pay, too, I bet."

If only you knew how much better, Flynn thought. He nodded at his father with a forced grin and finished the second half of his beer. Placing the empty bottle back in the cardboard six-pack container, he removed another, twisted off the cap and tossed it over the railing. A moment later came the faint sound of it clanking to the bottom of the empty pool, another agent of rust in the world.

"Maybe someday you two will run the whole operation," Harry said.

"That's not a dream we share, Dad."

Harry looked off. "Whatever it leads to, it's a hell of an opportunity."

Flynn thought he sounded like Andy. Or maybe Andy

sounded like Harry. Either way, they both sounded like a broken record. "It sure is," was all he offered.

"I hope you'll take full advantage of it," his father said after a moment, a sort of resigned lilt in his voice.

"I plan to do just that," Flynn assured his old man.

Harry kept his eyes on the horizon. "Guess you'll also be looking to move out of here, get your own place."

"Probably so."

Harry nodded and took another pull on his bottle. "That'll be nice for you. Easier to meet a woman that way."

"For you too," Flynn said with a small chuckle.

Harry looked at him. "Good things are coming to both of us, then."

They clinked bottles and drank.

It was the last conversation the two of them would ever have.

Manco Quinones, like his well-respected father, was first and foremost a businessman eager to tap into new revenue streams. He had done a thorough background check on Covington, of course, and found more than a few trusted men to vouch for him—a requirement in the drug trade. But Covington wasn't interested in drugs and Manco wasn't interested in making life difficult for the pale-skinned, shockingly redheaded English-man Covington sent from the north as his emissary. He seemed to be having enough trouble as it was.

"El soroche es malo," Manco said to him, before returning to his broken, but passable, English. "Altitude sickness, yes?"

The Englishman looked like he was about to lose his breakfast. His face was spotted with perspiration as he popped another aspirin. "It's fucking miserable."

"Better in a few days," Manco assured him, leaning back into the sofa cushions.

"I'm heading back tonight, thank Jesus."

Opposite the couch, behind the high-backed chair where the ailing Englishman sat, one of Manco's men looked up from his cell phone and nodded. "Todo el dinero está allí."

Manco smiled. "Our business is complete."

The redheaded Englishman stood and waved a shaky hand at the two large boxes he'd brought to Manco's home in Cusco from his contact in Lima. "As long as those get to where they're supposed to. Otherwise I'll have to come back and throw up all over you."

Manco laughed and bid the Englishman an uneventful trip back to America. He then returned to his father's warehouse with the two large boxes from Lima and repacked their contents, along with the Alpaca cardigans bound for Bannon Imports, into the specially constructed wooden crate with the false bottom.

Andy held up the keys to the delivery truck but hesitated before handing them to his brother. "Once everything clears customs," he instructed, "make sure the paperwork's in order before you leave."

"Everything'll be fine," Flynn said. "Relax."

"What the hell? You know I hate it when you tell me to relax. Besides, do I really need to point out that I'm talking to you as your boss, not your brother? A little respect wouldn't hurt."

After five weeks of toeing the line, Flynn was ready to step over it and never look back. But he was still on the clock and had to maintain the con a few more hours before he could punch out for good. "Understood," he said.

"I'm not trying to be a hardass," Andy said. "I just want to make sure there's no problems, so remember to check the bill of lading and compare it to our order form."

"Got it."

"And the Royal Baby fiber price didn't increase as much as the lower grades, so—"

"If the prices don't match with the final quote," Flynn interrupted, "call Hector right away so it can get straightened out."

Andy finally handed over the keys. "I guess you've got it all under control."

"Don't sound so surprised. I'm not always gonna be a screw-up." For the first time in over a month, Flynn's voice again wielded the acerbic tone that always felt like a weapon, or maybe a shield. Either way, it served to keep the brothers apart.

Andy held up his hands as if to ward off any further harassment. "Forget I said anything."

The sly grin flashed. "About what?"

Andy half-smiled, shook his head. "I've got an early dinner with Erin. I'll find out how it went tomorrow morning. How's that sound?"

Flynn spun the key ring around his index finger before catching the clattering keys tightly in his hand. "Sounds good," he said. "See ya in the morning."

Though, of course, he wouldn't.

Two hours later, Flynn stood on the loading dock of the US Customs Clearance Warehouse, just south of LAX, talking with customs agent Phil Jenkins, a profoundly round man with a few strands of sandy blonde hair hanging on for dear life atop his smooth scalp. As the two men watched the wooden boxes emblazoned with green customs stamps get loaded into the Bannon Imports delivery truck, any residual anxiety Flynn felt slowly evaporated like morning dew on a windshield. With every passing second, he could see success a little more clearly. As Thacker had insisted, it was all a piece of piss.

"So, how's your brother?" Phil asked with a familial ease.

"He's fine," Flynn answered, ready to leave.

"I was expecting to see him today. You know, help you learn the ropes."

"Well, it's not that hard. Just have to triple-check the paperwork, right?"

"I guess so," Phil said. "Anyway, I heard all about you from Andy. I'm glad to see you're doing so well."

Fucking Andy, Flynn thought. Always talking down about me. "Why wouldn't I be doing well?" he challenged the customs agent.

Phil shifted his considerable weight from his left foot to his right. "I didn't mean anything by it. It's just that Andy told me you were, you know…doing well."

"Mm-hmm," Flynn said. He nodded at the delivery truck. "You're sure all the crates made it through customs all right?"

Phil scanned the invoices in front of him. "Let's see… seven units from Cuzco, Peru, as per the bill of lading…customs declarations in place and all tariffs paid." He handed the paperwork over. "Looks like you're all set."

Flynn climbed into the truck. Turning over the engine, he offered a phony wave. "Thanks, Stan," he said.

"My name's Phil," the agent called out.

But the truck was already rumbling away.

Fifteen minutes later, Flynn pulled to the curb on an isolated side street. Thacker's hatchback was already up, ready for the transfer. Flynn cut the engine and jumped from the cab, moving quickly to raise the rolling door at the rear of the truck. The door reverberated like thunder as it jolted upward and disappeared into the back of the cargo hold. The two men climbed inside and worked quickly. There was no longer anything to discuss; it was now all about speed. The last thing they needed was for someone to happen by and get curious.

It took only a matter of seconds to locate the wooden crate with the letter "C" burned into the side. Finding it brought a sudden moment of stillness, as if they had been captured in a photograph commemorating their last moment as men of meager means.

"We're golden," said Flynn under his breath. Using a crowbar, he opened the lid off the crate to find a pile of Alpaca cardigans vacuum packed in thick plastic. He began handing Thacker the sweaters, who in turn placed them on top of another crate.

Flynn felt the bottom of the now-empty crate with his trembling fingers. He knocked on the rough-hewn wood with his knuckles and then nodded at Thacker, who anxiously worked his tongue into the space between his two lower teeth. Using a claw hammer to remove the nails holding the false bottom in place, Flynn gently lifted it from the crate. For a moment they could only stare in awe.

Looking up at them like startled old men confused by their surroundings were six solid-gold Incan burial masks. Flynn ran his hand along the edge of the broad nose of the first mask, then lightly brushed the cheeks of another, warming himself in their unmistakable power.

The Incas called gold the "sweat of the sun," and inside Bannon's delivery truck, it was as if the sun itself was glowing from the bottom of that crate.

"How'd Covington get these out of the museum?" Flynn asked.

"We're making sausage here, mate," Thacker said, mouth agape. "Better not to know."

Thacker squeezed past Flynn and knelt down to pick up a particularly fine mask with widely spaced eyes and a mouth turned upward mischievously at the corners. He studied it closely, longingly, the way a lover stares at diamond rings at the counter in Tiffany's.

"C'mon," Flynn said, his hand tapping Thacker's back. "This heat's killing me."

Thacker looked at him and grinned. "Then what do you say we use one of these when we bury you?"

"Only if you promise no one will dig me up in five hundred years and take it back."

They wrapped each mask in a blanket before placing them securely inside Thacker's car, then nailed the lid back on the repacked wooden crate inside the truck.

The whole operation took no more than fifteen minutes.

Standing in the near twilight, Thacker slammed the hatchback on his Toyota and turned to Flynn, letting out a small laugh of relief and appreciation. "I owe you for this one, Flynn," he said, his voice even and sincere. "I couldn't have made a score this big without you. You're the best mate I've ever had."

Flynn, however, was too preoccupied to fully embrace the sentiment. "We can talk later about how much we love each other. Right now, I gotta get the truck back to the warehouse.

I'm not convinced my brother trusts me enough not to be there to check up on things."

"Don't worry about him," said Thacker, his tone back to its usual hard edge. "You don't need him anymore. You're free."

That night Flynn drove along Mulholland Drive in his father's car, high above the twinkling lights of the city. Mulholland stretched twenty-one miles through the Santa Monica Mountains, a windy, mostly two-lane road with spectacular views of the Los Angeles Basin, the San Fernando Valley, and Hollywood. But Flynn wasn't interested in the views, or the celebrity houses dotting the road along the way. He was already late picking up Thacker before they were to continue on to the rented house in Topanga, the rural, artsy community in the Santa Monica Mountains where Covington had arranged a small victory party. He hadn't intended to take this slower route, but a leaky oil can had fallen off the back of a flatbed truck on the Ventura Freeway and caused a three-car accident in the center lane, forcing him to alter his plans.

Flynn's window was down, and a warm Santa Ana wind blew across his face, lulling him into a dream-like state of gratification. Sinatra crooned "That's Life" from the stereo, a particularly cruel joke that neither the DJ nor this particular listener was in on.

Every decision Flynn had ever made—every corner he had ever cut, every action, reaction and choice, indeed every road less traveled—had made all the difference. They had all led him to this very moment. But even now, with each and every fallen domino of his life stretched out behind him like a road map to nowhere, they alone had not lined up to finally push his Probability Index to one hundred percent. For that last domino to fall, he needed Ira Berger.

Ira was the owner of a chain of successful pharmacies that had afforded him every luxury he'd ever desired. But when his wife divorced him, he was left with only the house and its fantastic city views. It truly was one of the most beautiful homes on the street, but Ira's ex-wife had incessantly complained about the rigorous rise of steps leading from the street to the front door.

"Up and down, up and down! Every goddamned day, it's the same thing!" she customarily whined upon arriving home, usually from the tennis club that Ira himself never had enough time to enjoy. "It's exhausting!" Her nightly half-bottle of white wine only made the haranguing worse. Despite his ex-wife's selfishness and chronic negativity, Ira still loved her, even after she shopped away his life savings and cheated on him with the Sparkletts delivery man. Ira, at sea in the black waters of his unrequited love, became a drunk when she moved out and he rarely showered anymore. He also never cleaned his house. Only when the stench could no longer be tolerated did he bother to take out the trash. And if he was feeling particularly sorry for himself (and was particularly drunk), rather than drag the garbage bags down the long steps his wife had hated so much, he would stand at the top landing and toss the garbage bags as far as he could toward the curb.

Flynn rounded a tight curve along Mulholland, singing along with Frank. He had just turned up the radio in an effort to make himself sound better when a set of bright headlights flashed behind him. His voice fell away as he squinted in his rearview mirror. It was just a quick glance, but by the time Flynn looked back to the road, a family of raccoons had stalled in their tracks, their eyes glowing in the illumination of the headlights as they made their way toward the garbage spilling from the torn bag at the bottom of the long steps of Ira Berger's house.

Flynn yanked the steering wheel to the left as he pounded the brake with a rigid leg and heavy foot. The tires squealed in a vain attempt to gain traction. The car continued to skid, fishtailing sideways toward the steep cliff overlooking Hollywood. The sound was deafening. Then everything stopped.

The car was at rest, angled sideways like a crab, its driver-side tires over the brink, the drive shaft rubbing against the weeds and rocks of the cliff. Flynn was pinned against the door, with his head bobbing listlessly out the window like a spent jack-in-the-box. His left elbow radiated a sharp pain, and his legs shook with adrenaline. He took a few halting breaths, trying to find his bearings. He could see the sharp slope of the mountain falling away below him.

"Oh, shit…" he said, lifting his weight off the door.

Someone yelled in a high, anxious voice. "I wouldn't move if I were you!"

"I don't think I can get out," Flynn answered.

"Hold on!" the man called out.

Using the vertical strap of his seatbelt as leverage, Flynn pulled himself high enough in his seat to see over the edge of the passenger window to where the man stood. Their eyes met and Flynn read in his expression that the situation was as bad as he had feared. The man slowly inched his way toward the passenger side door with an outstretched hand. As he reached for the handle, Flynn hit the switch on his door to make sure it was unlocked.

When the lock flipped, the earth underneath him moved.

The sickening sound of dirt and debris sliding away from under the tires filled the air. Flynn's breath flew from his mouth as if trying to escape its fate as the car tumbled over the edge and disappeared into the darkness of the hillside.

Somewhere up the hill, Ira was crying over his lost love.

Frank was right. That's life.

CHAPTER FIVE

GRADUATING FROM ONE stage of life to another is a lot like New Year's Eve without the party. With no festive hats, confetti, noisemakers, or drunken people singing "Auld Lang Syne" to mark the occasion, one might not be aware it happened at all.

This was certainly true of Flynn as he lay heavily on the brightly colored sheet, slowly waking. His eyes fluttered a bit, but for the moment, he remained mostly asleep. His cheek was warm, though he grew increasingly uncomfortable due to a crease in the sheet that bunched under his neck. He reached down toward his back and pulled the yellow blanket up around himself, kicking his legs out, his bare feet extending to the end of the bed. He turned onto his back, but the new position afforded him little comfort.

As the haze dissipated and Flynn's senses sharpened, his eyelids lifted. He continued to lie there, focusing on the object floating above him. At first, he couldn't make out what it was, but the image gradually grew clear: a toy prop airplane, suspended from the ceiling by a thin wire. His bleary eyes traced the twin propellers, and the red, white, and blue USAF stickers coming unglued at the edges. *Why the hell is that so familiar?* Flynn wondered

With a flash of recognition, he realized why.

He shot upright, grasping tightly the Lone Ranger bedspread somebody had evidently placed over him. Trying desperately to remember what had led him to this most peculiar place, his grip loosened, and he listened intently. For what, he wasn't even remotely sure. A hospital page perhaps. Or maybe an anesthesiologist commenting through the drug-induced fog that the patient was coming to. But he didn't hear anything.

"Hello?" he called out.

Still nothing.

He climbed to his feet and ran his palms over the rough polyester pajamas he was, for some reason, now wearing. A faint memory hissed in his ear as he scanned the room. It was all there—the graphic novels strewn across the tiny desk in the corner, the bookshelf lined with Star Wars figurines, and the toy soldiers scattered on the floor, bloodless casualties of an eight-year-old boy's make-believe war. The final piece fell into place when Flynn spotted the stuffed teddy bear, Mr. Foo-Foo, sitting on a corner chair, stubby arms sticking out as if begging for an eternal hug. "What the fuck is happening?" he gasped.

The sound of tires screeching to a stop cut into the room from outside the shuttered windows. Flynn hesitated before slowly opening one of the pale-yellow slats to peer at the battered taxicab idling on a long cobblestone street that led off to more and more nothing. There was no light outside, but there was no dark either—only a clear broth of atmosphere. It was as though his childhood home was all that was left of the world, along with the taxi that was now clearly waiting for him.

"Sweetheart!" a voice called out from somewhere deep inside the house. It was a gentle voice, sympathetic even. And it tied Flynn's stomach into knots. He turned warily toward the closed bedroom door. The woman's voice called out again, "Sweetheart! Time to get up!"

Flynn took a few deep breaths to keep from hyperventilating and was able to force only one word from his parched throat. "Mom?"

He'd not seen nor heard from his mother in twenty-one years. Not since the day he climbed aboard the school bus to begin third grade and she said her very last words to him: "Remember to have fun."

When Flynn had arrived home from school that afternoon, he'd found his father sitting alone on the floor of the kitchen clutching a note. His eyes were red, but there were no tears. Flynn thought it was funny at first, his father sitting like that on the floor. But when Harry only stared at him, saying nothing, barely moving, the humor was quickly replaced by a pitiful worry.

"Is everything okay, Dad?" young Flynn asked.

"Your mother left."

Flynn tried to process why his mother going on some errand would cause such drama.

"Where'd she go?"

"I don't know."

"When's she coming home?"

Harry looked at the note a long while, then looked up at his son. "She's not."

Flynn's life was never the same. The note his father read to his sons later that evening explained little. Their mother wrote only seven sentences, less than fifty words to blow up three lives.

I'm sorry for leaving this way. I'm weak and tired and I can't do this anymore. You'll all be fine. I hope I will be too. I love you, boys. I understand if you don't want to love me anymore. P.S. I took the can opener.

Over the years, much time was spent in the Barnes household trying to figure out why she had taken that can opener. Finally, they decided she had run off to become a hobo and wanted to be the most powerful hobo riding the rails. Certainly, a hobo with a can opener would be revered as a God. It had been a dark joke, but it was at least one they could all laugh at. At the time, they did not appreciate the significance of their conclusion, but it proved to be the last thing the Barnes men would ever agree on.

Soon enough, Harry's back gave out, he lost his job, worker's comp ran out, the house was sold, and the two brothers ricocheted in opposite directions from the demolition of all they had ever known. They got word when Flynn was a sophomore in high school that Karen-Marie Barnes had died in a car accident outside of Mesa, Arizona. She'd evidently been living there alone for some time, working as a waitress at an Applebee's. By the time they'd heard about her death, she'd been buried for almost two months. Flynn thought it was, all things considered, a perfect death for the woman who had abandoned him without explanation. He'd never bothered to visit her grave. She would remain a mystery, her life forever a mirage. Only, now, she was about to walk through the door.

"Time to start your day!" his mother's voice rang out.

The handle turned, and Flynn cringed as the door creaked open. He took a step back, his skin tingling with anticipation. But into the room stepped not his mother, but a tall, lanky man wearing a single-breasted, peach-colored suit, who seemed to be somewhere in his mid-fifties. The man was going grey, yet still handsome in an aging schoolboy sort of way. He smiled kindly at Flynn.

"Hello there, the name's Langhorne," he said, closing the door behind him.

"Is my mother with you?" Flynn asked, his eyes moving between Langhorne and the door. "That was her I heard, right?"

"In a sense," Langhorne said. "Her voice, anyway. It was intended to make you feel more comfortable. Did it work?"

Flynn was sure he was about to pass out. "Not really."

"Sorry to hear that," Langhorne said. "We do our best, but mothers are always tricky."

Flynn's mouth hung open. "Where am I?"

"O and F," replied Langhorne, as if the letters meant something. He went on to clarify, "Orientation and Facilitation for the Recently Graduated."

"Graduated?"

Langhorne conceded the language barrier as he again clarified the terminology: "*Dead.*"

There was only one logical reaction to the news. Flynn bolted for the door. Blowing past Langhorne, he wrenched the door wide and flew to safety, running as fast as he could—right back into the very room he had just left. He stopped, breathing heavily. Confused. Dizzy.

"Well," Langhorne smiled. "Wasn't that fun?"

Flynn refocused as best he could, which is to say not very much at all, and then wasted no time before again taking decisive action. He bolted once more for the door, this time pausing at the threshold, lifting his foot deliberately before lunging forward. But once again his foot landed back into the room as if just stepping inside. Clearly there was no out, only in. His chin fell to his chest in defeat. He steeled himself before again raising his eyes to Langhorne, who seemed to be growing impatient.

"Please stop doing that," Langhorne said.

"This is insane."

"A perfectly understandable summation. But—entirely wrong."

"You're telling me I died?" Flynn asked. "And God sent me to my room?"

"This is the time in your life when you were the happiest," Langhorne explained. "Everyone goes to their happy place. Isn't that nice? And each Facilitator, like me, is responsible for preparing each happy place for every Orientation and Facilitation session, such as this one we're having right now."

Flynn shuffled sideways and sat on the bed. He took a few breaths as he looked around, letting it all settle in.

"Very good," Langhorne said. "Just let it wash through you."

For reasons he wouldn't have been able to articulate, Flynn's customary sense of suspicion drifted away, replaced by a calming acceptance. At once there was no stress, no worries, no questions. It was as if he was indeed eight years old again, safe and content. The world wasn't big yet, no burdens to carry, nothing to strive for that wasn't within reach.

Langhorne smiled. "There you go…"

The sense memories of Flynn's childhood flooded through him, and his body lightened. For the first time in over twenty years, he thought of his family and was at peace. He loved them and he was loved in return. No conditions. Pure. Blissful. A cleansing sigh rose and fell, and tears of happiness pooled in his eyes as a joyful laugh rolled out of him.

"This feels so good," he said, with no sense of embarrassment, only a warm pleasure.

"Yes," Langhorne nodded. "I'm honored to have shared it with you. But now, I'm afraid it's time for you to go."

"Go where?" Flynn asked, looking up.

Langhorne curled his lower lip and looked at him like a parent looks at a child who needs a shot. "*To Hell*. Sorry."

"What?" Flynn sputtered. "Wait a minute—"

"There's no time," Langhorne interrupted. "The taxi's already here."

Flynn jumped to his feet. "That's insane!"

"We're back to that, are we?"

"Maybe I wasn't the best person, I'll give you that. But I don't deserve to go to Hell!"

"That's what everyone going to Hell says."

Flynn held up both hands. "Stop!"

"Stop what?"

"Just listen, okay? Listen…"

"I *am* listening."

Flynn was scrambling now, trying to gather his feet under him and fight the sensation of slipping into quicksand. "Is it because of Jesus?" he asked.

Langhorne's brows stitched together. "Jesus?"

Flynn had vague memories of his grandfather's brief marriage to his second wife, who had insisted on scaring her step-grandchildren with stories of God's wrath and how he had his own son—*his own flesh!*—crucified so everyone could avoid going to Hell. He recalled her warning him about salvation, but he didn't remember enough of the details (about the crucifixion or his step-grandmother) to skillfully plead his case. But he did remember watching his share of televangelists while getting high with his buddies, so he said, "You can't blame me for not getting into that whole thing."

"What whole thing?" Langhorne asked.

"All that Jesus-y stuff! Have you seen those preachers on

TV? They've conned more money out of more people than I ever did, with all their personal jets and mansions and all that shit—I mean, stuff. So, if you guys are relying on them to convince people that we're supposed to—"

"Enough! We're not relying on anyone to do anything, I assure you. And you're not going to Hell because of Jesus. You're going to Hell because of you."

"For stealing?" Flynn said, sensing the futility of his pleadings. "Really?"

"Let's not kid ourselves," said Langhorne. "It's more than stealing that landed you in hot water. Should we just ignore the touchy matter of you putting twenty-seven cats into a woodchipper?"

"What're you talking about?" Flynn was coming completely untethered, but he was sure he would recall turning twenty-seven cats into feline mulch. "I never did that!"

"Yes, you did."

"I would never! I like cats!" he offered as proof, even though that last bit was, in fact, a lie.

Langhorne was having none of it. "There's no sense in trying to argue your way out of this, Mr. Spivey."

For the first time since waking to this horrifying predicament, Flynn saw a glimmer of hope. "Hold on, my name's not Spivey."

"Of course it is."

"No. It's Barnes. *Flynn Barnes.*"

"Lying about your name isn't going to work," Langhorne scolded him, looking out the window at the waiting taxi. "Now please, we have to get going."

With a burst of clarity that this was all some sort of terrible mistake, Flynn screamed, "Wait!"

"Oh, stop yelling," Langhorne said. "I'm right here."

Flynn crossed to the bureau and scooped up the one and only Little League baseball trophy he'd been awarded before quitting the sport altogether. He handed it to Langhorne, who was not interested. "Look at it!" Flynn demanded.

Langhorne glanced at the trophy. "The Mighty Mitts, that's very impressive. But please stop with all the theatrics, there's nothing that can be done at this point about—"

"Look closer," Flynn said, unable to hide his own growing annoyance. "At the name."

Langhorne lowered his gaze and stared in shock. "Well, would you look at that," he sighed. "Is this right?"

"Yes!" Flynn shouted. "It says it right there on—"

Langhorne held up his hand. "You really do need to stop yelling." He then went on as if there were a third person in the room explaining the situation. "Uh-huh," he said, looking off. "Oh, I see what I did. He was the cliff diver in Portugal. I'm sorry, what was that? Ah, yes, he should have paid closer attention to the tides. Can you send the taxi over? I'll be there as soon as we finish up here. This is exciting, isn't it?" This last question had evidently been aimed at Flynn, and Langhorne barked when he got no response. "I *said*, isn't this exciting?"

Flynn stumbled back onto the edge of the bed, emotionally spent. "I wouldn't say being dead is exciting, no."

"Not *dead*," Langhorne corrected him, replacing the trophy on the shelf. "You're a *graduate*. And you should be excited, because there was indeed a mix-up."

"So I'm not going to Hell?"

"Let's not get ahead of ourselves."

"Meaning what?"

"Meaning there's still some work left to do."

Flynn didn't like the sound of that. "On my part or yours?"

"Both of ours, actually. Seeing as you are Flynn Barnes, there's something we need to look at." He motioned for Flynn to sit. "Shall we?"

A fifty-inch television was now positioned at the foot of the bed. "You're giving me a TV as a parting gift?" asked Flynn.

Langhorne held a finger to his lips. "Have a seat and watch."

Flynn warily situated himself on the bed, folding his hands across his lap as the screen lit up with a message: *Flynn Barnes. This Is Your Life.* Once the title card faded, it was impossible for Flynn to look away; his focus was so intent, so dialed-in, that it was as though his consciousness had been grafted to the screen itself. His mouth hung open as a numbingly rapid series of images from his life flashed before his eyes—or were they *behind* his eyes? He couldn't tell. Either way, the TV lit his face like a thousand flickering candles. The images were in chronological order, from birth onward, but they were also strangely lumped together as one moment, as if space and time had no meaning (which of course they don't, another truth Flynn would learn). And now, rather than experiencing his life as a series of individual events strung together by time as he once had, Flynn was able to *absorb* them as a single thing (which, of course, they were). It was all over within a matter of seconds. Or was it an hour? Flynn wasn't sure.

When the screen went dark, he was stunned into an overwhelming sense of humility. "That was amazing," he whispered, tears again welling.

"Every life is," Langhorne agreed.

"And I like the way you don't edit out the sex parts. Can I watch that again?"

Langhorne shook his head. "I'm afraid not. It was merely

meant as a refresher course, as you'll be needing all that information."

"For what?"

"I'll explain when we get there," Langhorne said.

Flynn looked warily at him. "Get where?"

A spark flashed above, and Flynn was yanked ferociously upward, a rag doll soaring toward the ceiling.

He closed his eyes and screamed.

CHAPTER SIX

WHEN FLYNN OPENED his eyes, he was standing on a grassy hill, wearing a tailored black wool suit that seemed to have been made to his exact measurements (it had been). Other than a slight feeling of disorientation, as if he had misjudged the height of a step, there was no apparent physical effect from the trip. A soft breeze cooled his face. He blinked a few times in the bright sun and glanced toward Langhorne, who stood placidly beside him.

"Is this Heaven?" Flynn asked.

"Once again," said Langhorne, "let's not get ahead of ourselves."

"Well, if it's not Heaven and it's not Hell, where are we?"

"This is where you're being buried. Right over there."

Flynn looked in the direction Langhorne had nodded, where a small crowd of smartly dressed people milled around a freshly dug gravesite. "They're already burying me?" he asked. "How long was I asleep?"

Langhorne waved him off. "Don't worry about that. As I said, time works differently for graduates. Focus on what needs to be done. You're about to have what is officially called a Graduate Regeneration Encounter. But I like to call it 'taking a ride on the Oh Shit buggy.'"

Flynn was finally catching on. He pressed his fingers into his chest, half expecting them to pass right through. "I'm a ghost, aren't I?"

"Don't be silly. But you're not quite *you* either." Langhorne turned to face him. He raised a warning finger to make his next point. "Now, this is *very* important, so you need to pay close attention. You're—" He looked past Flynn.

"I'm what?" Flynn asked. "What am I? What's important?"

Langhorne scowled at him. "Shhh. *Please.*"

"Again with the call waiting," Flynn grumbled.

"I see," Langhorne said. "And how many graduated? Uh-huh. How did it happen?" He laughed. "You're kidding! Well, I suppose now, not *everyone* loves a parade. Listen, I have to go."

Flynn was staring down at the crowd around his grave, trying to pick out familiar faces.

"Flynn!" snapped Langhorne. "You need to pay attention when I'm talking to you."

"Why're you so on edge?" He pointed at the funeral. "I'm the one who died."

"*Graduated.* And with the unfortunate mix-up with the names, the entire schedule's been thrown off. Now don't worry, you'll figure out much of it on your own."

"Wait, you're leaving me here?"

"You'll be fine. Just do your best."

"How can I do my best if I have no idea what I'm supposed to do?" Flynn again glanced at the crowd around the grave. "And you never finished telling me what was so impor—" He turned back to Langhorne, but Langhorne was gone.

Flynn walked down the sloping hill. The sun had yet to dry up the morning dew, and it made the going unsteady. Or maybe it was nerves that caused the trepidation in his step. His uneasiness grew with each halting stride. It's gonna make for one hell of a funeral, he thought, when the guest of honor strolls up to thank everyone for coming.

As Flynn approached the gathering, he recognized some faces from the warehouse but could attach names to only a few. Manny was there, standing with what's his name and that other guy from the loading dock. They were talking to the three crones from the loft office. One of the crones—Mindy, or Mallory, or something like that—said something that made the men laugh, which bothered Flynn. All of these strangers had come to see him off, but none of them looked all that upset by it. Apparently they were there to support Andy, not to mourn him, and certainly not to pay their respect. *Who needs you anyway*, Flynn thought.

He spotted his father standing beside Andy and Erin. His brother and father were expressionless, but Erin looked as if she had been crying, which made Flynn feel a tad better. As Hoyt stepped up to offer a few words of condolence to Harry, Andy fidgeted, clearly anxious for the entire endeavor to end.

Jimmy Bannon's mother, Jane, a frail-looking woman with short brown curls and lightly freckled skin that customarily smelled of peach soap, stepped up after Hoyt finished and gave Andy a tight, motherly hug. She gave Harry a hug as well, but the old man did not raise his arms to return the kindness.

Flynn decided there was no reason to delay his big moment and waded into the crowd, nose pointed at his shoes, doing his best to conceal his face with his hand. It was only fair that Andy and his father should have first crack at fainting from shock.

The drama of the moment excited him. But with each person he shuffled past, it became more and more apparent that the moment held no drama at all. With each step, Flynn's chin rose, and his hand lowered slightly to reveal his face. But there was no acknowledgment of his presence. Nobody recoiled. Nobody gasped. Nobody so much as blinked. The wolf had entered the hen house and everyone just went right on laying eggs. He grew determined to scare the crap out of someone—*anyone*. As he passed each mourner, he smiled expectantly, waiting for somebody to scream out. But nobody did.

Flynn stepped into the center of the well-dressed crowd, hands at his sides, feeling more alone than he had in a long time. "You do see me, right?" he asked one of the mourners.

"Excuse me?" the man asked.

"I feel like I just told a joke nobody got," he said. "You don't recognize me, do you?"

"I'm sorry, have we met?"

"I don't know, maybe. To be honest, I don't remember you either."

"Matt Rudoff," the man said, offering his hand. "I work with Andy at Bannon Imports. How did you know Flynn?"

"Forget it," Flynn said, waving him off. "I'm just trying to figure all this out."

Matt looked sadly at him. "It never makes sense when someone dies so young, does it?"

Flynn rolled his eyes and continued on. Matt was right though. None of this made any sense. For some reason, he didn't look the same anymore. Fine. Langhorne said he'd figure things out, and he just figured out that much. But what now? If this was indeed his funeral and not some coma-induced hallucination, he had no idea where to begin. And, for that matter, *what* to begin.

With the low, polite conversations buzzing in the air, he found himself peering into the freshly dug grave at a shiny black coffin tucked into the ground like a giant watermelon seed. "That's freaky," he muttered.

He thought about jumping into the hole and pulling open the casket lid to make sure he really was in there. But if he jumped in, he'd have no room to stand beside the coffin, and he couldn't very well lift the lid if he were standing on top of it. *And lying inside it.* His head hurt from the existential confusion knocking around his tortured mind.

It was time to confront Andy and his father and, in doing so, put an end to this charade. Flynn turned from the grave and cut aggressively through the crowd, no longer bothering with the effort to blend in. But as he made his way resolutely toward his family, he spotted Thacker standing off to the side, away from the crowd, and immediately changed course.

Thacker's hands were shoved deep into the pockets of his rumpled black suit, which gave him the appearance of someone suffering a bout of boredom, rather than sorrow.

Flynn stepped up beside him. "I suppose you don't recognize me either, do you?" he asked.

"Sorry, no."

Flynn was keyed up to share his secret but instinctively recognized that when informing someone that you are, in essence, a zombie, it was best to do so calmly. "Okay, don't freak out."

"I'll do my best," Thacker said dryly.

Flynn leaned close. "It's me."

Thacker nodded, "Well, you'd know, wouldn't you?"

Flynn's excitement grew. "Listen closely. It's *me*, Ffff, Ffff—" He struggled to say his name, but his mouth and tongue refused to work. His lower lip curled inward and he toiled to get past the aborted "F" sound, managing only to spew a fountain of spit onto his chin. His face grew hot as he tried again. "Ffff…"

"You all right?" asked Thacker.

Flynn took a quick breath. "I can't say my name."

Thacker furrowed his brow. "You do seem to be coming off your trolley a little bit. But don't worry about it, I had an uncle who stuttered. It's no big deal."

"No, I don't have a stutter. I'm not sure what the problem is."

"While you figure it out," Thacker said, "I'm gonna go stand over there. It was nice meeting you."

"Wait, wait, wait, wait," Flynn said, his words coming out fast, matching the speed of his thoughts. "Let me try this. Do you have a piece of paper? A pen?"

"'Fraid not."

Flynn checked the pockets of his suit. "Damnit, me neither. How about a phone?"

"You wanna call someone to have them tell me your name?" Thacker chuckled.

"Can I borrow it real fast?"

Thacker looked at him with continued amusement, then pulled his cell from his pocket, unlocked it, and handed it over. Flynn opened the "notes" app and started typing. He only got as far as, "This is going to sound crazy, but I'm" before his thumbs stopped working. Every time he tried to land them on the letter F for Flynn, they bent and skittered away. The phone shook in his hands as his frustration mounted. No matter the effort, he could not type out his name. "This is fucking bizarre," he said, giving up.

Thacker took his phone back. "No argument from me,

mate. It's been nice chatting with you." He moved closer to the crowd.

Now alone, Flynn stretched his mouth wide and extended his tongue. Once out of earshot of his best and only friend, he tried again, and the word "Flynn" came flying past his lips. "I'm Flynn," he announced, but nobody was close enough to hear. He regrouped and was about to yell out his true identity for all to hear when Andy turned and raised his hand. "If I can have everyone's attention, please."

Curiosity as to what his brother would say overtook Flynn's immediate need to identify himself. He wandered over, staying at the back edge of the crowd as they formed a loose semicircle around the grave. Andy stood in front, as there was no preacher to give the eulogy. The Barnes family hadn't set foot in a church since the boys were little, even though their father was Catholic (or at least had been growing up).

Their mother had been a "Christmas Christian," as she called it. She liked all the trappings of Christmas—the tree, carols, decorations, and general good cheer—and insisted they attend a holiday sermon every year on Christmas Eve. The boys never complained, as they looked forward to the eggnog and sugar cookies the church served. But despite their mother's affinity for the season, the holy high never managed to reach the new year, and the tradition was dropped when she disappeared from their lives. Flynn wasn't anticipating much from his brother in the spiritual department, but he was keenly interested in what he would come up with to mark such a momentous occasion.

Andy paused and shuffled his feet. "My father and I appreciate you all coming," he began. "It's nice to know we aren't alone today."

Yeah, yeah, whatever, thought Flynn, get to the good stuff.

Andy continued. "This isn't easy for me, because I never seemed to know the right thing to say when I talked to my brother, and I certainly don't know what to say now. In a lot of ways, Flynn was a troubled man. He made a lot of mistakes. I'd like to think, though, if given the time, he would have…" His voice trailed off and for a moment he was in danger of losing control of his closely held emotions. "If he had taken the time to know all of you better," he said, clearing his throat, "he would have seen that a good life is made of good friends." Andy lowered his eyes to the ground and the crowd waited patiently for him to put his thoughts in order. Flynn knew the tears were about to arrive, which pleased him to no end.

Flynn looked at Harry, but the old man was staring off at a bank of clouds on the horizon. Andy again cleared his throat. Just when it seemed the silence would go on a while longer, Andy looked up and nodded. "I think I'm going to leave it at that," he said. "He was loved."

A few more throat clearings rose into the air to mingle with light sighs and indistinguishable mutterings.

From the back, Flynn yelled, "You gotta be kidding me! That's it?"

"Excuse me?" asked Andy.

"No, you're not excused," said the man nobody recognized, pushing his way forward through the crowd. "That's all you're gonna say? That he was loved? That is so lame! I can't believe you don't have anything else. Nothing from when you were kids? There's gotta be something!"

Flynn stood directly in front of his brother, who only stared in consternation.

"I'm sorry," Andy said. "Do I know you?"

Bile rose in Flynn's gut. All concern for the sensibilities of the living was gone. "I hate to ruin your little party by telling you this, but it's *me*! Ffff..." His face contorted as he strained to say his name. "Ffff, *Fuck*!" he bellowed, frustration again winning out.

A murmur of concern circulated in the crowd. Even Harry was listening now. Thacker couldn't help but laugh a little as Andy attempted to take control. "Maybe you should just—"

"No!" Flynn roared, silencing his brother. Calming himself as best he could, which was not much at all, he continued on. "I'm not allowed to identify myself. Fine." He looked into the sky and yelled, "Though a heads up would have been nice!" He again leveled his eyes on the crowd. "But I sure as hell *can't* live with what I'm seeing here." He hit his words hard, like a preacher with the spirit upon him. "I mean, come on! Flynn was a great guy...I said Flynn! Flynn! I can say it!" His face lit up with understanding. "That actually makes sense. I can say Flynn when I'm talking about him, not me."

"Sir," Andy cut in, "I appreciate you wanting to say something, but—"

"But nothing," Flynn said. "I was told I'd have to figure things out and that's what I'm doing. Now, where was I? Oh, yes. You all should *definitely* be crying *a lot* more than this, *especially* the women. You're gonna tell me that not one of you had a secret crush on him?" The women all shared a curious look and a shrug of denial. "Yeah, right," said Flynn. "And let's clear something else up—Flynn wasn't *troubled*, okay? He was actually quite carefree and easygoing. The type of guy you'd like to have around. And he was smart too. Very smart. Maybe not about math and all that shit, but you know, the *important* stuff. And he was a great athlete too. Basketball, baseball, street hockey, you name it." His voice outran his thoughts for a moment, before he hesitated long enough for them to catch up.

"And I'll tell you something else," he continued. "He was *funny*. And charming. Funny and charming. That's how I'd describe him. And, if I may, I'd add good-looking too. Maybe not, like, *model* good-looking, but well above average." Flynn had turned an emotional corner and was in complete control now—comfortable even. He slowed down his speech to make sure his words landed with the proper impact. "He made a few mistakes. So what? Who hasn't? Let he who casts the first stone…or something like that. I don't actually remember how that one goes, but you know what I'm talking about. Whatever mistakes Flynn made, he was tough enough—no, *brave* enough—to pick himself back up, dust himself off, and never give up. I think that's to be commended. To be *celebrated*. He should be looked to as an *inspiration*."

Flynn scanned the faces staring back at him, reminding them of their duty to solemnity. Only Thacker seemed to be on board with the unexpected eulogy. He was smiling and nodding, his tooth gap showing. The rest stood passively, exchanging wary glances. "What is wrong with you people?" Flynn went on. "Don't you have any idea what a loss this is? It's a tragedy of untapped potential that now lies in the cold, damp ground, never to be heard from again." He paused briefly for effect before dramatically kneeling to pick up a handful of black soil piled next to the grave. He examined it for a moment, as if he were holding the entire universe in his palm. "My God," he said softly, turning his hand to sprinkle the earth onto the coffin laying silent, six feet below. "His spirit will be missed." He paused a moment more, then stood up, his eyes boring into the open-mouthed faces staring back at him. "And you *really* should be crying."

Flynn studied the unsettled expressions before him. And then he heard it. Hannah from accounting began to cry. Her wet sniffles filled Flynn's ears as he pointed at her with an appreciative finger. "Thank you," he said. "That's great."

He turned back to Andy, who stood dumbfounded. Flynn cocked his eyebrow. Then he dropped an invisible microphone. "Boom."

The crowd dispersed and everyone gave a wide berth to the strange man who'd come to eulogize Flynn. "Friend from prison" was the general consensus shared quietly as they departed, which spurred Flynn to try again with Thacker, his actual friend from prison. But Thacker slipped away when Flynn watched Erin and Andy walk Harry to their waiting car. His father's car was in some junkyard by now, pulled from the bottom of the cliff below Mulholland Drive. Flynn imagined his body being pulled up with the wreckage, arms and legs flopping like the limbs of a rubber chicken, bloodless flesh the color of paste, his lifeless eyes fixed in his skull. The image brought him a wave of nausea he pushed away.

There was evidently no after-gathering planned, no celebration of a life not well lived: only a small dinner with immediate family hosted by Hoyt and Jane at their sprawling home in Brentwood. Flynn briefly considered ways he could horn his way in on the meal, but there was no logical path back into the family he was no longer a part of. So he merely stood there, watching them drive away, powerless to decide his next move. Lost.

Hannah from accounting stepped up beside him, her nose pink with emotion. "Excuse me," she said. "I just wanted to say, your words were beautiful."

"Thank you," Flynn said.

"I didn't know Flynn well, but your eulogy made me wish I'd taken the time to get to know him a little better."

"I get that." He smiled. "You don't have to hold it all inside. We're alone, you can admit it. You had a crush on him, didn't you? Attracted to the bad boy, right?"

Hannah wiped her nose, giving a slight laugh. "No."

"C'mon! Nobody? Not one woman in that whole warehouse?"

Hannah dug into her purse. "I don't think so," she said, pulling out a pair of mirrored sunglasses. "Maybe Keith. I caught him staring a few times."

"Really?" Flynn looked after the departing crowd. "Which one's Keith?"

"Older gentleman," she said, searching the few people remaining, "salt and pepper hair? I don't see him."

"Forget it," he said, trying not to sound disappointed.

"You're a good friend to speak about Flynn like that," she said. "I was very touched." She put her sunglasses on, and Flynn caught a fleeting glimpse of himself in the reflection.

"Oh my God!" he gasped.

"What?"

Grabbing her to steady the image, Flynn leaned in, inches from her face, mouth agape, unable to comprehend the unfamiliar moon face staring back at him in the glass lens.

"Please don't hurt me," Hannah whimpered.

Flynn yanked the glasses off her face and Hannah turned and scurried off. Flynn didn't notice her panicked escape, however. He held the glasses up with one hand while running his opposite hand over his lumpy cheeks, lost in his grossly unfamiliar features. The eyes reflecting back to him were set wide, toad-like, the lips thick, two large ears sticking out like open flaps of a cardboard box. He tilted his head back on his fleshy neck. "My nostrils are *huge.*"

CHAPTER SEVEN

FLYNN LEANED HEAVILY against the rear bench of the empty bus, eyes closed. The bus shifted gears and rumbled forward, then shifted again. Diesel fumes attacked his giant nostrils. Distraught with self-absorption over the events at his funeral, he didn't so much as flinch when he heard Langhorne's voice next to him.

"It takes a while to get used to."

Instead of asking how Langhorne had materialized beside him, Flynn simply accepted it as very low on the list of strange things that had happened to him recently. "I'm hideous," he said.

"Nonsense. You're very handsome."

"Who's handsome? Me or this guy?" asked Flynn, pointing at *the face*. "Because from the look of things I'm no longer Flynn."

"Sure you are. Haven't you ever heard that it's what's on the inside that counts? It's just against the rules for you to present any information that could identify your true self."

"That much I understand now. But what isn't clear is why you had to give me a foot for a face."

"Once you settle in, you can make any physical changes you'd like."

"Settle into what? What the hell am I doing here?"

"I don't know. You're the one who got on the bus."

Flynn stared blankly at him. "You're an enormous help."

"You're fully in charge of your decisions," Langhorne explained. "Graduate or undergraduate, people still have free will. Which is, honestly, why they have so many problems. You see, everyone rubs off on everyone else, altering each other's destinies with the tiniest of influences, sometimes for the better and sometimes—as in your case—for the worse. In the end, each person bears their portion of responsibility for the way the casserole turns out."

"Don't say *of course* like I should know what the hell you're talking about," Flynn said. "Because I have no idea what that means. I have no idea what *any* of this means."

Langhorne frowned. "That's because you're not listening."

"Oh, shut up."

"Fine, you're listening but you're definitely not hearing. It's not that difficult to understand if you pay attention."

Though the body was no longer his, it was still animated with a healthy dose of ego, and Flynn didn't appreciate the dig about the relative simplicity of understanding his predicament. He took a moment to calm down, then said, "You're saying I've somehow screwed up someone's destiny…"

"No, not precisely. That's still an undergraduate's way of thinking. The truth is, nobody can *screw up destiny,* as if it were something preordained. In fact, one can only *create* a destiny that may or may not be, as you so elegantly put it, *screwed.* Think of it like this: every contact between you and someone else is like a tiny Big Bang, creating a new reality each time.

Along with your own reality, you contribute your share, however large or small, to the *creation* of someone else's. And, as I've now said twice, you will be held accountable. If we were only concerned with your life, you'd have moved on by now."

Flynn took all this in, watching all those anonymous people on the street as the bus rumbled past. "So I'm supposed to change someone else's destiny?"

"Still not the right verbiage. Again, because life is in a constant state of flux, you can't actually change a destiny, but you can—"

"Create a new reality."

"It's more apt to say that you *contribute* to the creation of a new reality."

"Give me a break, Dr. Semantics. Whose new reality am I responsible for *contributing* to?"

"That ledger is too full to account for. The butterfly effect and all that. But, the issue isn't in the quantity, it's in the *quality*. Let's focus on that."

"Meaning the people I've affected most directly in a negative way?"

"Now you're getting it." Langhorne leaned back, hands folded in his lap. "And once you figure that out, you'll have to again affect their reality enough to avert whatever danger your actions have contributed to creating."

Flynn's discomfort rose—an emotional state that was becoming more and more familiar. "What sort of danger?" he asked.

"Again, that's your responsibility to figure out. But it could be anything. Remember, everything is in a constant state of flux."

The bus pulled over and five middle-aged ladies in matching hotel maid uniforms got on, chatting loudly in Spanish. Langhorne smiled at them, but Flynn was too busy sifting through his memories to even take notice.

"I have no idea!" Flynn said. "I bailed on my prom date in high school, maybe that's it. Maybe I ruined Laurie Gow's life forever by choosing to get drunk with my buddies rather than slow dance to some crappy Coldplay song."

"I rather like Coldplay," Langhorne said.

"Not my point!"

The ladies stopped chattering and looked toward the back of the bus. Langhorne continued to smile as Flynn blabbered on. "C'mon, man, so I put a thumbtack on Susan Currey's chair in the tenth grade. Would that really screw up her entire life? Did she become deathly afraid of sitting down and develop arthritic knees or something? Never achieved her dream of becoming a yoga instructor?" One of the ladies said something under her breath and the other five nodded. Flynn's exasperation grew. "Now that I think about it, it's all so clear. When I worked at the Gap, I sold a fat chick a pair of spandex bike shorts—I can only imagine the chaos that created!"

"I could be wrong," said Langhorne, "but I wouldn't guess it's any of those."

"You're the one who said it could be *anything*." Flynn waved at the window. "Look how many people are out there. I can't remember every foot I ever stepped on, which may or may not have altered the course of someone's life!" Flynn caught the women staring. "What?" he yelled at them, losing all sense of decorum.

The ladies quickly gathered up their purses and moved closer to the front of the bus. One of the women said something to the driver in Spanish, and while the driver spoke no language other than English, he understood her perfectly. With an annoyed hiss of brakes, the bus lurched toward the curb and came to a jarring stop. The driver irritably pulled his lever and the side doors swished open.

"I think he's trying to tell us something," Langhorne whispered.

"What tremendous insight!" Flynn snapped.

The two men stood and exited the bus, the doors swishing closed behind them. The fumes again filled Flynn's huge nostrils, but he remained motionless at the curb, refusing to hold his breath, inviting the toxic wash into his system as the bus rumbled away. "Perfect," he said.

Langhorne was as chipper as ever. "To figure out what you need to do next, perhaps just concentrate on the biggies. Focus on the times when you really went out of your way to affect another person."

Flynn was already tired of thinking about it. He half sat, half collapsed onto the curb, his feet landing in the gutter. Taking off the jacket of his tailored wool suit, he used the sleeve to wipe the sweat from his face, then dropped it next to his shoes. "Maybe I never tried to *help* anyone, but I never really *hurt* anyone either."

Langhorne did a silent calculation of his schedule, then sat beside Flynn on the curb. "You'd be amazed at the number of politicians who've told me the same thing. But you did. Otherwise, you wouldn't still be here."

Flynn looked at himself in Hannah's sunglasses once more before crushing the lenses under his heel in disgust. "What kind of angel are you? Shouldn't you already know what's going on?"

Langhorne shook his head. "I'm not an angel. Angels are concerned with your spirit. I'm a Facilitator. I'm only concerned with your soul. And as such, my role is to attend to you as you figure things out."

Flynn looked at the cars whizzing past, all with a clear purpose. He wished he, too, had someplace specific to go. Anywhere. But he didn't, not yet anyway. He stewed a moment more, then slowly spoke. "I guess if I'm gonna be honest, I do know of one *biggie,* as you call it."

"Excellent. Lay it on me."

"I recently helped smuggle some stolen Incan artifacts into the country. I'm not exactly proud of it, but I didn't actually hurt anybody. Unless I pissed off some five-hundred-year-old mummy."

"As a matter of fact, you did. His name's Tupacuti-Apo-Mayta, so definitely put that on your list. What else do you have?"

Flynn considered his other missteps. He sighed. "I recently did twenty-two months for stealing some guy's identity and taking the last two grand from his bank account to buy tickets to a Springsteen concert."

Langhorne stared hard at Flynn, as though forcing him to consider that his victim's pain amounted to something more than a series of numbers on a bank account. "As they say," Langhorne said, shaking his head, "elephants never forget."

Whatever wisdom Langhorne was trying to impart, the metaphor was lost on Flynn. "What's that supposed to mean?" he asked.

"I'm sorry, Flynn. I was having another conversation. Evidently an elephant trainer in Hamburg went to the prod one too many times." He stood up quickly. "I'm afraid we need to go."

Flynn was too tired and dejected to move.

"Come on," Langhorne encouraged him, offering a hand to help him up. "It only gets more exciting from here."

Flynn stood inside room 130 of the inaptly named Palace Motel, feeling sorry for himself. There was a creaky twin bed with a faux wood table beside it, on which rested a fat-bottomed lamp with a heavy lampshade that blocked most of the light. There was also a chair, but its discolored and frayed fabric looked so uninviting that it probably hadn't been sat in for years. The well-trod areas of the carpet leading from the door to the bed to the bathroom were worn through in places, revealing the plywood flooring underneath. The walls were painted the same brown as the carpet, which served to swallow what little light managed to escape from the lamp.

"This is Hell, isn't it?" asked Flynn.

"Not quite," Langhorne said. "Though we are still in Los Angeles, so I understand the confusion. This is merely a place for you to reflect for a while."

"I'm good. Let's just get this thing moving."

"I'm afraid it's somewhat of a *requirement* at this stage of graduation."

Flynn bristled at the thought. "Reflect on what?"

"That's up to you."

"You mean on the whole God thing, don't you?"

"If you'd like."

"I don't."

"Be that as it may."

"What's the deal with him anyway?" Flynn asked. "Does he prefer God or Lord?"

Langhorne's impatience was obvious, though he remained cordial. "Either is fine."

"How 'bout Allah? Or Jehovah? Ganesha? Flying Spaghetti Monster?"

"Any one of them will do."

"Personally, I would've stuck with Zeus. That was a cool name."

"All you need to concern yourself with right now is why you haven't moved on. To that end you can meditate, chant, pray, use whatever path you find useful."

"No offense, Langhorne, but the only path I'm interested in right now is the one that leads to the nearest bar."

Langhorne rested his hand on Flynn's shoulder. The feeling of his palm unsettled Flynn—it was the first time he'd actually touched him, and the sudden intimacy was awkward. Langhorne said gently, "Perhaps you should use the time to consider why nobody had anything to say at your funeral." He left his hand where it was, as if doing so would drive home his concern.

Flynn felt an unmistakable warmth through his shirt and his mood indeed turned more reflective. "Can I at least get a pizza?"

Langhorne stared at him, as though studying a new species of animal. "I'll be back as soon as I can."

Though physical hunger was no longer an issue for the recent graduate, Flynn's cravings remained. "I'm serious," he said. "Bring a pizza with you."

But Langhorne was already gone.

Flynn was at a total loss. He sat on the edge of the bed, then stood back up. He had no instinct with this sort of thing. *Reflection*, that is. If he had once possessed the capacity, he'd never given it much energy, thus dulling the part of him necessary for the act. He operated on the strict principle that truth could only be found in what he could see in front of him. At the moment, all he could see was a closed door.

He waited three and a half minutes before walking out of the motel room.

Late afternoon sun cast long shadows down Western Avenue. He glanced around, worried he would find Langhorne standing guard by the humming soda machine set inside its heavy black cage. He figured if Langhorne knew *anything* about him (free will and all that), he would be there, ready to shuffle him back inside. But he was undoubtedly alone.

He started north, toward the tall, distant buildings of downtown Los Angeles. He was surrounded by a burnt-out strip mall on one side and a long, heavily shadowed apartment complex on the other. With his starched white shirt and tailored slacks, he saw himself as a target, one certainly easier to break into than the well-guarded soda machine. That was truer than he realized. He got no further than the middle of the parking lot before being stopped short by the sound of his name.

"Flynn," a man's affable voice called out. "Flynn! Over here!"

As Flynn turned to see the owner of the voice, he found that while he might not be hard-wired for personal reflection, he did have a finely tuned instinct for trouble. He was already dead though, he figured. How much trouble could he get into?

He was about to find out.

CHAPTER EIGHT

THE MAN'S JAWLINE ran down from his high cheekbones like ski slopes, squaring off at the chin. Thick, sandy-colored hair was swept up and back over his scalp. His eyes glistened in the fading light like deep pools of spring water. He was perfect.

"How do you know me?" Flynn asked, approaching him across the parking lot.

The question brought a smile to the man's silken lips. Then a laugh. And with that laugh, the illusion of magnificence was irrevocably broken. Wispy breath floated from his mouth on a current of leaden, brown air. Like rotting twigs rising from a mossy bog, his teeth sat raggedly in his mottled gums. His tongue lay in this graveyard hollow of a mouth like a moldy pumpkin shell. He was, quite literally, decayed on the inside.

The man removed a pack of Marlboros from the pocket of his honey silk shirt, held it out for Flynn. "Smoke?"

"I'm good."

"You sure?" He lit one and took a long, deep drag, but strangely did not blow out any smoke. "Don't have to worry about the big 'C' anymore. Sort of takes the fun out of it though. No risk."

Flynn realized he had seen this man before. Well, not *him* as much as the beat-up taxi he was leaning against. "You were outside my bedroom window after I graduated, weren't you?" he asked.

"Yes, and it's a stupendous Happy Place you have there, with the whole childhood-home vibe. Gave me a warm fuzzy. Truly."

Flynn was more curious than afraid. In fact, he felt immediately comfortable with the taxi driver. "What do you need?" he asked. "I mean besides a Tic-Tac."

"The real question is what do *you* need."

"A pizza wouldn't hurt."

"Think big picture, Flynn," the driver said, stepping closer. "You wanna be a slave like Langhorne or free, like me?"

Flynn winced, breathing in the putrid breath wafting from the driver's mouth. If he had been granted that pizza, he imagined he would have lost it right there in the parking lot. "If you're so free," he said, leaning back, "why don't you see a dentist?"

This elicited another hearty laugh, which only made the stench worse.

"I like you," the taxi driver said.

"I'm flattered."

He took another long drag on the cig. "Langhorne gave you the rundown, I assume?"

"The rundown?"

"Of all that's required, now that you're a hotshot graduate."

"He touched on it," Flynn said.

"Bet he also wanted you to sit around like some monk on a mountain and reflect on your life, consider your place in the universe, all that boring stuff."

Flynn stood motionless, but his mind moved at breakneck speed. "You seem to know a lot about my situation."

The driver watched him closely, as if gauging the spinning wheels in Flynn's overloaded brain. "That's correct, I do. For instance, I know that all that meditation, prayer, and reflection is an utter waste of time and energy." He squinted. "And I bet you have no interest in what Langhorne's selling, because you intuit that having to chase down all the schmucks who blame you for their lives not working out is patently unfair. And you're correct, it is. It's also a shell game. Keep your eye on this one! He's the one you're responsible for! Watch him closely. Got him? Too bad, because it turns out you should have been looking at someone over here. You lose!" He laughed a spiteful laugh. "And then it's game over."

Flynn found the man's confidence enticing. "And what, exactly, is your game?"

The driver's expression turned serious. "I'm not playing games."

"Then what do you want?"

He dropped the cigarette onto the cracked asphalt and snuffed it out with the shiny toe of his black leather shoe. "I want what you want. For you to live on your terms, not theirs. Free Will with a capital F, capital W. Use it or lose it. It's up to you how this goes. It's the God's honest truth that you have a lot more control than Langhorne would have you believe."

Flynn ignored the naturally evolved instinct all humans possess, graduated or not. When confronted with a potential danger, it comes down to fight or flight. Flynn, however, opted for door number three: continued chatty conversation. "What do you mean more control?" he asked.

The driver looked pleased to see the fish rising to the bait. "It's up to *you* to decide what's best, not him."

"Uh-huh," Flynn said, his con-man mind trying to work out all the angles. "And what exactly do you get out of this?"

"Nothing. I'm just a working stiff doing my job driving graduates to their next stop. Where that turns out to be isn't up to me."

"It's up to me," Flynn said, playing along.

The rotted smile returned. "Capital F, capital W."

"What would I have to do?"

"For now? Just take everything under advisement. Think about what you truly want. And how 'bout while you consider, I get you out of this roach motel and set you up someplace with a little class?"

Flynn didn't say yes, but he wasn't walking away either.

"No strings attached," the driver went on. "If everything feels right, we'll talk some more. If not, you're on your own."

The idea of options and control sparked a fire in Flynn. It made him feel *alive*. When his ego was engaged, life was as it should be, and nothing engaged Flynn's ego as much as freedom to do as he pleased. But his guard was still up. "I know how this works," he said. "My old man had me watch every *Twilight Zone* ever made. I accept your offer and I end up with a pig face or something, right?"

The driver took out another cigarette and tucked it behind his perfectly symmetrical ear. "Have you looked in a mirror lately?" he asked, laughing.

Flynn self-consciously ran his hand down his chubby cheek and glanced back at the motel, feasting on the thought of doing as he pleased. "No strings?"

"Scout's honor," the driver said.

Flynn figured the driver was a long way from being a boy scout, but still he asked, "What kind of place you have in mind?"

The taxi pulled to a stop and Flynn stepped out in front of the Hotel Marigold. This was a different taxi, however, one he had ultimately flagged down after a forty-five-minute walk. When dealing with persons who may or may not be the living dead but whose innards are undeniably decomposed, he believed it best to demonstrate a measure of caution and restraint. Not too much restraint, of course, or he wouldn't have accepted the hundred-dollar bill the desiccated driver offered him for cab fare. And he wouldn't now be standing in front of the nicest beachfront hotel in Santa Monica.

The Marigold stretched half a city block, its frontage lined with skinny, arching palm trees, like paeans to the slender beauties Flynn anxiously imagined sunbathing each morning in lounge chairs around its glittering pool.

He walked up the travertine tile path leading into the brightly lit Shangri-La but was hesitant to enter. He had no bags, no reservations, and no identification to announce his arrival. All he had was the word of a cab-driving corpse that he could, in fact, sleep in one of the hotel's finest suites, no questions asked. Any attempt to give his real name to the front desk would only end with the concierge offering a tissue to wipe the spit from his chin.

Standing there, trying not to look conspicuous and wondering how to attack the problem, Flynn shoved his hands into the front pockets of his suit. Feeling something, he pulled out what he first thought was a credit card. Examining it, he found that on one side was an electronic strip, and on the other were the words Suite 701.

"Can I help you, Sir?" asked one of the white-gloved bellhops.

"No," Flynn said, holding up the room key, "I was just waiting for…someone. But I think I'll go ahead upstairs."

"Very good, Sir," the bellhop said, pulling open the glass door etched with a giant cursive M.

Flynn warily stepped into the polished-floor lobby, where he was immediately met by another white-gloved bellhop. "Welcome to the Marigold, Sir," said the second bellhop.

Flynn again held up the passkey. "Yeah, I'm, uh, staying in suite seven oh one."

"Very good, sir. Is there anything you need?"

Flynn didn't press his luck. "No, I'm cool. Thanks."

"Have a good night, Sir."

Flynn walked on, but turned back to say, "I might need some towels or something later."

The bellhop nodded. "Just call housekeeping and they'll take care of it right away, Sir."

"Yeah, I'll call housekeeping. From my room. Suite seven oh one."

"Yes, I remember."

Flynn's confidence grew as he moved to the bank of elevators at the far end of the lobby. Nobody paid him any mind as hotel guests wandered past, on their way to an early dinner or to see the sights. His anticipation rose along with the illuminated numbers of each floor he passed. On the top floor, he walked down a long hallway and fed the keycard into the slot of suite 701, smiling as five green lights streaked across the top of the lock with a happy beep. The sound of success.

Pushing open the door, he stepped onto the custom-woven carpet, then continued through the immense room (taking note of the complimentary fruit and muffin basket on the coffee table), past the open double doors that led to a master bedroom with a four-poster bed, and finally arrived at the French doors leading to a balcony large enough to accommodate a small party. He yanked the doors open and felt the sweet kiss of salt air as the sun bid adieu to the continent with a blaze of glory on the horizon of the great Pacific.

"This is more like it," Flynn said, breathing deeply.

Facing the sandy expanse before him, taking in that rarified air high above the common folk, the multi-colored lights of the Ferris wheel on the pier to the north shinning bright in the gloaming, he imagined himself a president, Pope, or king—or best of all, a movie star—the world bending to his considerable will.

Then, like a cockroach through a hidden pipe, an unwanted thought crept into his mind. He flashed on another balcony, one not overlooking smooth sand and white-tipped waves but an empty, rust-stained pool with a discarded beer bottle cap at its pitiful bottom. He pictured his father sitting alone in his rickety beach chair, staring off at nothing.

Flynn refused to let the image linger. *Everyone's on their own*, he told himself. *All that changes is the view.*

He took a bubble bath in the eight-foot hydrothermal massage tub and ordered room service filet mignon with thin-cut french fries and lobster tails with garlic butter. He found an Armani suit hanging in the closet with a fat roll of twenties, fifties, and hundreds in the pocket. The taxi driver had more than kept his word; he had exceeded all expectations. Flynn's grin widened. It was go time.

The city outside was bustling with many options for a man with an apparently unlimited supply of money, and because Flynn's belly was full, his attention focused on satiating another sort of hunger.

Another cab ride brought him to the Sunset Strip in Hollywood. The strip at night had an energy of its own, a buzzing mix of electrical currents. Some of the live wires were the wannabes who dreamed of being famous, of having their movies or TV shows or albums featured on the giant billboards lit up like beacons of hope along the famed street. Other wires were the sort-of-ares and tabloid celebrities with no interest in staying out of the gossip pages, intent on the dimmer switches of their egos turned as far to the right as passing interest would allow. Still other wires were the hustlers and the players, whose game was to siphon as much juice out of the system as possible.

Flynn climbed from the taxi in front of House, one of the hip hotspots that rises or falls in popularity depending on who walks in and out of its doors. There was a short line of high-heeled hopefuls, immune to the shame of waiting behind a velvet rope, and a shaggy gaggle of bored paparazzi hanging out on the sidewalk, smoking cigarettes and jawing with each other as they waited for someone of note to arrive. Flynn, clearly, was not anyone of note. He surveyed the situation and concluded there was only one way *the face* was going to get past the gatekeeper standing guard at the front door. After some haggling, Flynn handed him five, crisp, hundred-dollar bills and promised never to come back again. The doorman stuffed the bills in his pocket and the velvet rope was lifted.

Flynn waded seamlessly into the packed crowd inside, but it didn't take long to realize that although he had gained entry to the sacred space, with *the face* leading the way, it was a truly lost cause. Every opening line was met with either a disinterested stare or dismissive rejection. Even telling his potential conquests he was a movie producer didn't help. Whoever said "No man is an island" had obviously never been to LA.

After one hour and four drinks, Flynn was ready to give up, go back to the Marigold hotel and see what was on pay-per-view to satisfy his inflamed desires. Then he saw her. She sat alone at a table in the corner, innocently sipping a drink and watching her friends dance. While she was attractive, with dark hair and large, nearly equine eyes, it wouldn't be until last call that she got any play. For the jaded men inside House, she was more "two-in-the-morning pretty" than "ten-thirty pretty." But when she smiled at Flynn, he was so thankful that he never bothered to look for a clock.

Scarlett leaned heavily on Flynn, giggling drunkenly as they entered suite 701 of the Hotel Marigold. Flynn drew her close, their hips grinding together. Her lips tasted like strawberry daiquiris and her skin had the faint scent of perspiration. Feeling her body pressed against his sent a wave of lust through him and he pulled her into the bedroom, where they tumbled backward onto the giant bed like a knotted ball of arms and legs. She rolled onto her back and Flynn was on top of her, struggling to remove his coat while kissing her neck. Sitting up as he straddled her legs, he finally got his arms free and tossed the coat to the floor. He pulled off his shirt, sucking in his gut as he lowered himself onto her. They kissed passionately, deeply. Running his hand up her toned leg, he found her breast and teased it with the tips of his fingers. Rising up onto his forearms, he stared into her hazel eyes. "You're beautiful," he told her.

She smiled, and then simply melted away. *Literally*. Her skin turned translucent in the soft light, then slid around her face like hot wax on a plate. Her eyes receded into her head and her button nose dissolved into her gooey cheeks. The wax shifted and new features quickly formed, congealing instantly into a familiar visage. "Thank you," Langhorne said.

"Oh shit!" Flynn screamed. He pushed himself up, lost his balance, and fell off the bed, landing hard on his back beside his discarded coat.

"I can't believe you left the motel," Langhorne scolded him, sitting up. "You should *not* be accepting gifts from the taxi drivers, no matter how enticing they may be."

"You could've given me a heart attack!" Flynn yelled, adrenaline pumping so ferociously that his skin itched.

"Impossible," Langhorne said. "You obviously don't have a heart."

"You didn't have to put your tongue in my mouth," Flynn moaned, spitting on the carpet.

"This is exactly the type of selfish behavior I've been warning you about."

"She was into it!" Flynn defended himself. "I mean *you* were into it."

Langhorne stood up from the bed and adjusted his suit. "She had too much to drink and you acted with no regard as to how it might affect her." Flynn looked up at him with a pained expression, but Langhorne was in no mood to feel sorry for his pathetic charge. "Despite what the taxi driver might have implied, there are rules that must be followed. Including rule number one thousand three hundred seven, subsection B."

"Rule one thousand three hundred seven?" Flynn said, incredulous.

"Subsection B. *No graduate will have intimate knowledge of an undergrad.*"

"How the hell was I supposed to know that?"

"You would have if you'd stayed put in the motel and

waited for me to explain everything—but even without going over the rules, I thought I was very clear that every action you take affects the world in ways large and small. And you will—"

"Bear the responsibility for my part, I got it. But this whole 'butterfly effect' deal is totally unfair. One small thing I do today blowing up a whole life twenty years later? It's chaos!"

"It's more elegant than that," Langhorne insisted. "You're still thinking of existence in a linear way, instead of accepting that the past, present, and future are all one moment that lasts an eternity."

"Tomato, tomahto, Langhorne. It's still cause and effect that screwed up somebody's life and landed me here with you."

"Yes, but, as it is only this moment that exists, determining responsibility is much simpler than you imagine. And if you would be still and focus, stop thinking about only yourself, it will be much simpler for you to determine what needs to be done."

Flynn let his droopy eyelids fully close. "I know what needs to be done."

"What?"

Flynn climbed to his feet. "I need to take a shower." He went into the bathroom and closed the door.

CHAPTER NINE

THE HOTEL MARIGOLD'S café extended outside onto the patio. Beyond a low flagstone wall ran the Ocean Front Walk, northward to the Santa Monica pier and southward to the Venice Boardwalk. Just past the walkway was a separate path for bicyclists and rollerbladers, and beyond that a wide expanse of sand dotted with a blue line of lifeguard stations looking over the undulating Pacific Ocean. At this early hour there weren't many people out, only a few exercise fanatics and a handful of eager tourists. As a gift, Langhorne had allowed Flynn to remain at the Marigold rather than return to the roach motel on Western, explaining that, unlike the taxi driver, he truly did have only his best interests in mind.

Flynn sat at a corner table, a patio umbrella shielding him from the morning sun, feeling once again like a movie star—a star evidently being wooed by two competing studios. He took a sip of freshly-squeezed orange juice and said to Langhorne, "I'm sorry about last night. I was, you know, I had just died, and I was trying to cheer myself up."

Langhorne swallowed a bite of bacon and shook his head. "*Graduated.*"

"And I'm gonna start focusing, I promise."

"And following the rules? No more sex with undergrads? No more running around without permission?"

"It's like I'm still on parole. But, yeah, sure. Whatever it takes to get all this squared away and move on." Flynn took a bite of his over-easy eggs. "I figure a good place to start would be by tracking down the dude whose identity I stole, see if I screwed him up in any way."

"Excellent idea." Langhorne patted at his clothes. "Now where did I put that book?" He removed a small brown leather notebook from his inside coat pocket and handed it across the table to Flynn. "You'll need this."

Flynn read the cover: *The Happy Graduate Rule Book*. "Is this when you tell me not to say Beetlejuice three times in a row?"

Langhorne blanched. "Oh, you should never do that."

"Really?"

Langhorne smiled. "Not really. But there are rules against summoning spirits. Make sure you read over that section. I had intended to give the book to you after you spent some time in personal reflection; it's much more useful once you have a firmer grasp on your intentions. At the very least, you would have known better than to seduce an undergrad."

The book was the size of a notepad and thin, no more than an inch thick. But no matter how many pages Flynn flipped past, there was seemingly an unending supply of more. The issue for Flynn wasn't the physics of such a phenomenon, but that each page was filled with dense blocks of black ink; only the edges of each page showed any white. "I think the last happy graduate used the wrong highlighter," he said, turning the book so Langhorne could see.

"I'm sorry," Langhorne said, pulling out a pair of glasses. "You'll need these."

The black reading glasses had thick frames matched in loathsome bulkiness by the lenses themselves. "Haven't you people heard of Ray-Bans?" Flynn asked.

"They're a bit short on style, but they do the trick."

Flynn put the glasses on and immediately felt their considerable weight. They were so heavy, in fact, he needed to tilt his head back to keep them from sliding off the end of his nose. Looking at the rollerbladers along the bike path, Flynn blinked a few times. Instantly, he felt as though he were on the deck of a heaving ship. If he had been standing, he would undoubtedly have fallen over for lack of balance and depth perception.

"They're not recommended for distance," Langhorne informed him. "I suggest you look down."

Flynn lowered his line of sight, pushing the slipping glasses back up the bridge of his nose, and then jutted his chin forward to keep them there. Bringing the book up a few inches, his eyes finally focused on the page. Where once had been nothing but blocks of impenetrable black, perfectly clear letters emerged, word after word, paragraph upon paragraph, with endless subsets and footnotes on each page. It would take months, if not years, to get through it all.

He ripped the glasses off his face. "You gotta be kidding me with this shit."

"It's a bit overwhelming," Langhorne conceded. "But you'll catch on." He pushed his chair from the table and stood. "Take the book with you when you track down this fellow you stole from and refer to it as needed."

"Take the book? Aren't you coming with me?"

Langhorne ate his last piece of cantaloupe and wiped his hands with a napkin. "I'll have to catch up with you later. Right now, I have orientation with a young man from Oklahoma who urinated on an electric fence."

Though he wouldn't admit it, Flynn wished Langhorne would stick around. He glanced again at the rulebook, wondering how he would ever be able to retain any of it. When he looked back up Langhorne was gone, and in his place stood a concerned-looking waiter. "Will there be anything else, Sir?" the waiter asked.

Flynn whipsawed his head around, trying to catch sight of the departed Facilitator. "Did you see him leave?"

"Who's that, Sir?"

"The guy I was eating breakfast—" Flynn let the rest die on his tongue. He saw then that his was the only place setting, as if Langhorne had never been there at all. "Forget it," he mumbled. Suddenly, the reaction of the hotel maids on the bus made much more sense. In deference to Flynn's delicate sensibilities, the waiter smiled kindly and headed off.

Flynn settled himself, placed the glasses back on his nose, tilted his chin up and began to read.

The tract houses were nicely kept. Every lawn was shorn with steadfast uniformity, save for a rather broken-down, two-bedroom surrounded by a chain-link construction fence at the end of the block. Basketball hoops sprouted in front of most of the houses, as if some "driveway recreation" law had been passed requiring a garage hoop ratio of three to one on every block. Mature sycamore trees lined the street, offering nice shade, though their thick, meandering roots intermittently buckled the sidewalk. Flynn walked up the sidewalk reading the rule book, black glasses balanced on his wide face. Every so often he tripped on the uplifted walkway, steadied himself, and continued on.

He flipped a page of the rule book and let out a sigh. Rule twelve-hundred-and-five prohibited him from simply giving his victim a bunch of money. He ran a searching finger down the page. And no dice on rigging the lottery, either.

Racing toward him on the sidewalk were three twelve-year-old boys on matching BMX bicycles, pedaling furiously with their stick-figure legs. When it became clear the path would not be obediently cleared for their hard-charging assault, one of the boys yelled a bit less helpfully than he could have, "Watch out, dork!"

Flynn looked up from the rule book and his eyes swelled behind the bulky lenses, the sudden change in depth perception sending his equilibrium sloshing like a half-empty pail of water. As the first of the kids wheeled past, Flynn shuffled sideways, trying to steady himself, but tripped on a ragged crest of cement. He fell into a heap on the ground, sending the glasses flying from his face. The other two kids swerved around him, spokes whirring, and they all continued on, laughing at his expense.

Flynn yelled, "You're lucky rule twenty-seven prevents me from kicking your puny little asses!"

He gathered up the glasses and rule book and put them in his pocket. With newfound determination (and clear vision), he rechecked the address he had found after a simple Google search and marched up to the house of the man whose life he may or may not have destroyed by clearing out his bank account. Settling himself, he knocked on the door.

It had been over two years since Flynn had last confronted his victim in court and he was a bit apprehensive about facing him again. *It's a nice house,* he thought in an effort to lighten his sense of foreboding. *He can't be doing so badly. All the* same, he was thankful for *the face* and its guarantee that he wouldn't be recognized. But when the door opened, it was not his victim who stood before him but a small-framed, bony old man with brown spots on his bald scalp that looked like flattened chocolate-chips. "Who're you?" the old man asked.

Flynn had to think a moment. With all the changes he'd been dealing with, actually naming himself anew had not occurred to him. Standing there, with the old man staring him down, he grew flustered and could only come up with "Bob." His inflection went up when he said it though, as if asking a question rather than stating a fact. The old man's overgrown eyebrows stitched together, and he asked Flynn if he was sure. Flynn briefly considered changing his name to something cooler, like Ace, but decided it would be strange to do so. And he had no interest in adding to the strange quotient.

"Bob," Flynn stated again, this time more definitively.

"What can I do for you, Bob?"

"I, uh, I'm looking for Scotty Schaffer."

The old man's expression lightened. "Ah, you mean my son."

"Is he here?"

"'Fraid not. He moved out a little over a year ago."

"That's just perfect," Flynn groused, hope for a speedy resolution fading.

The old man's expression turned suspicious and his demeanor shifted accordingly. "Are you a friend of his?"

Put on the spot, Flynn did what he did best. He lied. "I am. I'm an old friend from school." Good. Keep it general, let the mark fill in the details. Grade school, high school, veterinarian school, it didn't matter. Whatever the mark offered, that's where he knew him from.

The old man stepped out onto the porch and brushed his hand over the back of his leathery neck. "You went to Grant with Scotty?"

"That's right…Grant."

"High school was a long time ago."

High school! Okay. Now throw in some detail. Really sell it. "I was actually a grade behind him, but we hung out together, especially during his senior year."

The old man chortled. "You must have been one of those marching band kids he was always packing around with."

"Exactly! Trombone for life."

"You're still playing then?"

"Every chance I get. Not often enough, though. I have some elbow issues. What about Scotty? He still playing?"

The old man bit a small piece of skin hanging off the cuticle of his thumb and then blew it away with a small puff. "'Fraid not." His voice trailed off, leaving Flynn to fill in a hole he had no way of knowing the size of.

"Is he still living in the neighborhood?" he asked.

The old man gazed down the street with a fond remembrance and then shook his head. "No, he ran into some financial difficulties and moved out to Idaho where his aunt lives."

"Is that right?" Flynn said, his stomach lurching.

"He needed some distance after his girlfriend left him. He was convinced they were gonna get married, but she got real upset on account of his business goin' bankrupt. You can appreciate how hard that can be on a relationship."

"Oh, crap."

"He had one of those mobile dog grooming vans. Primping Pups he called it."

"But he came out of it okay, right?" Flynn asked, his mouth dry.

"Well, it was a bad time for him." The old man paused a moment, as if going on was difficult. "Unfortunately, he put his hand through a bathroom window out of frustration after running into trouble with some two-bit crook 'round the same time. Got some pretty bad nerve damage and lost the feeling in his fingers." The old man shook his head at the memories flooding back. "It was a damn stupid thing for him to do. With everything else going to shit, playing the clarinet was about the only thing that brought him any pleasure at all. I'm sure you know all about the pleasure music can bring a person. Of course, now that's all gone."

Flynn stumbled to a dusty porch bench, burying his head in his palms, picturing the lonely, broke, one-handed clarinetist trying to find work grooming dogs in Idaho.

"You all right?" the old man asked.

"No," Flynn said, wiping his sweaty palms through his unkempt hair.

"I didn't mean to upset you."

"It's not your fault. It's mine."

"If it's something to do with my son, I'm sure he'd be happy to talk with you if you give me a number."

"It won't do any good at this point."

"You never know. I'll have him call you as soon as he gets back from his honeymoon."

Flynn looked up. "Honeymoon?"

"They went to St. Barts. Two weeks. 'Course she'd been there before on one of her modeling gigs."

Flynn quickly stood. "He married a model?"

"Samantha, yes. She's one of those Sports Illustrated swim-suit girls."

"Holy shit!"

"She's a good cook, too. Makes him very happy. But between you and me, I'm not convinced she would've fallen for him if he hadn't hit it so big with that Bitcoin nonsense."

"Bitcoin?"

"The virtual currency; they're mining it or trading it, or something like that. I don't understand how it works, but my sister got him started out there in Idaho when he moved in with her. Made millions. Craziest thing I ever saw. Turns out, that move to Idaho was the best thing ever happened to him."

Flynn was instantly transformed. Like a spent balloon shot full of helium. "Yes!" he shouted, jabbing his fists wildly into the air. "In your *face*, destiny!"

The old man reared back with a quick laugh, surprised and pleased. "I suppose that's one way of putting it."

With the twin drugs of relief and joy overwhelming the synapses in his flushed brain, Flynn grabbed the old man by the shoulders and kissed his spotted bald scalp. "You just made my day, pops! Or my year, or lifetime or whatever. With time it's all one thing anyway, right?"

The old man blinked at him. "I'm afraid you lost me there."

"You'll understand some day," Flynn assured him. He stepped back and squinted. "Actually, could be pretty soon by the look of things. Do me a favor and say hey to your son for me next time you talk."

"Of course, yes. What was your last name again?"

Flynn shrugged. "Does it really matter?"

"Well, yeah."

"Then let's say…Intrilligator."

"Bob Intrilligator?"

"Sure," Flynn laughed. "Why not?" He jumped off the porch and excitedly ran off, stopping short to turn back and ask one final question. "By the way, do you know what issue of Sports Illustrated Samantha was in?" Before the old man could answer, Flynn decided this wonderful turn of events might earn him some much-needed karmic bonus points and he didn't want to blow it. "You know what, forget it! Doesn't matter."

Flynn ran off, leaving the old man to stare after him, utterly confused. He watched the lumpy-faced friend of his only son run wildly up the street until he was completely out of sight. "Crazy musicians," he grunted as he walked back into his house and closed the door behind him.

CHAPTER TEN

THE KING'S DRAGON was packed, all attention on the moon-faced man holding the darts. He, in turn, reveled in the cheers rising up from the excited crowd. Flynn had set out to find Langhorne but had given up when his thoughts turned to beer. And now, halfway to fall-down-drunk after discovering an interesting footnote on page six hundred and five of *The Happy Graduate Rule Book*, he stood on the toe line, prepared to display an amazing newfound prowess.

With the crowd spurring him on, he whipped a quick succession of three darts toward the board exactly seven feet, nine-and-a-quarter inches away. Thwap! Thwap! Thwap! The first dart landed squarely in the bull's-eye, the second stuck in the end of the first, directly between the flights, and the third stuck into the end of the second, creating one long arrow.

The astonished crowd erupted in merry favor of this modern-day Robin Hood. Flynn turned triumphantly and waved toward the bar. "Drinks are on me!" he shouted above the din. The crowd erupted again, offering an avalanche of pats and handshakes as he wound his way to the bar.

"Hell of a show!" the bartender said.

"A perfectly useless talent," Flynn said as he sat down.

"Are you that talented at everything you do?" a woman behind him asked.

Flynn spun around to see a tall brunette with heavy-lidded eyes smiling at him. He patted the small book in his pocket. "I guess that depends on what the rule book has to say about it."

She giggled, leaning closer, her low-slung blouse revealing a steep valley of milky skin. "How 'bout that drink?" she asked.

Flynn chuckled. "Nice try."

Her playful smile faded a few degrees. "Excuse me?"

"I'll get you whatever drink you'd like," Flynn drunkenly said, "but I'm not falling for this again."

"Falling for what?"

"Oh, please. How stupid do you think I am? Dart groupies don't exist. And another thing, if I may? You enjoy pretending you're a woman a little too much."

The brunette's expression soured. "What's your problem, asshole?"

An uneasy concern crept into Flynn's voice. "Langhorne?"

She slapped him, then pushed her way back through the crowd.

"That didn't go very well," the bartender said, placing a fresh beer in front of Flynn.

"A little misunderstanding is all." Flynn tested his jaw and found it fully functional.

"If you're still buying though," came Thacker's familiar voice as he sat beside Flynn, "I'll have a Guinness."

"Hey! Thh, Thh, Thh—" the name couldn't get past the back of his teeth. "Wait a minute!" he said, thinking for a moment. "There's no reason I'd be able to say your name, because you never gave it to me, did you? Flynn would know, but not me."

"It's Thomas, but everyone calls me by my last name, Thacker."

"Thacker!" he drunkenly yelled out. "See? Now I can say it! And I can say my name now too, it's Bob. I couldn't remember it at Flynn's funeral because I got so emotional I went out of my head for a while."

Thacker's eyes widened. "Are ya sure you're back?"

Flynn's sloppy laugh exploded. "Oh, I'm back. Trust me."

"You're a strange man, you know that?"

"You have no idea."

"Small world, seeing you again."

"You come here a lot?" Flynn asked.

"Once or twice. Flynn told me about it."

"Yeah, me too." He took a deep drink of beer and plopped his glass back onto the bar. "Damn, I needed this."

"Been under some stress, have ya?"

"You have no idea," Flynn said, the alcohol pumping up his emotions. "It's not just Flynn's death, though that was a real kick in the ass, wasn't it? No, it's all the *thinking* and *reflecting* they want you to do that gets to me."

"Who?"

"Them! Everyone!"

"If you say so," Thacker said.

"I'm sure it's supposed to be all about *learning* and *growing* and *understanding* and all that shit. But it drives me nuts."

Thacker reached for the Guinness as it was placed in front of him. "You're a married man, are ya?"

Flynn sighed. "No. I just miss the life I used to have when there was nobody to worry about but myself."

Thacker chuckled. "You sound like Flynn."

"Yeah, well, you could say there was a time when he and I were inseparable."

"That right? I'm surprised he never mentioned you," Thacker said, studying him closely. "He and I were damn close." He shook his head. "It was a hell of a thing seeing him buried. But as they say, I'm sure he's in a better place."

"Not necessarily."

Thacker again stared, trying to figure him out.

"I mean," Flynn explained, "sometimes I feel like he's still here."

Thacker lifted his glass. "To Flynn."

Flynn raised his own nearly empty glass. "To Flynn, the best guy I ever knew."

Thacker's grin evaporated and his expression morphed into a mask of shock. Or maybe it was fear. "Oh, damn."

"What's the matter?" asked Flynn.

Thacker set down his Guinness and rose with a start. For a moment it seemed as though he was going to run off but decided against it. Flynn stood up beside his friend as three men approached through the boisterous crowd. One was a black man, maybe five-nine in boots, with an almost childlike appearance despite a thick goatee surrounding his mouth. The other two men were much larger, both at least six-three. One had bright red hair that fell flat against his chunky head. The other, the lead man, had shoulders wide enough to hang drapes from and the hardened body of a quarry worker, or possibly a dragon slayer. It was apparent they weren't there for the happy atmosphere. They moved slowly, like dark clouds moving in to blot out the sun.

The lead man stepped close to Thacker, his bright eyes

focused intently. *Chillingly*. It wasn't hard to imagine him as a glacier covered with skin; if he exhaled, frost would billow.

"Hey, Mr. Covington," Thacker stammered. "I was gonna come see you, I swear."

Hearing the name jolted Flynn into sobriety.

Covington spoke, his lips barely moving. "You were supposed to come see me four days ago." His Manchester accent was still pronounced despite all the years he'd lived in America. "Instead, I had to track you down to this piss-poor idea of a proper British pub."

"I know," Thacker said, quivering. "I'm sorry."

"I would hope so," Covington said. "Where are my goddamn masks?"

Flynn leaned closer to get a better look at Thacker. "What the hell is he talking about?" he asked.

The goateed thug shoved him back on his heels. "This doesn't concern you," he barked. The goatee was much stronger than he looked, or maybe Flynn's borrowed body was much weaker, but either way Flynn was badly overmatched.

Thacker's eyes remained fixed on Covington. "I don't know how to tell you this," he said, his voice begging forgiveness. It was an attitude Flynn had never seen in his friend and wouldn't have believed existed in him. Thacker swallowed hard, "I don't know where they are."

Flynn lost himself. "What?"

Covington remained ramrod straight, only his head turning toward the bothersome intruder. "Who the fuck are you?"

Flynn had no answer. His mouth again stopped working, this time due to fear, rather than some arcane rule he barely understood.

"He's nobody," said Thacker.

Covington grabbed him by the arm. "Enough of this shit. Let's go."

"Let me explain," Thacker said. "I've been trying to figure out what happened, but I have no idea where—"

"Shut the fuck up," Covington said, yanking him away from the bar.

"Wait!" Flynn shouted, stepping forward. This time the goatee met his advance with a well-placed jab to the gut, dropping him to his knees. He gasped for air, which brought a tremor of pain to his chest. Unable to straighten up, Flynn noticed a purposeful shuffle of feet around him. With another uneasy inhale, he was able to lift his head enough to see a burly man in a flannel shirt hovering over him. The man had the goatee by the throat, squeezing tight with knotted knuckles.

The goatee struggled to pull free from the grip, but the burly man merely regarded him like an irksome pimple set to be popped. More men from the bar stepped up to surround the action.

"Everyone take it easy!" the bartender yelled, remaining in relative safety behind the bar. "We don't need this in here."

Covington, still with his own vice grip on Thacker, remained calm, almost indifferent. "Listen to the man," he said, a distinct warning in his voice. "This doesn't concern any of you."

"The hell it doesn't," retorted the burly man. "*He's buying.*"

A roar of agreement sounded out from the crowd as someone within the mass of drunken humanity lifted Flynn to his feet. "I'm okay," he assured them, gracelessly spitting onto the floor as he continued to struggle to regain his breath. The burly man released his grip, and the goatee was now the one gasping for air, the bulging vein on his forehead slowly receding.

Covington, sensing the moment, again yanked Thacker away and started toward the entrance. On instinct, Flynn reached out to grab Thacker's free arm, gaining only a slight, tenuous hold of loose cloth.

Covington felt the tug on his shirtsleeve and the glacier at once turned into a volcano. He spun back and violently pushed Flynn with his free hand, sending him thudding against the edge of the bar. Flynn gathered himself quickly and again lurched forward but was swallowed by the surging crowd as the room became a whirlpool of pushing and shoving.

Someone grabbed Covington from behind and he lost his grip on Thacker as both the goatee and the redhead were clawed away from their boss by the professional drinkers of the King's Dragon Pub. But the three intruding Englishmen had been in these situations many times before and were well prepared for battle. All three were on the London police hooligan list for Manchester United soccer matches and possessed well-honed brawling skills. With a flash of aggression, the redhead and the goatee let loose a flurry of quick jabs and tight left hooks, sending the unlucky men close to them to the floor.

Other men quickly filled the space, throwing haymakers that connected only out of blind luck. But the Englishmen merely cracked fists with greater authority and enthusiasm, the more of their own blood they tasted. Bodies flew in all directions as eyes were gouged with precision and groins were grabbed and twisted into submission.

Pushing his way through the fog of testosterone, Flynn reached Thacker, but Covington arrived at the same moment and drove his elbow into Flynn's teeth, knocking one clean out of his mouth with a spurt of mucous and blood, sending him to the ground beneath the dartboards.

Seizing the moment of distraction, Thacker made his move for the front door, but Covington was too quick. Like a striking snake, he grabbed Thacker's neck from behind and used the fleeing Brit's own momentum to drive him forward through the crowd like a battering ram, followed by the other two hooligans, who were actually *smiling* with bloody joy at the havoc they'd instigated.

It had taken only a few moments of anarchy for the King's Dragon regulars to retreat and salvage what remained of their wounded egos. Most of those who lingered at the front of the out-muscled pack decided the best course of action against the hard-fisted intruders was to puff out their chests and yell obscenities as loudly as they could. In fact, only one person remained with any real ammunition.

Flynn stood with six darts clutched in his hands. Covington was seconds away from making his escape with Thacker, as Flynn pivoted his elbow forward like a precisely engineered lever and let the dart loose. The dart soared on a perfect arc above the heads of the intoxicated crowd, before coming down deeply into the soft flesh of Covington's neck. The massive Brit yelped in pain as the goatee yanked open the front door of the King's Dragon. Covington took another half-step toward freedom before the second dart spun down to stab him in the back of the head. Blood trickled under the collar of his shirt and he cried out in agony, but his hold on Thacker never loosened.

Two more darts were launched like miniature ICBM's, one finding Covington's left tricep, the other his right.

Under the stress of the air assault, Covington finally lost his grip on Thacker, who made a move for freedom. But the goatee tripped him, sending him hard to his knees. Like wild dogs, the hooligans regathered their prey and hustled him outside, but not before two more darts shuttled through the door with them. As the door slammed, the goatee's anguished yelps trailed back into the pub.

Pushing his way through the hyped-up throng, with cheers rising for his marksmanship, Flynn pushed his way to the exit. Bursting through the door, he ran onto the sidewalk just in time to see Thacker being hustled into a waiting car.

"Thacker!" he yelled as the car peeled away. His focus intensified as he gave chase, unwilling to give up on his friend.

Flynn jumped from the curb into the street, taking two long strides before the earsplitting blare of a horn stole his attention. He had no time to react before a city bus barreled over him, crushing him into the pavement.

CHAPTER ELEVEN

Flynn awoke in his childhood bedroom, staring up at the toy plane hanging from the ceiling. His right leg itched under his cowboy pajamas. He scratched it gingerly, expecting to find it mangled from the collision. But there was no pain, and no apparent damage to his body. And it was his body, he noticed. He'd returned to his old, corporeal self, but it gave him no pleasure.

He impatiently flung off the Lone Ranger bedspread and paced the room. He could not fathom what had happened to the masks. If Thacker didn't know where they were, who had them? "Come on, Langhorne," he yelled, "Where the hell are you?"

Unable to wait or remain still, he yanked open the bedroom door and ran forward, and of course found himself stepping right back into the room.

Langhorne was standing next to the dresser, smiling at him. "It's a neat little trick, isn't it?"

"Where have you been?" Flynn asked. "I've been waiting for like—" He couldn't calculate the amount of time he'd been waiting because as a graduate, the import of time as a meaningful measurement was gradually receding. "You should be here when I need you!" he snapped.

"I had an ice floe break apart in Norway," Langhorne explained. "It got very busy."

"Do you have any idea what's going on?"

"Yes. And rule number sixteen thousand two clearly states, 'You are not a ghost, so do not step in front of any fast-moving objects.' I really thought you'd have that one down by now. Maybe we should go over the rule book together."

"Forget the rule book," Flynn shouted.

Langhorne shook his head. "We don't do that."

"Haven't you ever heard that rules are made to be broken?"

"Okay, I admit, I promised you hands-on attention and I haven't delivered. From now on I'm going to give you my full—hey! Black Beauty!" He picked up a horse figurine from the dresser.

"That's the Black *Stallion*," Flynn corrected him. "And can we please focus?"

Langhorne returned the horse to the bureau and set his face intently, "Sorry."

"Everything got screwed up," Flynn said, again pacing the room. "It wasn't the guy I stole from who's in trouble. In fact, you need to cut me some slack on account of the favor I did that lucky son-of-a-bitch."

"It's all taken into account, I assure you."

"It's *Thacker* I have to worry about. Something happened and he never got the masks we smuggled from Peru to this dude Covington who stole them from some museum down there."

"Yes, I know."

"You know?"

"Of course."

"Then fucking help me! Tell me what's going on!"

"I've explained to you how this works. You need to take responsibility for your behavior and choices, and then figure it out for yourself. All I can do is facilitate your efforts and keep you updated on the Probability Indexes, which will undoubtedly change anyway."

"I'm getting tired of this shit, Langhorne. Can you at least tell me where they took Thacker? Can you *facilitate* that much?"

Langhorne took a deep breath. "I'm afraid it's not good."

A shudder swept through Flynn. "Oh God," he said, sitting on the bed as if what was to follow might send him to the ground. "They killed him, didn't they?"

"No. Mr. Thacker hasn't graduated."

"Then, where is he?"

"He's been admitted to Saint John's hospital in Santa Monica."

Flynn imagined the beating that landed Thacker in the hospital. Covington's anger was undoubtedly stoked by the events at the King's Dragon and he would have released his fury on the only target he had—all that enraged energy flowing through his fists until his hands ached and the fire in his belly was extinguished.

Flynn stood up from the bed. "I have to see him."

Langhorne considered him.

"What now?" Flynn asked, impatiently.

"Perhaps we should consult the rule book first."

"Are you saying there's a rule against me going?"

"No, no. But, just like the rule book helped you discover a graduate's capacity with throwing darts, perhaps there's something in there that will help at the hospital."

Flynn immediately regretted the darts. They had only

added fuel to Covington's unhinged sociopathy and had done Thacker no favors. Whatever Langhorne had in mind, Flynn was intent on making sure it wouldn't later come back to bite him in the ass. He reached for *The Happy Graduate Rule Book* on the bedside table and put on the chunky glasses.

"What exactly am I looking for?" he asked.

"Try page seven hundred and twelve," Langhorne suggested.

Flynn flipped through the book and read. "Yeah," he said, nodding. "That would be great. That's some nice facilitating, Langhorne. I appreciate it."

"Thank you."

And then a spark flashed above, and Flynn was once again yanked upward toward the ceiling.

A heavyset nurse in soft white shoes padded her way up the intensive care corridor of Saint John's hospital. The quiet hall smelled of cleaning solution, pain, and worry. She passed an orderly pushing a linen cart with a squeaky wheel and continued on toward the nurse's station, where her stash of Butterfinger candy bars was hidden under the counter.

She bit into the crunchy chocolate and peanut butter just as the tall, deeply dimpled doctor rounded the corner, glancing into each room as he went. "Afternoon, doctor," the nurse said, quickly swallowing her secret treat.

The doctor nodded absently. "How ya doin?" The nurse gawked at him curiously. Having not taken the time to adequately prepare, Flynn had forgotten his new role. His voice dropped to a warm baritone. "I mean, good day to you as well."

The nurse had seen the administration memo detailing the hospital privileges granted to the visiting doctor, but the memo hadn't mentioned how handsome he was. The phone rang at the station and she placed her hand on the receiver without picking it up or averting her eyes. "Is there something I can help you with?" she asked with a smile, unaware she had a large globule of chocolate staining her two front teeth.

"Thomas Thacker?" Flynn asked.

She pointed to the Intensive Care Unit opposite the station.

As Flynn walked away, she picked up the receiver, her eyes never rising above the tight catch of scrubs framing his perfectly sculpted ass.

Inside the room were four beds, only two of which were occupied. On one lay a sleeping middle-aged man hooked up to a heart monitor; a meaty scar ran the length of his bloated torso. The severely angular nurse attending to the man's damp wound dressings glanced up briefly before continuing intently with her work.

Flynn crossed to the opposite end of the room, where Thacker lay unconscious, a saline drip IV snaking into his left forearm. A bandage covered much of his forehead, and a deep split on his lower lip had been sewn together, the five black stitches poking out like laces on a football. His eye sockets were swollen, and his left cheek was deeply bruised in an uneven purplish pattern. Flynn studied the damage and saw only his own failings as a friend.

It took him a few moments to find his words in the presence of so much pain. "I'm gonna do whatever it takes to help you," he said. "I promise."

The nurse behind him cleared her throat, and Flynn instinctively grabbed the chart hanging next to the bed.

He glanced at the nurse, then flipped open Thacker's chart, pretending to scan the information. When his eyes met the page however, a curious thing happened—his mind actually *interpreted* the information it gathered. He read over the chart again, paying closer attention. "Looks like they've got you on Lasix, forty milligrams," Flynn found himself saying. "That's fine, but I would have put you on twelve-point-five Mannitol." He flinched with the realization that he actually knew what the hell he was talking about. Throwing darts was child's play compared to his refreshed abilities. "How cool is this?" he whispered under his breath.

He flipped another page on the chart, hoping to find something more to test his newfound intellect, when the erratic beating of the scarred man's heart monitor pierced the soothing hum of the room. Flynn lowered Thacker's chart, turning toward the commotion. "That doesn't sound very good," he said. At once, the bed alarm, the heart rate alarm, and the blood pressure monitor all began blaring with an insistent cacophony of warning. A distant PA announced, "Code Blue, ICU. Code Blue, ICU."

"He's in V-fib!" the nurse called out. Now a fluid melody of action and vitality, she began CPR, using her full weight to press down on the dying man's scarred chest. "Let's go," she said to Flynn, all business, no panic.

"They'll be here in a second," Flynn said, pointing through the double glass doors at the station nurse on the phone.

"Get the defibrillator!" the nurse said, still pumping the man's chest.

Flynn's mind blanked. He followed the nurse's eyes to the defibrillator cart opposite him. *Think. Think.* And when he did, it was as if a levee broke away. An ocean of serotonin washed over him, and an encyclopedia of knowledge flooded his brain, begging to be let loose. At once, his mind lurched and shifted from neutral to high gear.

He dragged the cart to the side of the bed as four more nurses rushed into the room. "Charge de-fib to two hundred," he barked at the new arrivals. "Increase dopamine to ten. Give him Eppi, one amp. Start lidocaine and increase his oxygen to a hundred." The team worked in unison, one setting IVs, another administering oxygen, another rifling through a large red chest of medications, pulling what was ordered. When the paddles were fully charged, Flynn grabbed them from one of the newly arrived nurses and shouted "clear" before placing them on the man's chest. *Fwap!* A powerful electric current splintered through the bloated mass like an infinite multitude of torpedoes targeting the rapidly fading heart. The man's body jolted in response, but the monitor still pinged with relentless urgency. "Again!" Flynn reset the paddles on the man's chest. *Fwap!* The man's body heaved, then instantly calmed, as did the pinging of the monitor. "He's back in sinus," said the nurse who had been performing CPR, glancing up to record the man's T-wave activity. "His pressure's up."

Flynn noticed yet another five nurses, doctors, and respiratory therapists had arrived. "Take that, Ms. Chapman!" he said to them all. They each gave a quizzical squint. "Tenth grade biology teacher," he said. "Gave me a D-minus."

As the attending physician, a bespectacled man with bad breath and a reedy voice, pushed his way to the bedside and began running the code, assessing the patient and giving further orders, Flynn burst from the ICU, bravado wafting from him like a pungent cologne, the authority to heal raising him to new heights of arrogance.

He practically bounded down the hall, winking at every nurse that had the pleasure of passing him by. *The face* was gone and in its place was the finely chiseled facade of the ultimate daytime television stud. Saint John's had a new resident, and he was damn ready for his fan mail.

He should have left the hospital to begin figuring out how he was going to tackle the Covington problem, but his ego was in charge now, not his newly calibrated brain. He found a nervous young woman in her room and calmed her with a performance of God-like authority he cribbed from an Alec Baldwin movie he'd seen on an airplane. "After the biopsy," he explained to the woman, after looking over her chart, "we'll check you for CMV, Aspergillis, and TB. In the meantime, you're on mega-doses of steroids, cyclosporine, and FK five-zero-six." He then gave her his best soap opera stare. "Don't look so worried. All that mumbo-jumbo just means that I'm not going to let anything happen to you."

Leaving the woman behind, he moved on to a faltering, seventy-eight-year-old grandfather holding hands with the only woman he had loved for over fifty years. "Your echo-cardio-gram shows severe mitral-valve regurgitation," Flynn informed him. "Until the valve can be replaced with a porcine graft, you'll be on Beta-blockers to keep your pressure stabilized. We'll keep an eye on it, but we don't expect any problems."

"Yes," the pale grandfather said, "that's what our regular doctor told us. But my wife is so worried."

Flynn cupped a steady hand under the woman's chin, raising her watery eyes to his. "Remember," he said to her, "hope is a good thing, maybe the best of things, and no good thing ever dies."

She sighed. "That's beautiful."

"I've heard that before," the grandfather said. "Isn't that a line from The Shawshank Redemption?"

Flynn shook his head. "I don't think so, no."

And so the day went. He checked in on several more lonely patients, stepped between a group of doctors huddled around a light box to point out the irregularity on an x-ray they surely would have missed, flirted with a few nurses, and generally had a fine afternoon.

There was, however, one patient beyond his help. Flynn found him in a darkened room covered with a white sheet, waiting for some bored orderly to wheel him down to the morgue. There were no personal effects in the room, no family photos, no half-read magazines or books on the counter, not even the drooping remnants of a flower bouquet to announce that someone had once cared. After a long day's flurry of exhilarating encounters, Flynn was struck by the abject loneliness of the moment, the unsettling quiet of the physical endgame of life. A fleeting sense of loss passed through him as he lifted the sheet and stared.

An elderly black man with skin so ashen it was nearly white lay on the bed. His eyes were deeply recessed and his lips dry and cracked. With frail hair curling out of his withered scalp, he looked like a shrunken head from New Guinea. "Don't know if anyone was here to see you off," he said. "But congrats on your graduation."

The old man's eyes popped open and rose forward from the recesses of his skull, his lips blooming red as they came to life. "Having fun?" the body asked. Flynn shuddered and fell to the ground, the bedsheet still clutched in his hand. The body sat up and grew taller, its features elongating into Langhorne's familiar face.

"What's wrong with you!" Flynn shouted, struggling to free himself from the sheet tangled between his legs. "Stop doing that!"

"Physician, heal thyself," Langhorne said, smoothing out his peach-colored suit. "You do understand you're not *really* a doctor?"

"What's the big deal? I wasn't hurting anyone. In fact, I helped save some dude's life. I'm sure he didn't mind me playing doctor."

"And Mr. Thacker? How's he?"

Flynn stood and tossed the sheet onto the now-empty bed. "Beat to hell, but he's gonna be fine. He should be out of the ICU tomorrow and moved to a regular bed for observation."

"Very encouraging," Langhorne said. "Unfortunately, it's not all good news."

"Meaning what?"

Langhorne's expression turned plaintive. "I'm afraid there's something you need to see."

CHAPTER TWELVE

AN LAPD OFFICER met Detective Paul Putman in the parking lot of Bannon Imports and led him inside.

In the breezy space below the raised warehouse door, a gathering of employees huddled like scared children. "Excuse us," the officer said.

As the crowd shifted and the officer led a detective through, Hannah from accounting whimpered. "Who would do such a thing?"

Crates, boxes, and scales were overturned, and most of the shelving units were swept clean. Thick reams of wool were scattered across the floor like felled trees in a graveyard comprised of sneakers from China, readymade garments from Bangladesh, jeans from Vietnam, and leather jackets from Italy. It was a veritable United Nations of textile destruction. The metal steps leading to the loft were strewn with the ravaged contents of the office, including a massively dented file cabinet that looked as if it had been beaten with a baseball bat. Uniformed officers sifted through the mess, snapping photos and cataloging the damage, while others interviewed workers.

Flynn moved past Hannah and the others and trailed behind the officer leading the detective through the damage, lingering within earshot as they approached Jimmy Bannon. Jimmy slumped in a folding chair at a righted table, holding an icepack to the side of his head. His left eye was badly swollen with a red bruise that was on its way to purple. His lower lip was cut, and though it was no longer bleeding it would probably need a few stitches. Andy and Hoyt stood behind Jimmy, worriedly taking in the proceedings. In all of the commotion, none of them noticed the handsome doctor who was pretending not to eavesdrop.

"Mr. Bannon," the officer said as they approached, "this is Detective Putman."

Both Jimmy and Hoyt said hello at the same time.

"I'm Hoyt Bannon," Hoyt clarified. "This is my son, Jimmy."

Putman gave them both an amused nod. He was probably close to Hoyt's age, but with his jet-black hair and smooth black face, he looked fifteen years younger. "How're you feeling?" he said to the younger Bannon.

"Okay."

"Then I guess you feel better than you look."

Jimmy smiled and winced at the sharp pain it brought on.

"Have you been seen by a paramedic?" Putman asked.

"Yes, sir," Jimmy said. "They said I might have a concussion."

"I'll make this as quick as I can. It's my understanding you were the only one here this morning?"

"Yes."

"What time was that?"

"A little after five."

"Are you always here that early?" the detective asked.

"No. It's because we have inventory." Jimmy looked at his father apologetically. Hoyt put a reassuring hand on his son's shoulder and left it there throughout the remainder of the interview. "It should have been done by now," Jimmy continued, "but we've had some problems, so I've been working overtime to catch up. As soon as I opened the door, they grabbed me and pushed me inside."

"How many were there?"

"Three."

"You get a good look at them?"

"Not really. I can tell you that two of them were really tall and the third guy was short, and had a goatee."

"He was black, I understand? The shorter one? The other two were white?"

"We already went over this with the officer," Hoyt interjected.

Putman smoothed out his already smooth tie. "I'd like to hear it myself," he said. "Let me get through this, so your son can get some rest." He looked back to Jimmy. "I ask because the officer you spoke to mentioned that you thought they might have had Jamaican accents?"

Jamaican? Flynn wanted to scream.

"I don't know, maybe?" Jimmy said. "I thought British at first, but it wasn't like James Bond or the Queen or something. It sounded different, you know? But only the one guy was black, so I guess it'd be weird if they were all Jamaican."

"There are white Jamaicans," Putman said.

"Really? But one of them had red hair, so…"

"There's redheaded Jamaican's too. It's a place, not a race."

They're not fucking Jamaican! Flynn fumed.

"What did they say to you?" asked Putman.

"Asked me for the keys to the loft office, but I didn't have them. Then they asked about a safe. We have one upstairs, but I didn't have the key to that either. I don't think they believed me, because the one guy, the one with the goatee, started hitting me." He hesitated and his eyes briefly twitched to Andy, then back to the detective. "They were also talking about Flynn having worked here."

Andy's jaw clenched. Flynn stepped closer, straining to hear.

"Your brother," Detective Putman said to Andy.

"Yes, sir," Andy said. "He worked here for a few months."

"After getting out of prison," Putman said, his observation carrying an unmistakable, and appropriate, suspicion.

Andy sighed. "Yes."

"I understand he recently passed?"

"A week ago," Andy said. "He drove his car off the road up on Mulholland. It was an accident. He hadn't been drinking or anything. It was just bad luck, I guess."

Putman nodded, offered no condolences. "What was he in prison for?"

"I'm guessing you already know that, too."

"Humor me."

Andy's jaw flexed again. "He was a thief."

The concise summation staggered Flynn. His entire life, everything he was, distilled to its very essence. He was a thief, nothing more, nothing less.

"Excuse me," a voice came from behind, stealing Flynn's attention. He turned to see the uniformed cop step up. "Do you work here?" the officer asked.

"No, I work up the street," Flynn said, easily slipping into another lie. "I was passing by and saw all the commotion. What happened? Is everyone all right?"

"This is a crime scene, sir," the officer said. "They had a

break-in. If you're not an employee, I'm gonna have to ask you to leave."

There was nothing left for Flynn to discover, so with a quick glance back at his brother, Hoyt, and the detective still grinding away on Jimmy, he walked out of the warehouse.

It was a hot day, which added yet another layer of misery. He wandered aimlessly, perspiration turning to sweat as he made his way up the sidewalk, lost in that shadowed section of his mind he rarely visited, let alone wallowed in—the part that housed feelings of regret. What if Jimmy had been killed by Covington and his men, he wondered. That would have been his fault. He did his best to push the notion away. And what if it hadn't been Jimmy? What if it had been Hannah, or Manny, or one of the secretaries, or Hoyt, or Andy? So many people he had indirectly put into harm's way. Shame pulsed through his body, confusing him. The pulses were as unfamiliar as the skin that he was presently wrapped in. Everything, his entire existence, felt foreign to him. It was as though he'd been struck by a virus circulating discomfort, spiking a fever one moment, then casting chills the next. So he did what came naturally—he tried to rationalize his way out of the unwanted feelings of guilt and responsibility.

This wasn't even his body. His body was in a box buried six feet underground, so how could he know these were truly his feelings? Since this wasn't his body, how could he know if it was even his own mind that was worrying so much? And if this wasn't his mind, how could he trust that these were even his thoughts? His stream-of-consciousness effort to straighten out this conundrum went on. If it wasn't his body, nor his mind, nor his thoughts, then he wasn't truly involved at all. But if he, Flynn, the true Flynn, was not intricately involved, then it would be a complete waste of everyone's time to convince him that he was. Well, not a waste of Flynn's time, because if this wasn't his mind or his body then he's evidently off doing something else. But if this really wasn't Flynn's mind or his body, then where was Flynn? Was there some reality beyond personal perception?

This is precisely why Flynn never allowed himself to think too deeply about things: it only confused him further. Though thinking of himself in the third person was jarring enough to convince him that only his own mind would find it unsettling in the first place.

As he walked, cars whipped past, horns blared, distant voices trailed in and out, birds chirped, planes flew overhead, people passed by, but none of it distracted him; he could not outpace his thoughts. Eventually, he became convinced that while his *body* had flown the coop, it was indeed his own *self* working to separate itself from any feelings of responsibility. What now?

Jimmy was ultimately fine, he rationalized—a few bumps and scrapes is all—and there was little use going on about things that could have happened but did not. But Thacker. Unlike Jimmy, he had been beaten close to death. So Flynn focused on the fact that Thacker had *wanted* to go into business with him. It was Thacker who pushed the plan into action. And it was Thacker who had involved Covington. Under those terms, what happened to Jimmy was more Thacker's fault than his. But without his own involvement, Flynn thought, the whole plan would never have been put in motion. Crap.

In the end, no matter how hard he struggled to worm his way free from responsibility, he could not reject the reality facing him. At least partly because of his actions, Thacker was in the hospital, Jimmy was badly beaten, and Bannon Imports had been trashed. He took a deep breath. Now, what to do about it?

The noxious odor of engine exhaust assaulted his senses. A rusty taxi cab pulled to a stop a few feet away. The driver climbed out, lighting a cigarette.

"You're looking good there, Flynn!" The driver laughed a raspy discharge of fetid smog to match what spewed from the taxi. "Or should I call you Doctor Barnes now?"

"I was wondering when I'd see you again," Flynn said, pleased with the opportunity to get out of his own (borrowed) head.

The driver smiled, exposing his rotted gums. "Figured anything out?"

"Working on it."

"That Bannon kid sure got a raw deal." He leaned on the taxi's hood and lit a cigarette. "Bet you wish you could have prevented it. But how could you have known? Truth is, whatever it is you think you're gonna do about any of this, you're gonna fail. Remember, it's all a—"

"Shell game," Flynn said.

The driver went on casually. "It's actually more than that. I've seen it a million times and it's always the same. Making you figure out whose life you screwed up is only the beginning. Even if, miracle of miracles, you keep your eye on the right shell and figure out who you're supposed to help, the game comes with so many petty rules you won't be able to get anything done."

The familiar comfort with the driver washed over Flynn, calming him. The driver said everything with such certainty—an enviable quality—Flynn immediately assumed he was correct. It was like talking to an old friend who knew all his secrets, knew his mind better than even he did. Without much thought, he said, "I'm guessing you have a few suggestions?"

"Just one." The driver leaned forward. "Rules are made to be broken," he said, smiling knowingly. "Those were your very words, Flynn."

Flynn was not surprised the driver had that information: he seemed to know everything about him. He nodded.

"And it was very insightful," the driver went on. "In fact, no truer thing has ever been said. Except maybe, 'If the glove doesn't fit, you must acquit.' Where I come from, we really like that one, too."

A gnat of suspicion swirled into Flynn's thoughts and he casually waved at it by asking, "So you're gonna help me just to prove what a swell guy you are?"

The driver teased him with just enough information to keep him interested. "I wouldn't necessarily put it that way. Though I am a swell guy. I will say this much—I can give you what Langhorne can't." He let the offer hang like a string of yarn dangling in front of a cat.

Flynn knew he was being baited. "And what's that?"

The driver grinned. "A guarantee you'll succeed."

Flynn was drawn to the casual promise, to the ease and clarity of it. The driver inched forward and spoke to the base root of who Flynn Barnes was.

"Come with me right now and there will be no more rules, except for the ones you make. You can stop worrying about your brother, or your dad, or Erin, or that skinny little turd with the braces who should have learned a little self-defense. And you can definitely stop worrying about being *redeemed*. I promise you, redemption's overrated. In your heart you know you have nothing to be redeemed for anyway. Honestly, people like you do better in Hell. And it's not like it's depicted in the movies with all the fire and brimstone. Sure there's some of that, but overall, it's actually very nice, especially in the spring. Trust me, so-called *redemption* is the worst thing that could happen to a groovy guy like you. You'd miss out on all the fun. Instead, you can live for all eternity doing *whatever* you want, *whenever* you want. You'll be freer than you've ever thought possible."

Flynn's borrowed heart beat faster. The appeal of an after-life lived on his own terms was palpable, though he tried to remain casual, if not detached. "I'll give it some thought."

"Please do. Just don't take too long to decide." The driver tilted a thumb back toward the taxi. "All my boss cares about is the number of fares I book, and I'm gonna collect a fare from you one way or the other."

Flynn's cheeks flushed hot as the cocoon of kinship tore a little with the warning. "What do you mean by that?"

The driver laughed, spewing more rancid vapor from his belly. "I mean the meter's already running, my friend," he said.

"Flynn!" Langhorne's stern voice rang out. Flynn turned to see Langhorne striding up the sidewalk toward him, his face clouded with anger.

"Did you hear what he said to me?" Flynn asked quickly, irritably. The taxi driver was already inside his cab, pulling away.

Langhorne stepped closer. "I warned you not to talk to him."

Flynn's mind reeled. "What did he mean he'll be collecting his fare one way or the other?"

Langhorne's eyes looked dull and tired as he stared at him.

"Cut the bullshit," Flynn said. "I'm sick of this Facilitator red tape crap. It's time you told me the truth about what's going on."

After a long moment of silent consideration, Langhorne said, "I agree."

Flynn sat on the warm sand beyond the patio of the Hotel Marigold, staring at the waves crashing on shore, oblivious to the naïve undergrads lounging around him on their soft beach blankets, concerned only with their tans. The ocean seemed to spread out forever, but he knew it was merely an illusion. He knew that everything he saw would someday come to an end. "When you said I created a new destiny for someone," he said, "you weren't kidding around."

Langhorne remained standing behind him. "I wanted to wait until you were ready to accept the totality of your situation," he said. "But, the rules are quite clear. You must be held accountable."

Flynn dug his heels deeper into the sand. "I guess that's only fair. After all, someone *is* going to die because of me."

"*Graduate*, Flynn. Though it doesn't have to play out that way."

"No pressure there. Just create a new path for whoever it is I've affected or get sent to Hell."

"For a quarter of an eternity, yes."

Flynn turned and squinted at him. "A quarter of an *eternity* doesn't make any sense."

"You really do need to stop thinking about time the way undergraduates do," Langhorne gently reminded him.

Flynn realized he wasn't only trapped inside a new body; he was trapped inside an invisible box. "I'm starting to think, as a *graduate*, that maybe the taxi driver has it right." Standing abruptly, he wiped the sand from his hands and legs. "Maybe I can use all the help I can get."

Langhorne moved to face him directly. "Yes," he said. "And in exchange for his help you will indeed save whomever is in danger. But you must understand this clearly: in return for the taxi driver's assistance, you will go to Hell for *all* eternity. And even for a graduate, that is a very, very, long existence. His meter is indeed running, Flynn, and you don't have the luxury of waiting to act. But the driver only wants you to decide quickly because he wants to hook you before you have a shot at redemption. Redemption is the one and only human endeavor that keeps them up at night."

Flynn was tired of Langhorne's measured practicality. "At least he's offering me *something*! Since we're finally laying our cards on the table, let's be totally honest here and admit that you're not that much help. I mean, what the hell's your problem? Why can't you tell me who's gonna *graduate* so I can take care of it?"

"Because I don't know. I explained that to you already. Every soul, whether they are graduates or undergrads, has free will. As a result, life is in a constant state of flux. We work only in probabilities. I can only tell you that, on their current trajectories, *someone* in your sphere of influence is going to graduate. But, as of now, we don't know who it is."

"Can you at least tell me which Probability Index is rising?"

Langhorne remained still. "All of them."

Flynn suddenly recalled the sensation of watching his life flash on the big screen television, and a simple truth finally became clear to him. Projecting a desired result onto the future was impossible. All that existed was the moment he was in;

everything else was ego. He was finally thinking like a graduate, one who fully understood there is no difference between
the past, present, and future. In the end, they are all the same.

So, he did something he had never done before. He
remained still. He cleared his mind. He stopped wishing for
an outcome. The best he could do was to act with a pure heart,
to do what he could in that moment, the only one that truly
existed, to cause no harm.

CHAPTER THIRTEEN

THACKER HAD BEEN transferred from the ICU into a semi-private room that he shared with a sixty-year-old colon cancer patient who spent most of the day asleep. For his part, Thacker would occasionally wake from his own slumber with a full erection and demand to see a nurse. "Can't you do *something*?" he'd ask.

Flynn was glad to see the blood once again flowing in his friend and was confident the rest of his body would soon follow suit and be up as well. Until then, Flynn dutifully followed his brother to work, mindful of Covington possibly paying another visit. And he would also follow his father, though the old man rarely left his apartment. Harry Barnes only sat in his beach chair on his tiny balcony, drinking his cheap beer and staring off like a decaying statue waiting to be torn down.

Flynn spent many hours watching him from the mouth of the alleyway next to the weathered apartment building. Doing so brought a peculiar sadness, and at times he longed to be up there with his father, for no other reason than to share his silence. For the first time Flynn could remember—including the months he was confined to a prison cell wondering if his father would visit—he actually missed his old man.

Eventually, inevitably, he went to the grave where his body had been laid to rest. There was no clear reason behind his going, at least not on a conscious level; he was simply drawn to it. He stared at the blue-grey headstone engraved with the words, *Flynn Barnes. He was loved.* He wasn't sure he believed it. Tolerated, yes. Maybe *endured* was more like it. But why the hell would he be *loved?*

He spotted a funeral gathering on the opposite hill, so he left his grave and crossed over. The scattered crowd barely gave him a glance. Some were dressed smartly in conservative black suits and dresses, others in casual, carelessly wrinkled slacks and untucked shirts. A few of the men were even in shorts. The members of the shorts brigade were obviously drunk and laughed loudly at some private joke between them. When they did so, an older woman clutching a handkerchief to her nose began to softly cry. She reached out to a young man that Flynn judged to be about twenty years old, probably her son. In a cruel response to his mother's gesture, the young man pulled away and kicked at some of the dirt next to the freshly dug grave. The mother cried harder, then made no noise at all, her silence somehow making the unfolding drama all the more loathsome.

Flynn wandered close to the giant wreath resting on a wooden stand. At the center of the wreath was a picture of the deceased. He looked to be in his late forties, with a bushy mustache dividing his wide face. His forehead was lined with deep grooves and was lumpy, like freshly turned soil. From his expression, it was apparent the lines crisscrossing his face had been formed by years of insistent scowling.

"Why'd they use such a crappy picture?"

Flynn turned and was surprised to see the owner of the voice was the same man whose picture was on the wreath.

The dead man spit onto the ground. "I look like shit," he said.

At first Flynn thought he was talking to him, but the man was not. "It's the only one they had of you," the stunning, six-foot-tall woman standing next to him explained.

"Well, it sucks," the man said. "They should've used the one of me water skiing."

Flynn's attention was torn between his fellow graduate and the intoxicating beauty of his companion. Her ombre-colored hair fell across her face, and she used her long, porcelain fingers to brush it behind her perfect, shell-shaped ear. Her gently curving breasts heaved with a sigh and her lips turned coyly upward at the corners. Her eyes met Flynn's.

Embarrassed, he quickly shifted his attention to the mustache man, who was still fuming. "What the fuck are you looking at?" the man demanded to know.

Flynn shrugged. "I don't see what you're complaining about," he said. "The picture looks exactly like you. At my funeral, I got stuck with a foot for a face."

The man turned to the woman. "What the hell is this clown talking about?"

The woman smiled wide and Flynn involuntarily gagged. Her teeth—what was left of them—dangled, all yellow and brown, from her rotted gums at odd angles, like bent and rusted bicycle spokes. Her cloudy breath could have been carved with a knife as it snaked over a pitted, festering tongue. "Don't worry about him, sweetie," she said with a flirtatious smile. "He's not important, only you are. So how 'bout it? You ready to have a little fun? From now on, you can do anything and everything you want. There's absolutely nothing to stop you."

The man took one last look at the sobbing woman still

clutching the handkerchief to her nose, then to the young man who continued to kick at the dirt. "Let's get the hell out of here," he said. "I couldn't stand these people when I was *alive*."

It dawned on Flynn that the man's face hadn't changed because he wasn't going to be sticking around. Evidently not everyone got a second chance. As the woman led her fare toward an idling taxi, she reminded the man that he wasn't really dead, he was a graduate.

When Flynn returned to his suite in the Hotel Marigold and discovered that Langhorne had disappeared once again, he realized that if he had any real chance to succeed, he'd need to learn to do a few things on his own. Jumping from body to body, for instance. Being able to shape-shift at will would certainly make the surveillance of Thacker and his family much easier. He pulled out his copy of *The Happy Graduate Rule Book*, loaded the bulky glasses on the bridge of his nose, and got to reading.

To learn everything the book catalogued within its magically expanding pages, with all of its subsections and footnotes, would take an unfathomable amount of time (no matter how it was measured), so he focused on chapter six, "Appearance and Voice." He quickly discovered that manipulating matter was no simple thing, as there were hundreds of footnotes on organic chemistry alone—not to mention the sub-chapters detailing the physics involved with the relativistic effect in regards to quantum theoretical calculations. After skimming over the even denser text that detailed the rules of altering the wave-particle duality of matter, he decided to wing it.

Standing before the mirror in the bathroom, he ran through the mental checklist he'd made, double-checked footnote eleven thousand and four in the rule book, closed his eyes, and did his best. At first he felt no different, other than a faint sensation of his back tingling, and considered the possibility that he had failed entirely. Then he opened his eyes and screamed. He had failed only partially. The body had changed, but it had reformed without skin. His reflection in the mirror was a red mass of blood vessels, nerves, bones, and muscles. With no skin to hold them in place, his internal organs shifted and he used a shaking hand to push what he guessed was his stomach and liver back into place. Within seconds, blood began spewing in all directions, soaking the counter and dripping onto the white, tile floor. Fortunately, the rule book had instructions written in glowing block letters on how to reverse such a calamity, and Flynn quickly employed them.

After collecting himself by lying down with a cold washcloth on his forehead, it took a few more deep dives into the rule book before he tried again. Each subsequent effort brought him closer to a working understanding of a basic corporeal reconstruction. Effort number two delivered a new body with the appropriate amount of skin, but with three heads—each one growing out of the other like a totem pole. He snapped a few pictures as a keepsake, then tried again. The third attempt ended with a missing torso (the neck and head growing out of the waist, no arms), and the fourth with all the customary body parts, but with one arm sprouting from the chest, the other from the back, and legs facing the wrong direction (when he tried to step forward, he moved backward and slammed into the wall).

At this point he almost gave up, deciding it best to wait for Langhorne. But after yet another consultation with *The Happy Graduate Rule Book*, he tried for a fifth time and, at last, came away happy. Content with his new corporeal self, he headed back to Saint John's hospital in Santa Monica with a renewed sense of urgency.

This time when he walked the long, echoing hallways, the nurses took no notice of him. Doctor Studbody was gone, replaced by a saggy-bottomed janitor with jangling keys on his belt and a dirty mop of greasy, black hair. Flynn was relieved to be rid of the good doctor, as it was distracting to be constantly pulled in every direction with cries of concern every time he visited his friend. Now, nobody bothered him with their arcane medical discussions and problem diagnoses, which was just as well because he could no longer tell the difference between a defibrillator and a toaster oven.

He entered Thacker's room and was immediately met by the frowning face of a nurse irritably removing sheets from an empty bed. "I called you guys with a code brown ten minutes ago," she complained, waving her gloved hand at the clock.

"Code brown?" Flynn stammered.

"Yes. Mr. Richards had an accident and made it only half-way to the lavatory."

One whiff of the pungent air and Flynn the custodian needed no further clarification on what a *code brown* entailed.

"Where's your bucket?" the nurse asked, already fed up with him.

"I forgot it," answered Flynn weakly.

"Well, *please* go get it," she demanded, making the word *please* sound like a vulgarity.

He looked past the overly taxed nurse and saw that Thacker was not in his bed. In fact, he was nowhere to be seen. Pushing past her into the room, he held his breath against the horren-dous smell. "Where's Mr. Thacker?" he asked, assuming the smeared trail of feces on the floor leading to the bathroom had driven him from the room, along with the loose-bowelled Mr. Richards.

"Why are you worried about *him?*" the nurse said. "Get your damn bucket!"

"Look here, Nurse Ratchet," Flynn said. "If your patients are pooping on the floor, then rub their noses in it to get them to stop but leave me out of it. Now where's Thacker?"

The nurse dropped the soiled sheets and reached for the phone. "That's it, I'm calling your supervisor."

Flynn pulled his shirt over his nose and slammed his hand on the phone cradle, disconnecting her call. "Tell me where he is," he demanded. "And I promise you'll never see my face around here again."

The nurse recoiled, but at the end of a twelve-hour shift, she had no fight left in her. "I have no idea where he is," she said. "He just got up and left, despite his doctor's orders."

"When?"

"This afternoon," she explained further. "Right after his friends came by for a visit."

Flynn instantly understood. He lifted his hand from the cradle, allowing the nurse to hang up the phone. "They weren't his friends," he informed her.

The door swung open and a whistling custodian entered, pushing a yellow bucket, mop at the ready. Without a word, Flynn brushed past him and headed back up the hallway. He had his own mess to clean up.

The city of Los Angeles is exactly five-hundred-and-three square miles in size. Add in the surrounding areas that make up Los Angeles County, and you're up to four thousand, seven hundred square miles. That's a haystack big enough to hide a shitload of needles. But Flynn only needed to find one, and he recognized that to do so successfully, he could no longer rely on the city bus system. He dug out the remaining cash given to him by the taxi driver and put it to good use.

Flynn maneuvered the jet-black Porsche Carrera around slower traffic as he sped south along the 101 Freeway. The engine roared as he cranked it up to ninety, his attention slipping only once, when Langhorne appeared next to him in the passenger seat. "Perhaps you should slow down," Langhorne advised, clutching the sides of his seat. "Lest you be held responsible for more graduation parties."

Flynn eased off the accelerator. "Where have you been?"

"Two different crews tried to rob American Federal Bank at the same time; they made quite a mess of themselves."

"Speaking of messes, can you swing by the hotel and clean up the bathroom before housekeeping goes in and has a heart attack?"

"Yes, I was made aware of the issues you had. Skin can be difficult. You're looking well now, though. Very impressive. So, where are we going?"

Flynn exited the freeway at Laurel Canyon and raced down the off-ramp. "I've gotta get to Thacker before Covington does. They paid him a little visit at the hospital, and he took off without telling the doctors."

Langhorne braced himself against his seat as Flynn hung a sharp left. "I see," he said, grimacing. "And may I ask where you got the car?"

"Premier car rentals," Flynn said. "I figure if I'm going out, I'm going out in style." He shifted gears, scuttling around a slow-moving Honda. "The problem is, I never went to Thacker's apartment before I died—I mean *graduated*."

"Thank you."

"Anyway, I had no idea how to find him."

"So your plan is to drive around the city like a madman until you accidentally run him over?"

"I tried to find an address online, but had no luck. Then I remembered something."

"What's that?"

"The hospital," Flynn said, breaking for a red light. "Admittance records. I made another quick change into the mid-level bureaucrat you see before you and pulled his file."

Langhorne considered the very image of nondescript middle management sitting next to him—rumpled suit, thinning hair severely parted, dark circles under the eyes—and nodded. "Well done."

"I'm finally getting the hang of this."

"That you are."

With the last light of day seeping between the cracks of the city, they pulled in front of a row of 1970s-era apartments. Flynn pointed toward a squat, royal blue building with overgrown, cobwebbed bushes obscuring its front. "Right there. That one's Thacker's. Number seven."

"Very nice," said Langhorne. "Now what?"

"What do you mean, now what?"

"Do you have a plan to keep him safe?"

"Of course I have a plan."

Flynn shut off the Porsche's engine and sat motionless, staring through the windshield at Thacker's apartment. Neither man spoke.

"Is this it?" Langhorne finally asked.

"No, this isn't it!" Flynn insisted. "Obviously, I'm first gonna have to make sure he's here."

"Of course. Then what?"

"Then figure out what happened to the masks. If I can find them and get them to Covington, Thacker's off the hook."

More silence.

"That's more of a *goal* than a plan," Langhorne pointed out.

"Look, man, if you'd like to facilitate something here, then go ahead and do it."

"The way I see it, you need to get close enough to Mr. Thacker to find out what happened. But he has no idea who you are, so he's not going to simply invite you in to discuss it."

Flynn nodded. "That's more of a *summation* than a plan."

"I do have a suggestion," Langhorne said. "I'm just not sure you're going to be happy with it."

After Langhorne facilitated a quick inspection to make sure Thacker was indeed home, it took another three hours before he finally made an appearance. Flynn's patience was wearing thin in the cramped quarters of the Porsche, but as he fought off crushing boredom, having long ago exhausted his patience with talk radio, his determination finally paid off when the liquor store down the block proved to be a siren call his friend could not resist. After so much time in the hospital, Thacker had had no opportunity to replenish his stock, and now, with the cover of darkness as an ally, he furtively made his way down the narrow steps of his building and hustled along the sidewalk toward the neon sign of Gill's Liquor Mart.

In the crisp light of the tiny store, Thacker made straight for the back refrigerator and pulled two six-packs of Bass Ale from the shelf, then proceeded quickly to the counter. The Vietnamese clerk took note of the cuts and bruises on Thacker's face but said nothing. As he rang up the sale, the only other customer in the store, the one who had followed Thacker inside and feigned interest in the latest issue of *People* on the magazine rack by the counter, smiled at the anxious Englishman.

Thacker looked over the milky-skinned creature standing before him. With firm tits and a well-rounded ass filling out her black latex mini dress like perfectly fluffed pillows, she seemed to have been made to order to his exact specifications. Which, of course, she had been. After all, following Langhorne's suggestion, it was Flynn who put the ass in the assembly, and he knew just how Thacker liked it.

"I hope the other guy got the worst of it," Flynn said, indicating Thacker's battered face with one fire-engine-red fingernail.

As he always did in times of high expectation, Thacker worked his tongue in the space between his teeth. "Fraid not," he said. "I'm a lover, not a fighter."

Flynn fidgeted in his high heels and leaned on the counter, providing Thacker the proper angle to visually calibrate the majesty of his chest. "I was hoping you'd say that," Flynn said, his feminine voice lilting and vanilla-scented perfume wafting. Thacker smiled and Flynn silently hoped he could get through the rest of the night without throwing up.

Leaving the bright lights of the liquor store behind, they walked together up the sidewalk, past the glistening black Porsche where Langhorne again sat, curiosity keeping him from his mounting duties. To his eye, it was *Flynn* in the latex mini dress wrapping his leanly muscled arm around Thacker's waist, his hairy legs moving with the particular gait of the experienced woman. Langhorne watched them until they disappeared into the apartment building. "This should be very interesting," he observed before once again fading away, off to greet a poor sap in Munich who had graduated in the throes of an LSD high after mistaking an industrial fan for a giant butterfly.

CHAPTER FOURTEEN

THACKER OPENED THE apartment door for his dream girl. "Make yourself at home," he said with a playful slap on Flynn's bubbly rear end. "I'll get some glasses."

"Glasses," Flynn cooed stupidly. "How fancy."

Thacker disappeared into the kitchen and Flynn took in the room. It was sparsely furnished—a leather sofa, coffee table, and a couple of chairs facing a fifty-five-inch flatscreen television—all of which looked new and top end. It wasn't surprising, given Thacker's ego and the fact that he'd spent the previous three years in a shithole. But there was also much evidence of Thacker's crooked life, which did surprise Flynn. Apparently, his friend had not put much effort into going straight. Stacks of Bluetooth speakers, PlayStation consoles, cell phones, laptop computers, GoPros, and video games, all in their original boxes, were piled high on a folding table along the far wall.

Flynn called out, "You win all this stuff on a game show or something?"

Thacker's voice trailed into the room. "Actually, I was a professional football player. You know, *soccer*," he said. "I recently retired and those are gifts from my sponsors."

Flynn was impressed with the casualness of the lie, though insulted by the easy assumption that "she" was stupid enough to believe it. He shook his head. *Men,* he thought. "If you were such a big-shot athlete," he called out, dutifully playing his role, though not wanting to let Thacker so easily off the hook, "why are you living here? Shouldn't you have, like, a mansion or something?"

After a slight hesitation, Thacker's voice came back with a hearty laugh. "This isn't my flat, love. It's a friend of mine's." He returned with the beers. "I'm staying here temporarily while I renovate my house in Malibu."

"I love the beach!" Flynn said, giggling. "It has sand and stuff."

"Then I'll have to have you up when the place is done," Thacker said, handing over a glass of beer.

"Don't you have any Budweiser?" he asked, pouting like a simpleton.

"Yes, I love American beer as well," Thacker continued to lie. "Unfortunately, my flat mate insists I buy only imported."

Flynn shrugged, playfully tossing his blonde hair off his fleshy white shoulders, as Thacker led him to the couch, sitting as close as possible, short of landing on his lap. He offered a toast. "To chance meetings."

They clinked glasses. "The best kind, right?" said Flynn.

"Cheers." Thacker grinned, leaning close for a kiss.

Flynn quickly brought his finger to Thacker's expectant lips. "What happened to your face?" he cooed, like a concerned girlfriend preparing to kiss the boo-boo all better.

"Nothing to worry about," said Thacker, pulling Flynn's hand down.

"Poor baby," Flynn fussed. "If you want to talk about it—"

Thacker leaned in for a second stab at her swollen lips. "I'm more interested in *your* face than mine."

Flynn nimbly turned his head to the side, cringing at the sensation of his best friend's tongue working its way up the nape of his perfumed neck. "That's so sweet." Flynn quivered, holding his breath. One of Thacker's hands found Flynn's right breast as his other slid smoothly up his thigh. Flynn stiffened, as did Thacker, though his stiffness was more centrally located.

"You mind if I use the little girl's room?" Flynn asked.

Thacker pulled back with a lascivious grin. "Of course, love. It's right down the hall. I'll put some music on."

"What a fabulous idea," Flynn said, retreating swiftly down the hall.

Locking the bathroom door behind him, Flynn worked to catch his breath and slow his madly thumping heart. He looked in the mirror and the revelation of seeing his reflection in the soft light shocked his nervous system into submission. For a moment, he could only stare at the contours, curves and shapes of his new body, enthralled with the way his eyelashes danced and his red lips glistened. "Wow," he said. Even as a woman, he remained such a *guy* that he was turned on by his own image. He pulled his breasts out from the tight latex dress and bounced them up and down, then side to side, staring.

Ozzy Osborne singing "No More Tears" wafted into the bathroom, bringing Flynn's attention back to the situation at hand. He listened to Ozzy's distinct vocals, followed by a rush of grinding guitars, and marveled that Thacker had chosen the ex-front man of Black Sabbath as *mood music*. "Oh yeah, that's a turn on," Flynn mumbled, tucking his breasts back into the dress.

He exited the bathroom, determined to get as much useful

information as he could from his horny friend, and returned to the living room. Thacker was nowhere to be found. Turning down the stereo, he called out, "Hello?"

"In the bedroom, love!" Thacker called from down the short hall.

Flynn made his way toward the bedroom like a prisoner heading to the electric chair. *Dead man walking*, indeed. His reeling mind worked to find a foothold, any way to get Thacker to talk about the masks without having to see him naked. Of course, Flynn had seen him naked before—prison showers are not for the demure, after all—but *context* had much to say about shared intimacy. Flynn decided he would be willing to show some skin to solve the mystery of the missing masks, but one thing was certain: if any actual *sex* was to be had, it would only be between himself and his own reflection back at the Hotel Marigold.

Reaching the end of the hall, Flynn rounded the corner into the bedroom and stopped. Stopped everything. Stopped moving, stopped thinking, stopped breathing.

Thacker lay on the bed, propped up on his elbow, shirtless, wearing leather shorts that hugged his hairy thighs. "You ready for a little rumpy-pumpy?" he asked, playfully rolling onto his back. His left foot rose into the air and wiggled.

"Holy shit," Flynn groaned.

"What's the matter, love?" Thacker said. "You're up for this, aren't you?"

A tide of nausea rose in Flynn's gut. Seeing his brutish friend in this manner was like an eight-year-old seeing Santa Claus take off his fake beard and masturbate with one of his elves. "Sure," he managed. "And I can see that you're up for it as well."

Thacker glanced at the bulge in his leather shorts and grinned. "Brilliant."

"Let's just take it slow," Flynn suggested, breathing deep. "Make it last."

"I like the sound of that," Thacker said, rolling onto his side. Flynn's stomach knotted as Thacker reached across the bed and opened the drawer of the side table to bring out a bright red spanking paddle. "How 'bout we warm up with this?" he suggested, ever the gentleman.

"You have got to be—" Flynn stopped himself. At once a new plan crystallized. He needed to take control of the situation, and Thacker had unknowingly shown him the way. He reached out and yanked the paddle from him. "On your knees!" he demanded.

Thacker's expression twisted with faux concern, his carnal enthusiasms spiking as he crawled onto the bed on all fours. "I have been a bad boy," he said.

A tide of disgust rose, threatening to overflow into Flynn's throat, but what needed to be done, needed to be done. Kneeling at Thacker's left flank, he warily tapped his friend's ass with the paddle.

"Harder, baby," Thacker said.

Flynn grimaced, but spanked him again, this time with more force.

"Harder!" Thacker barked.

"Please shut up!" Flynn snapped, whacking him again with considerable force.

"There you go," Thacker said.

"Tell me why you were beaten."

"Because I was *bad*," Thacker said again, his voice tinged with naughty guilt.

"Not by *me*," Flynn clarified. "By your business associates."

Thacker turned back. "Why're are you asking about—"

Whap! Flynn again brought the paddle solidly to his ass. "No questions!"

"Oooh," said Thacker, again facing front. "You like the rough stuff, do you?"

"Yeah, that's right. It gets me hot," said Flynn. *Whap!* He spanked him again. "Now tell me all about those naughty men who hurt you."

This unexpected turn of events loosened Thacker up appreciably. "They think I have something of theirs."

"But you don't?" Flynn swatted him again.

Thacker caught his breath before continuing. "It's just gonna take a little more convincing," he explained, swaying his rear end back and forth. "In the meantime, it might get a lot *rougher* for me."

Whap! Flynn spanked him with as much force as his skinny arms could muster. "So who *does* have what they're looking for?" he asked.

"Who gives a shit," Thacker said. "All I know is you've got what *I'm* looking for." Unable to contain his lust any longer, he swung around and lunged forward. Flynn instinctively shuttled to the side, giving a little shove that used Thacker's momentum to launch him off the side of the bed. He landed with a pathetic thump on the floor, like a pile of discarded laundry. "What the hell's the matter with you?" Thacker asked, truly confused.

Flynn climbed from the bed and helped Thacker to his feet. "It's hard to explain, but we have to do this together."

"I *know*," Thacker said. "But you keep stopping every time we get started."

An aggressive knocking came from the front door of the

apartment, startling both men. As the banging continued, Flynn moved to the window, searching for any means of flight, losing sight of Thacker as his friend pulled on a robe and exited the room.

Flynn followed a panicked moment later, arriving steps behind Thacker at the slightly ajar door, held in place only by the taught pull of safety chain lock. "Get the hell away from there!" Flynn said, imagining a shotgun blast ending this farce once and for all.

"Relax, love." Thacker unlatched the safety chain. "I'll get rid of him. It's just my mate, Donny."

Flynn's expression soured. Thacker had never mentioned anybody named Donny.

Thacker opened the door and Donny stepped into the room. In every way, he was an unremarkable specimen. His fat neck supported a strangely rounded head, which in turn supported a few wisps of yellowish hair reminiscent of the silk strings on a husk of corn. He looked like Charlie Brown a few years out of trade school. But while there was nothing particularly remarkable about his appearance, there was something familiar about him. Flynn just couldn't quite place where he had seen him.

"What the hell's going on?" Donny said. "I've been trying to call you."

Upon hearing the voice, Flynn's spine weakened, and the joints of his softly feminine body loosened as though its assembly was about to completely fall apart. His thoughts flashed back to the night he graduated, his car resting on the edge of the cliff along Mulholland Drive, Sinatra singing "That's Life."

It was Donny whose eyes had met his as he reached for the passenger door. The reality of that night flashed even more clearly. Donny had not been there to help. He hadn't reached for the car in a failed attempt to open the door and save him; he had reached out to *push* the car down the abyss, assuring Flynn's death. And now Flynn was staring at his killer in his best friend's apartment.

"Why the hell didn't you tell me you were leaving the hospital?" Donny demanded of Thacker.

"Covington paid me another visit."

"I told you he wasn't gonna buy your bullshit for long."

"It's fine. I bought some time from him and thought I'd use it out here instead of lying in that damned bed."

Donny looked past him to the sour-faced blonde taking in their conversation. "Yeah, I can see you're putting it to really good use."

Flynn wanted to scream out, to acknowledge his assassin, but he knew it would be impossible. The rule book would not allow the words to pass his lips.

"We'll talk about it later," Thacker said. "Not in front of company."

Donny's face reddened. "I don't give a shit about your *company*. I'm tired of doing all your dirty work for you. We've got to move those masks now."

Flynn's breasts heaved under the tight latex dress, his flesh suddenly on fire. He stared at the only friend he had in the entire world as Thacker harshly blasted back at Donny. "*I'm* running the show, you got it? It's all figured out and we'll take care of it in the morning. Now get the hell out of here."

Flynn's shock made way for his anger. "You son-of-a-bitch," he roared, fully realizing now the truth of his murder. "How could you do this to me?"

Thacker turned to him, puzzled. "What's that, love?"

"Must have been too hard with the whip," Donny said with a smirk.

"Were you planning this the whole time?" Flynn yelled.

Thacker shook his head at the blonde's unexpected ferocity. "I just met you half an hour ago. I didn't even know he was gonna show up. Don't worry about it, he's not staying."

Flynn punched Thacker in the face, doing no damage with the blow beyond breaking a nail.

Donny laughed. "This bitch is crazy."

Flynn turned to Donny, his waifish fists clenched, again ready to strike. "Fuck you!" he wailed.

"Forget it, lady," Donny said, grabbing Flynn's arm as it impotently swung forward, twisting it behind his back. "That's his thing, not mine."

"Take it easy, Donny," Thacker said, sounding only slightly concerned, no doubt resigned to the reality that his evening was to be cut short.

Flynn strained to look back at Thacker but could not turn far enough in Donny's overpowering grip. His head snapped backward on his neck as he was violently pushed from the apartment into the hallway. The momentum took him all the way to the opposite wall as he brought his hands up to brace himself.

"See you around, sweetheart," Donny cackled behind him, slamming the door shut.

The sounds of the surf crashed onto the shore a few feet from Flynn, and the lights of the Hotel Marigold glinted in the distance behind him. He lay on his side, cheek resting on his outstretched arm, beer cans scattered around him, a half-empty bottle of Tequila held loosely in his opposite hand. His damp, blonde hair stuck to his cheeks and his mascara fell in thick clumps from his reddened eyes. Sand wedged itself under his latex dress, rubbing his doughy skin raw. He did not know what time it was but figured it must be close to two in the morning.

He'd replayed the scenes over and over; all the time he and Thacker spent in prison with nobody but each other to rely upon. The memories bit hard: all the deep talks, the laughs, the blocks of friendship constructed with each shared moment. In his alcohol haze, Flynn managed fleeting glimpses of Thacker's gapped-tooth grin and his own face turned to his friend with beguiled enthusiasm. Had it all been a lie? Had Thacker been planning to betray him from the beginning? Had he been a chump the entire time?

"Hell of a sense of humor you got there, God," he whispered, rolling onto his back to stare at the stars. "I know you're up there pulling the strings. I *know* it. You did this to me as punishment. It's all a fucking joke. *Free will*, my ass," he said. "Free will, my perfect…sexy…ass."

His eyes slowly closed as he listened to the waves relentlessly crash onto the shore, forever pounding and pounding and pounding like the punishing drumbeat of eternity.

CHAPTER FIFTEEN

FLYNN AWOKE UNDER cool, satin sheets in the ocean-front suite of the Hotel Marigold. A pleasant breeze caressed his freshly washed skin through the billowing, white drapes that shaded him from the morning sun. His eyes fluttered open to find Langhorne sitting opposite him in a high-backed leather chair he'd failed to ever notice before.

Flynn sat up and stretched the stiffness from his bones. He eyed Langhorne with suspicion, pulling the sheets up to cover his naked breasts. "How did I get back here?" he asked.

"I brought you," said Langhorne, standing. "The beach is no place for a young lady to spend the night alone." He smoothed the creases on his suit a moment. "I'm sorry about Mr. Thacker."

Flynn looked at him suspiciously. "Did you know all along?"

Langhorne didn't answer.

Flynn rolled back over. "You knew."

"We all must follow the rules, Flynn. Even the Facilitators."

Flynn wasn't sure if his emotions were partly fueled by the estrogen that came with the body, but either way, he could not shake his gloomy mood. "He was my only friend."

"As it turns out," Langhorne said, "you didn't have any friends."

Flynn's eyes fell closed. "Thanks for cheering me up."

"So, now what?" Langhorne was clearly not interested in feeding Flynn's melancholy.

"For starters, I'm thinking about killing the bastard for what he's done to me."

"That would be—"

"Against the rules," interrupted Flynn as he abruptly rolled out of the bed. "Yeah, I got that. But the way I see it, if he *is* the one who's gonna graduate because of me, I'll go work on my tan and let it happen. And I'd appreciate it if you could at least arrange his graduation to be something slow and painful."

"It's your prerogative to feel that way," Langhorne said, "but I can arrange no such thing. Besides, we should take into consideration that Mr. Thacker's path to graduation is not your responsibility after all."

Flynn's shoulders dropped with a sigh. "Either way, he's gotta be directly *involved* in all this, right?"

"Fair deduction."

Flynn ran his fingers through his long, silky hair. "Whatever he's up to, he's not gonna share it with me just because I look good in a dress."

Langhorne held out the rule book and glasses. "I'm sure something in here will help."

"Forget it. I don't need it. A man doesn't spend the night inside the body of a big-titted slut, paddling the pasty ass of his own murderer without figuring out a thing or two."

Langhorne moved to throw open the drapes, flooding the room with light. "And what exactly did you figure out?"

"That this is all a big joke."

"You've surmised that all of human existence was designed solely for laughs?"

"I haven't the slightest idea *why* it was designed. I'm not the one in control here."

"Then who is?"

"God!" said Flynn. "And he's *fucking* with me."

Langhorne shook his head. "God is not a *he* or a *him* or a *she* or a *her,* for that matter. I'm afraid you're thinking like an undergraduate again. I was really hoping we were past this."

"Oh, stop being so condescending."

"What choice do I have? And it is a *choice*, Flynn. I can and will react to you in any manner I want. And right now, my reaction is that you're behaving like you haven't learned anything since you graduated."

"Come on, Langhorne. You're honestly saying God doesn't have anything to do with this?"

"No, that's not what I'm saying." Langhorne's tone grew impatient. "What I *am* saying is that God is not a *cruise director*. God does not plan your day for you. And God most certainly does not *fuck* with people. This concept might be difficult for undergrads to accept, but you are no longer an undergrad and I must say, your attitude is annoying. You are not a pawn in some divine chess game. This is, in fact, life. *Your* life. And you're free to do with it what you'd like. As is Mr. Thacker. *That's* how it works.

"You do not need *permission* to act in the manner you choose. And again, neither does Mr. Thacker. Nor do the multitudes of souls who have graduated before you and will graduate after you. For the piddling few undergrads living on earth, it's a manageable problem. But facilitating graduates in their headlong movement into eternity? That's a delicate jigsaw puzzle. Therefore, rules are in place to make sure Facilitators work on a level playing field. Is any of this sinking in? Just as undergrads must make do with the laws and rules *they've* put in place, *we* have our own rules to follow. The difference being, of course, that our rules make sense, whereas undergrad rules are often incongruous, haphazardly applied and built on faulty logic. I'm not placing blame: they do the best they can with what little information they have. I am, however, placing blame on *you* for your behavior. Moving forward, I can only suggest that you suck it up and stop complaining."

Flynn seemed too exhausted to take in more of the lesson, and Langhorne was falling further and further behind schedule, so he merely sighed, and held out the rule book. "Now take this and do with it as you'd like."

Flynn waved him off. "I don't want any more rules."

Langhorne's expression darkened.

"What?" asked Flynn, at once feeling self-conscious.

"You can *choose* that eternity if that's what you want."

"What do you mean I can choose it?"

"Just that. You must be aware by now that you can leave all of these restrictions behind and spend your eternity in a place without any rules, if that's what you truly desire. You wouldn't be the first to do so. And you won't be the last. Some people do better in a place where they're free to do whatever they want. It's in their nature, I suppose." He paused. "Is that your nature, Flynn?"

Flynn thought carefully. *Maybe it is.* At least, Langhorne clearly suspected as much. This was a challenge, then. Langhorne had thrown down the gauntlet and wanted to see if Flynn was honest enough to pick it up. But Flynn wasn't honest about much of anything; that was surely his nature. So, he chose to believe this challenge was something different, a call to his better, stronger-willed self, an opportunity to rise above what he had always been. Whatever it was, he was too tired to argue points of which he had only a vague grasp. Part of him felt ashamed that as an undergrad, he had never considered who he truly was, and it dawned on him that spending more time in reflection might have been a good idea, after all.

He snatched the rule book from Langhorne and lay back down on the bed without another word passing between them before the harried Facilitator left to explain the situation to a first-time bungee jumper in Costa Rica.

Flynn's eyes bulged and strained behind the glasses as he lay on the bed with the rule book, contemplating his next move. Throughout the day Langhorne came and went, as did room service. The physical contours of being a busty blonde proved to be too much of a distraction, so Flynn—honing his new-found skill at shapeshifting—opted to return his physical self to that of the man he was upon checking into the Hotel Marigold. *The face* polished off a sixty-dollar medium-rare porterhouse steak with fries, three micro-brewed beers, a heavenly slice of blueberry pie, and one glass of milk, all while struggling through the rule book's endless footnotes and clauses. Deter-mined to ignore his battered emotions, he focused on what needed to be done immediately; figure out what Thacker was up to and keep him from causing more harm.

The image of Jimmy Bannon and his bruised face flashed in his mind. My fault, Flynn berated himself. A slide show passed before him of everyone who could be in mortal danger in light of Thacker's conspiracy; a lineup that included every damn person at the warehouse. Who knew if Covington would return again in search of his masks? And then he thought of those even closer to him: Andy. Harry. Erin. Hoyt. Had his involvement with Thacker set their paths irreversibly toward graduation? He paced the floor, pushing the images of his one-time family from his mind, as they only worked to muddy his concentration with unwanted remorse. Back to the bed, rule book in hand, he read.

Langhorne returned once again from his appointed rounds and sat in the leather chair reading Carl Sagan's *Cosmos*. Occasionally, he chuckled under his breath.

Flynn glanced over as he flipped a page of the rule book. His sore eyes scanned to the bottom of page six hundred and two before stopping abruptly on the second paragraph of subsection five, clause four, paragraph nine. He read it three times to make sure he understood it, excitement growing with each devoured word. Once convinced he had indeed properly digested their meaning, Flynn sprang upright in bed.

"I got it," he exclaimed. "Rule seven thousand and twenty."

Langhorne laid *Cosmos* on his lap and looked upon his charge like a proud papa. "That could work very nicely."

Flynn swung his legs out, landing his feet firmly on the floor. "I'm gonna do it. It's weird, but I can't afford to waste any more time."

"No, I should think not," Langhorne said, picking a speck of lint from the knee of his trousers.

Flynn picked the last cold french fry off the room-service tray and popped it into his mouth. "Okay," he said, collecting himself. "Wish me luck."

"Go get 'em," Langhorne said.

A light above them flashed and Flynn soared upward.

Thacker drove his Mazda hatchback north on Reseda Boulevard, Metallica scorching from the speakers, bass turned high.
He banged his hands on the steering wheel with each thumping
downbeat of drums, lip-syncing "Enter Sandman". He was so lost
in his performance that he failed to notice the police officer pull up
behind him on his squat motorcycle, flashing his blues and reds.

After a glance in his rearview, Thacker shut off the stereo.
"Shit." His heart took over for the thumping drums and he
eased off the gas pedal. Unless they were wearing latex and
knew his safe word, Thacker had a problem with anyone holding a position of authority over him. He held a special dislike
of anyone with a badge. While a parent could ground him, a
teacher could flunk him and a boss could fire him, only a cop
could take away his freedom. Cops made him *care* about his
behavior, which only made him hate them all the more.

Thacker's jaw flexed under the weight of his grinding teeth,
as he had no idea why this particular *fucking pig* had singled
him out. He hadn't been drinking, driving recklessly, or speeding. And odd as it was, the car he was driving wasn't stolen.
Ordinarily he would argue belligerently even if guilty, just out
of principle. But on this day, he had an appointment to keep
that would lead him to riches and he didn't want to be waylaid
by a civil servant with a small dick (as he regarded all police
officers, male or female). Obediently, he drifted to the right and
practiced the subservient frown of the intimidated citizen. His
irritation increased as a fly zipped through the opened window
and buzzed under his nose, causing him to swerve further to
the right, nearly striking the curb with his front tire.

The motorcycle cop lurched forward, as if indicating his
irritation. But Thacker's worry and feigned submissive stance
proved unnecessary as the officer roared past, sliding between

the lemmings ahead as they pulled to the side to form a law-abiding path for his safe passage. Thacker cursed his own paranoia and pulled back into the street.

He kept the music off—the mood ruined—as he approached the deserted parking lot of the *U-Store-It* storage facility, where he made a quick turn and parked.

The San Fernando Valley was approaching ninety degrees as he entered the narrow lobby of the cavernous building. A sweating twenty-something lazily pushed a flatbed dolly past him, heading for a clutch of other dollies in the parking lot near the front door.

"What's up?" the man said.

"Not much," Thacker answered, and the conversation ended.

Thacker and Donny had chosen *U-Store-It* because, while there were a handful of security cameras on each floor, only one or two employees were present at any given time. And none seemed to pay much attention to who came and went. So as Thacker stood in the elevator, slowly moving up to the fifth floor, he knew he was not being noticed with any interest.

He was, however, entirely mistaken.

He exited the elevator and headed down the dimly lit corridor. The air was stiff and felt ten degrees warmer than in the lobby. His nose itched as he headed for the last storage unit on the left, where Donny sat waiting, eating from a bag of powdered mini doughnuts.

"You're late," Donny said, wiping his sugar-coated fingers on his pants. "I'm sweating my ass off."

Thacker dug a set of keys from his front pocket and moved to unlock the solid hinged bolt on the door. "You'll be paid well for your time," he said, swinging open the thick wood.

The two men stepped inside, but they were not alone.

They were followed into the cramped space by the very same fly that had buzzed Thacker moments before. The fat-bodied fly zipped past, sticking its six hairy feet to the far wall near the ceiling. The bulbous head swiveled as it peered down, seeing the storage unit as a sort of mosaic of hexagonal segments. This was all somewhat disconcerting to the fly, because up until that day, it had walked on two feet, could not stick to smooth surfaces, and, in fact, couldn't get far enough off the ground to touch the rim of a basketball hoop. Until that day, it had been a recently graduated *human* with a full load of personal problems—not the least of which was that his greedy best friend had him killed, thus forcing him to turn into a damn *insect* in order to determine what else was in the works to screw up his afterlife. So now Flynn walked upside down, eyeing a room full of stolen electronics and the men who had done him in.

"You're leaving the rest here?" asked Donny, popping another powdered doughnut into his mouth.

Thacker moved a stack of e-readers and pulled back a blue tarp to reveal a clear plastic bin holding the missing gold masks. Seeing the masks, Flynn's buzzing grew louder as he circled once and landed again on the wall.

"There's no reason to move 'em right now," Thacker said. "We just need the one to get Covington off our backs."

Flynn's comprehension of rule seven thousand twenty (and all of its subsections), which detailed the necessary steps to successfully become a *Musca domestica*, was limited, as annexes D-H were fairly dense in their written instructions, so his transformation, much like his first attempts at taking on a new *human* form, had not been completed in an entirely useful manner. In his haste, he had not taken the time to learn how to retain his human auditory perception, and now it was impossible for him to actually *understand* what was being said inside the cramped storage unit. Instead, as all flies do, he merely picked up the vibration of Thacker's and Donny's voices. Further complicating things, as a fully functioning fly, his focus was elsewhere. Watching the two men discuss their plan, Flynn's antennae flicked forward, and his translucent wings fluttered, again carrying him into the air. The tiny halters located behind his main wings steadied his balance as he shot forward to land gently on the one thing that mattered most to him at that moment—the powdered doughnut in Donny's hand.

With a newly discovered instinct for such things, Flynn proceeded to throw up. His digestive juices swathed a tiny section of doughnut between his front legs, quite efficiently dissolving it into a pasty liquid. *This is absolutely repulsive,* he thought, sucking up the gooey meal with his long proboscis. He found that, despite the aesthetics involved, he actually favored the taste and promptly vomited again on another portion. He then lowered his sponge-like mouth to slurp it up.

Oblivious, Donny raised the doughnut and popped it past his sugar-coated lips as Flynn darted upward to land on the opposite wall, his belly now warm and full. "You really think Covington will fall for it?" Donny asked, spewing white powder like dust off a shelf.

Thacker removed one of the gold masks from the plastic bin and held it up for consideration. "Why not?" he said, using his forearm to wipe a trickle of sweat from his temple. "Flynn's family already thinks he was a total fuck up. Who's gonna question it?"

Though Flynn couldn't comprehend a word between the men, the smug grin creasing Thacker's face refocused his antennae. He processed the sensory information into a lighting fast motor response that sent him into a flurry of agitated activity. Buzzing into the air, he circled above the two men before taking a more direct course of action.

As Thacker wrapped the mask in a blanket and placed it into a duffle bag, Flynn once again shifted his halters for balance, beat his wings at a rate measured in milliseconds, and dive-bombed with spectacular force directly into Thacker's left eye.

"God dammit!" Thacker wailed.

"What?" asked Donny.

Thacker squeezed his eye closed as a tear seeped out and rolled onto his cheek. "I think a fly just nailed me." Flynn's wings buzzed again, louder than before, as he shifted his tiny shoulders and turned back on a tight loop, hitting Thacker once more with a resounding vehemence, this time in the right eye. "Ah! shit—" Thacker yelped, dropping the duffle bag to the floor, momentarily blinded.

Flynn was astounded by how quickly he could process sensory information into immediate action. Suddenly, it made sense to him why it could be so difficult to swat a fly. He dive-bombed again, and despite Thacker's impotent waving of his hands in front of his face, Flynn the fly's tiny brain easily calculated the direction of the impending threat and simply outmaneuvered its pathetic defense. He repeatedly slammed into Thacker's sweat-stained cheek with a series of tiny popping sounds.

"Jesus," said Donny, scrunching his brow. "That's one pissed off bug."

"Don't just stand there with your thumb up your ass," Thacker said. "Kill the damn thing!"

Donny stood motionless, with his hand poised for a quick, decisive smack. Flynn landed enticingly on Thacker's head, just above the temple, and waited. Sensing his moment, Donny brought his hand down with a resounding slap.

"Watch yourself ya bastard!" cried Thacker, recoiling from the impact of Donny's palm.

"He's a quick little fucker," said Donny, laughing.

Thacker, having lost track of the possessed fly, again waved his hands in front of his face. With blinding speed, Flynn shot forward to find a safe haven that, for the moment at least, silenced his strident buzzing.

"Bloody hell!" Thacker cried out.

"What?"

"It went up my nose."

"That's disgusting," said Donny, reeling.

Thacker pressed his thumb to his left nostril and strongly exhaled from his right. Despite being well anchored in a forest of nostril hair, Flynn could not resist the force of the discharge and was once again buzzing the air around the increasingly distraught men. As Thacker used an aggressive finger to do some housecleaning up his violated nose, Flynn turned his attention to Donny. Zeroing in on his fresh target, he rammed into Donny's forehead, reset, and rammed him again. He then buzzed into his left ear, exited, circled around his Charlie Brown head, and buzzed into the right.

"I think it wants the doughnuts!" Donny shouted, dropping the bag.

But Flynn paid no further attention to the treats. He mercilessly continued his savage assault as the men recoiled, swatting aimlessly. Eyes, ears, and noses were assaulted with vigor. Donny shuffled backward in clumsy retreat and slipped, falling hard against a stack of laptop computers, sending them tumbling to the ground. Thacker pivoted toward the door, managing only to kick over a stack of PlayStation consoles, which crashed to the floor.

Then, all at once, it was silent. Neither of the men moved.

"Where'd it go?" Donny asked, hesitant to stand and face another round of attack.

Thacker arched his neck upward and located the thick-bodied fly with its armor of metallic green, hovering above him like a kamikaze. Flynn locked in the coordinates of his final approach as Thacker's hands came up to form a roadblock in the space between them. But it was useless. Flynn shot forward, his shrill buzzing amplified in the compact storage unit. Down he went, knowing as all kamikazes know that this was to be the end. Thacker yelped and then absolute silence.

Thacker's face twisted in anguish. "Holy shit," he said, gagging.

Donny, holding his breath, stared up from his position on the floor.

Thacker looked at his partner with disgust etched into his contorted face. "I swallowed it."

Donny pulled back. "What the fuck, man?"

"I can feel it! It's crawling!" He gagged and wretched. "It's crawling down my throat." Thacker's stomach lurched and, as if a faucet had been thrown open, bile surged into his throat like water into a pipe. He used his tongue as a stopper and bit hard on his back teeth. "I'm gonna honk up," he said.

"No!" Donny yelled, flailing to stand. "No!"

Thacker moved for the exit but tripped on his fallen comrade. Donny bellowed for him to look away, but it was too late. The stopper was pulled, flooding the contents of Thacker's stomach all over his partner's head. A second later, Donny again tasted his half-digested powdered doughnuts as they reversed course and surged north from his belly. Due to his unfortunate position splayed out on top of Donny, Thacker had no choice but to taste them as well.

Flynn threw off his Lone Ranger blanket and stood on his childhood bed, using it as a victory stand as he joyously spun the prop plane hanging from the ceiling. He then leaped to the floor and punched the air like a shadow boxer taking out an unseen opponent before raising his hands in triumph. "I am the greatest of all time," he yelled.

Langhorne stood watching him, his mood decidedly more sedate.

"Of course that means I'm the greatest *flyweight* of all time," Flynn said. "And now that I know where the masks are, all I have to do is—" He noticed Langhorne sorrowful expression. "What's the matter with you?"

Langhorne continued to stare gloomily. "I'm afraid I've also found an important piece to the puzzle."

CHAPTER SIXTEEN

FLYNN WAS UNSETTLED. Not because of the trip—he'd grown accustomed to the sensation of leaping from one place to another—but because of where he had landed. The grass was as green as he remembered, and everything was in its place: the low fence along the southern stretch of yard, the sloping arc of brick patio, the maple tree with its long branches begging to be climbed. But it was all so much smaller than his memory allowed. "Do you recognize it?" asked Langhorne.

"Of course." Flynn eyed the two Huffy mountain bikes lying in the grass. "This is my yard when I was a kid."

"Indeed, it is."

The sun reflected off a toy sheriff's star at his feet and Flynn collected it with a thoughtful shake of his head. "You guys don't miss a thing."

"You know why we're here, don't you?" Langhorne asked.

Flynn squeezed the badge tightly in his palm and looked to a faded deck chair resting at the edge of the patio. The faint sound of laughing children trickled in on a breeze. It was the laughter of two young boys. Flynn's body at once grew heavy, as if he'd been filled up with sand. He could not bear the weight. He almost fell, nearly submitted to his lurching emotions. The voices grew louder, and he dropped the sheriff's badge to the ground. He stood, motionless, as the ghost-like image of his father appeared in the chair.

Harry Barnes was young, younger than Flynn ever remembered him being. The road map of lines he had grown accustomed to were smoothed out, his father's skin tanned and his hair thick and dark. He sat with a goofy grin spread across his face. It was the sort of grin reserved for parents of young children who don't yet know how special they are, don't realize how much they give just by *being*. And how much they are yearned for and missed by growing up so fast.

With a flash that further unbalanced his very core, Flynn realized that when his old man sat in his frayed robe on the tiny balcony of his decrepit apartment, staring out at nothing, this yard was the image he held in his mind. And in those moments of worldly detachment, his father's gaze landed not on some distant, unrealized thought, but rather on the sweet, innocent faces of his sons.

As if tiny holes at his fingertips and toes allowed the sand inside him to flow out, Flynn lightened, feeling as if he could float away. He longed to be his father's child again. "We were happy once," he said. "Before my mom left, when we were still a family. Every night when he came home from work my father sat right there watching us play."

"I know," said Langhorne.

"This is for him, isn't it?" he said. "This is his Happy Place."

"Dad!" Andy's voice came from somewhere behind the garage. "Watch out! The bad guy's coming!"

Whenever they played, Flynn always cast himself as the outlaw, the desperado in the black hat, arriving in town to upset the townsfolk and outdraw the sheriff. Andy would often claim he was faster on the draw and had vanquished his rival, but Flynn never went down a loser. Even if he was hit first by his brother's imagined bullet, he'd somehow manage to fire off his cap gun and claim victory. Andy, ever the rule follower, would obediently suffer the consequences. It was young Flynn's secret that he would have liked, just once, to be the good guy, to be the hero. But the roles had been cast and he played his part well. Harry would cheer, no matter the outcome, never voicing an opinion on who shot first or who had survived the duel. He'd only smile and applaud his two boys, looking as happy as a man could be.

And now Flynn was prepared to see the seven-year-old incarnation of himself come tearing around the corner, chasing the hero of the story into submission. He scanned the yard, eyes flitting through the shadows cast by the thick branches of the giant maple tree, but nobody came. The voices of his childhood had fallen silent, leaving only a dissolving memory in their wake. When he looked back to the deck chair, his father was gone.

"What's going on?" he asked.

"You need to hurry," Langhorne said, clear warning in his voice. "Preparation for graduation has begun. You're running out of time."

Flynn scanned the idyllic mirage that was once his home, searching in vain for an island of solid ground on which to gain an emotional foothold. But no safe haven could be found. For the first time since graduating, he cried.

Harry sat on the sagging couch watching NBA highlights on ESPN. He sipped his beer, gave a small belch, and as he tapped his thumb on the remote, his hard-delivered pleasure came to a sudden and grating end. The images on the screen stuttered, froze, and were abruptly replaced with a kaleidoscope of bright, twitching colors. "Son-of-a-bitch," he barked at the lost signal, spending a fair amount of energy rocking himself forward to set his beer can on the coffee table.

Andy came out from the back bedroom. "What's the matter?" He had been there for half an hour, and his father's cursing was the first words he'd uttered since saying hello.

"Damn cable went out," grumbled Harry, shuffling over to fiddle blindly with the connections on the rear of the set. "What the hell am I gonna do now?"

"I don't know, maybe something that requires the blood to actually circulate in your body."

"Screw it," Harry said, giving up on the connections he could barely see anyway. "I'm gonna get another beer."

Andy watched his father pick up the can of Coors from the coffee table and down the last of it. Harry then placed the empty can back where it had been and wiped the residual moisture from his lower lip.

Harry noticed his only remaining son staring at him. "What's the matter with you?"

"I'm finished going through Flynn's stuff."

"And you didn't find a damn thing, did you?"

Andy shook his head. "No."

Harry steadied himself as he took a half-step forward. "I told you. He was doing the best he could, trying to turn his life around. You saw all his hard work as well as I did. He was *trying*, goddamn it! I don't give a crap what some damn detective said. Flynn had *nothing* to do with that break-in at the warehouse."

"I know he was your favorite," Andy said, his tone thick with resentment. "But let's at least be honest about who he was."

"I know who my son was!"

"Then say it! At least give me that, so I know you're capable of seeing reality."

"My son is dead. That's enough reality for me."

Harry heaved a harsh cough, and his face grew paler. He took a deep breath, rubbing his hand down his throat as if to help push the air into his lungs.

"You all right?" Andy asked.

The doorbell rang, as if announcing the end of a boxing round.

Harry waved him off with an annoyed flick of his hand and made his way across the room. He opened the door and asked gruffly. "Can I help you?"

Flynn stared at his father but said nothing. He wanted to reach out and touch him, as if to make sure he was really there. But he had to settle for knowing that his father was safe from harm and would be as long as he watched over him. "Having trouble with your cable?" he asked.

Harry eyed the Warner Cable uniform on the chubby man with the tool belt hanging low on his wide hips. "How the hell did you get here so fast?"

"We've been having trouble in the whole building. Your landlord called and I've been dealing with your neighbors for the past couple of hours," the cable man explained. "You mind if I come in?"

Harry was not accustomed to having visitors and rarely wanted people in his apartment, but the cable guy was held in higher regard than almost any other station in life. "TV's right over there," he said, stepping aside. Flynn entered the apartment, stopping short upon seeing his brother fuming in the corner.

"Great," said Andy. "Nothing's as important right now as making sure the television works."

"Don't mind him," Harry said to the cable man.

"I'll be as quick as I can." Flynn looked around, unsettled by the sensation of being in the same room as his family.

Harry said to Andy, "If you're done here, why don't you go ahead and leave? Go tell those people down at that damn warehouse you didn't find anything, so they're gonna have to figure out another way to tarnish your brother's good name."

"You really are blind, aren't you?" Andy said. "Flynn hasn't had a good name for over twenty years."

"That's bullshit," Flynn said.

His brother and father turned to stare, as if wondering why the cable guy would have any opinion on the matter.

Flynn nodded toward the television, "The amount they charge for cable, and it's always going out." They stared blankly at him. "I'll just get to work." Pulling the TV table away from the wall, he knelt behind the set and removed a tiny flashlight from his tool belt, pretending to fiddle with the cable box connectors.

Harry headed for the kitchen.

"Dad," Andy said, lowering his voice. "I wasn't trying to tear down Flynn's memory. I was only—"

"He was your *blood*," Harry snapped, pointing a rigid finger. "Why can't you forgive him for his mistakes?"

"I *always* forgave him," Andy said. "*Every time* he messed up, I was there. I gave him money, support—hell, I even made sure he had a job. And it was never enough for him. No matter what I tried, he never wanted to be around me."

Flynn listened intently, waiting for Harry to respond, to continue defending him. But the longer the silence stretched, the more obvious it became that his father would not argue the point.

"He was the only family we had left," Harry finally said.

"He didn't want to be part of our family," Andy said. "He didn't care about you *or* me. He only cared about himself." He retrieved his jacket from the back of the couch. "I loved him too, Dad. He was my kid brother. But I lost him long before he died."

Harry looked at his oldest son, his soft grey eyes clouded.

Andy allowed a rueful smile to part his lips. "You remember when we were kids playing in the back yard? All those crazy gun fights he and I had?"

Flynn, face hidden behind the television, looked up.

Harry nodded after the shared memory, "Of course." His voice was heavy and slow, as if it took considerable effort to drag the words out. "I loved watching you out there."

Flynn's heart raced as his thoughts turned to the Probability Index and some red-tape-loving Facilitator who was making plans to meet his father for the first time. The mere notion of it caused a flood of nausea to rise in his gut.

"That's how I want to remember him," Andy said, wiping at his eyes, "because it was the happiest time of my entire life."

Flynn's mind reeled. *Andy.*

His brother crossed to the door. Neither man said anything more, both arsenals depleted, both defenses worn away.

Harry watched in silence as Andy pulled the door closed behind him.

The images on the television continued to stutter and blink, but for Flynn the picture was finally clear.

CHAPTER SEVENTEEN

FLYNN'S RENTED PORSCHE stayed a few car lengths behind his brother's BMW as they made their way down Vineland Avenue toward the 101 freeway. It was a testament to the amount of tension he was dealing with that, even as he fretted over all the ways Andy's graduation could come to pass, his thoughts continued to drift back to his father's television. He hadn't had time to fix Harry's cable outage before leaving to follow his brother, and he knew the amount of distress it handed the old man. Losing a son *and* his television signal in such a short span would undoubtedly be a heavy burden on Harry Barnes's health.

Andy turned left on Tujunga Avenue and took a right onto the 101-freeway onramp. Flynn figured his brother was most likely heading back to work at the warehouse in Santa Monica. That was fine by him; if it was Covington and his men, or Thacker and Donny, that was pushing his Probability Index ever higher, they probably wouldn't risk anything in a public setting. But what horrible event had been put in motion by Flynn's actions that would lead to his brother's graduation?

Andy moved to the far right lane and took the winding ramp off the 101 to the 405 South. At just past two-thirty, the traffic was still moving, and Flynn followed easily, taking note of all the cars doing the same. Every driver sharing the road was now a suspect, a potential inbound missile that would blow up Andy's life and send him to his Happy Place. It was lunacy to try to assess the threat level of every person who came close to his brother. There were four million people living in the city of Los Angeles, ten million in the entire county, and Flynn would go nuts trying to contain them all.

As they drove into LA's Westside, the when, where, and why of Andy's graduation remained a mystery Flynn couldn't crack. All he could do, he decided, was stay close enough to avert disaster when the moment came. But how? He needed a game plan.

They arrived at the warehouse and Flynn parked on the street, keeping an eye out for incoming threats. Sunlight bounced off the pavement, and soon the heat inside the car became unbearable. He sat at the curb, wiping sweat from his face, worrying that he would not have the stamina to remain vigilant. Two laborious hours passed before Andy left the warehouse and climbed into his car. Flynn, happy to be moving again, followed him to a 24 Hour Fitness center, where another interminable hour passed with no noticeable threat to his brother's life, then through a Chick-Fil-A drive-thru, and finally, to the small craftsman home in Venice Andy shared with Erin.

Flynn pulled to a stop a few houses down, watching as Andy parked in the driveway and carried the chicken dinner inside to his fiancé. He cut the engine and considered how the hell he was going to get through another day in such a manner. And what about when Andy wasn't driving? To effectively protect him, Flynn would surely have to get closer than an adjoining car.

The city was growing dark and the porch lights were

coming on. In the gloaming that slowly swallowed the street, a pair of headlights on a black SUV illuminated behind Flynn. As the SUV passed, he realized he hadn't been the only one following Andy home.

He glanced at Donny as he drove past, the melon-headed killer not giving him any attention as he, too, watched Andy Barnes disappear into the house. Flynn's heart pounded as Donny continued on, his taillights retreating like warning flares into the coming night. He fought the initial impulse to follow, deciding it was best to stay put. His worry, though, continued to run along at full pace. Had Donny come alone? Was there someone else inside the house waiting for Andy? Was his brother inside right now, getting killed? *Shit.*

Using the few skills he'd mastered from the rule book, Flynn made a quick change, climbed from the Porsche, and walked intently up the street, not hesitating as he turned up the walkway to the craftsman home and rang the doorbell.

"Who is it?"

Flynn recognized Erin's voice. "Flower delivery for Erin Bannon," he said.

The door opened and Erin smiled at the pimply-faced teenager in the Farrah's Flowers shirt.

"Evening," Flynn said.

Her smile faded into a confused stare. "You have a delivery for me?"

"No. I mean, we do, but I came by to let you know that we ran out of flowers."

"You ran out of flowers?"

Flynn leaned to see past her, where Andy stood looking on from the hallway. "Yes, but we're getting more in a couple of hours, so I can bring them by then."

Erin chuckled. "Okay."

"We needed to see if you're going anywhere tonight?" he asked, relieved to see everything inside the house seemed safe and squared away.

"I'm sorry?" she asked.

"If you're going to be home for the flowers. If not, I can bring them tomorrow. You'll be home then, too?"

Erin glanced back at Andy, then again smiled at the delivery boy. "Nothing special planned. You can bring them whenever."

"So, you *are* gonna stay home?"

Her expression wavered a little. "That's the idea."

"Great. Have a good night."

"You too," she said, closing the door.

Flynn walked back up the sidewalk, still trying to crack the reason Donny had needed to know where Andy lived. Had he been there solely for reconnaissance? If so, reconnaissance for what? What were they planning? He settled back into the Porsche for a long night.

Darkness descended as Flynn considered his options. Barring the misfortune of Andy's graduation arriving randomly—say as a result of an icy block of frozen human waste falling from a passing airliner thirty thousand feet above and landing with cruel accuracy upon his head (a rather disconcerting event Langhorne had mentioned encountering)—he was certain that with focused diligence, he could successfully prevent whatever Thacker and Donny had planned. Though he did check the rule book to make sure that a frozen piece of poop crushing his only sibling—an occurrence he in no way could be held responsible for—would release him from some responsibility. After a bit of cross-checking and footnote following, he found it would, indeed.

In the meantime, his mind unspooled as many scenarios as it could, each one ending with him playing the hero and thwarting the enemy. In his fantasies, it was easy to succeed when he played all the parts. The reality was that Thacker and Donny—not to mention Covington and his men—would undoubtedly stray from whatever script Flynn constructed. After all, free will was still a major player. As the hours slipped away, the burden of measuring all the angles grew heavier, tiring the machinery of Flynn's mind, and somewhere around two in the morning, he finally fell asleep.

The sun glowed weakly through the thick marine layer of early morning when Flynn awoke inside the Porsche. His breath was hot and his feet cold as he sucked the soggy film of sleep off his tongue. Turning the engine over, he cranked the heat up and looked at the house, as still and quiet as it had been the night before. He was about to nod off again when Langhorne arrived in the passenger seat with a cup of coffee.

"I'm impressed," Langhorne said, handing him the steaming hot paper cup. "I really thought you would head back to the hotel when the temperature dropped last night. Your focus is to be commended."

"No Egg McMuffin?"

"Sorry, no."

Flynn shut off the engine and delivered a stinging swallow of coffee to the hollow depths of his stomach. "You know what the funniest part is?"

"There are funny parts?" asked Langhorne.

"Oh yeah," said Flynn, stretching the bulbous knot at the base of his neck. "Sitting here last night, trying to figure out what I need to get done, it occurred to me that I spent my entire life running away from my family, and now I'm spending the afterlife chasing after them."

"Ah," Langhorne nodded. "You meant funny *interesting,* not funny ha-ha."

"It would have made things a bit easier if you'd told me my old family yard was Andy's Happy Place."

"I never said it was your father's. You're the one who needs to work through everything."

"I'm trying, believe me. But I've wracked my brain and I'm not any closer to explaining how it would help Thacker or Covington to see Andy die."

"You mean graduate."

"Oh, shut up. I'm tired. Do you have any idea how uncomfortable it is sitting all night in this car? If I'd known I'd be on a stakeout, I'd have rented a minivan."

"I suppose Andy will be leaving soon, and you'll have a chance to start moving again."

"It's Saturday. If no deliveries are scheduled at Bannon's, he might not leave at all. I want to look around their backyard and house, see if anything looks suspicious. It's weird that Donny was here, you know?"

"I heard about the flower delivery trick last night. Perhaps they could finally arrive?"

Flynn yawned. "I'm not gonna learn anything from their front porch."

"You could again use the cable going out trick," suggested Langhorne.

"Damn, Langhorne, that's the type of idea that'd flunk you out of Facilitator College."

"Do you have something better in mind?"

"Thought of it last night," Flynn said, picking up *The*

Happy Graduate Rule Book. "Rule sixteen thousand and five. I've already arranged everything—got the look down that I'll need, but still haven't figured out how to successfully leap on my own. I'm afraid if I try I'll end up on a camel in Mongolia."

"I'm happy to facilitate," said Langhorne.

"I appreciate it." Flynn swallowed another sip of coffee and explained his plan. When he finished, he placed the cup on the dashboard. "All right." He clapped his hands together. "Ready when you are."

The dented pick-up truck rumbled down the street in a cloud of diesel fumes, heading toward Andy's house. Inside the vehicle rode three gardeners in hunter green shirts, sitting shoulder to shoulder as ranchero music bounced softly from the radio. The man in the middle strained to hear the music over the engine's hoarse stammer. "¿Sabes lo que es interesante?" he asked. "This music's not bad." He patted down his heavy black mustache with thickly calloused fingers. "Especially when you can understand the words."

The other two men glanced at him, then looked at each other. The driver shook his head, still not accustomed to the odd addition to their crew. Their regular third man had tweaked his back while wrestling with his sixty-pound Shepard mix and had showed up unable to work. They had hastily agreed on Miguel, one of the day workers who congregated outside the Home Depot up the street from their regular man's place. Several houses were on the schedule, three in the hills of Bel Air with massive lawns, and they needed the extra hand. Of course, neither had any idea that today would be Miguel's first day on the job. Ever.

The truck pulled up in front of the house in Venice

and parked. As the three men climbed out, the two regulars immediately went to work. The lead gardener, Octavio, lowered the gate at the rear of the truck, and his partner, Oracio, helped unload the trashcan, hose, mower, and rakes, throwing the occasional uncomfortable glance toward their eccentric coworker. For his part, the new addition continued to stare at the house, eyeing the gabled roofline and the dormer windows on the second story as if lost in some internal struggle. Octavio stepped close with a perplexed stare and handed him a leaf blower.

"Gracias," Flynn said. Taking the blower, he crossed the lawn to the flower bed along the front porch. He absently moved the blower back and forth over the white calla lilies and blue irises as he stood on his toes, peering through the front window.

Straining to see further back into the house, he searched for any movement at all. In his singular focus, however, he had forgotten a major component of the job. The blower had yet to be turned on.

Down the driveway, the two gardeners watched Flynn's peculiar mime act. "I think the new guy is stoned," Oracio said. Octavio nodded in agreement.

Leaving the flower bed behind, Flynn made his way to the side gate and walked along the side of the house. Reaching the kitchen window, he rose up in his rubber-soled boots and peered inside. Andy and Erin were sitting at the table, still in their pajamas, eating breakfast and reading the paper.

Erin, English muffin rising to her mouth, spotted him and offered a friendly wave. Flynn smiled and waved back, pleased to see the two of them sharing a simple moment of normalcy and comfort.

As he stood there, staring through the window, Erin's smile faded. She gave Andy a subtle kick under the table. Andy lowered the sports section and Flynn pretended to scrape some crud from the window with his thumbnail before slowly slinking from view.

He kneeled in the dirt under the window, satisfied that everything was indeed going as well as he could hope. The warmth of the morning sun felt good on his deeply tanned face, and it began to relax him. His eyes were drawn to the yellow marigolds among the rose bushes. The *Tagetes patula*, he thought, had been planted to help fight off rose pests. He ran his fingers through the soil and held some of the dry earth in the palm of his hand as if it were the world's most valuable possession. Using his forefinger to move the soil gently from side to side, he considered the need to add compost and peat moss to the earth beneath his feet to increase the humus level— that would help hold in moisture. He found that he liked being a gardener and regretted not taking note of the earth around him when he was still an undergrad. Sitting there, in the midst of a tiny collection of nature he had never before bothered to notice, he was surprised by his newfound capacity for reflective contemplation. His unexpected rumination on life and gardening would have continued, too, if not for the faint sound of a door creaking open in the back yard.

Dropping the dirt, he walked back toward the street to look for the other gardeners. Oracio stood with the hose, chasing a tumble of leaves down the driveway, and Octavio mowed the front lawn. *If Andy and Erin are in the kitchen and the gardeners are out front, then who the hell pushed open the back door?*

He quickly made his way around the corner of the house, hoping, if not expecting, to find nothing more than a stray cat squeezing through a carelessly unlocked door. But there was no cat. There was only Donny, that fucking balloon-headed bastard, slowly making his way from the house through the rear bedroom door that had sounded its creaking alarm. He was turned away from Flynn as he backed into the yard, clearly unaware he was being watched.

Donny turned on his heel and met Flynn face-to-face, with no idea the mustached gardener before him already knew his name. Though for reasons he could never understand, the gardener could not use it.

"Hola, pinche pendejo," Flynn greeted him, stepping close to halt Donny's hurried advance. "Qué pasa? ¿Porque estás aqui?"

Donny, ever the professional, remained casual, almost indifferent. "No hablo, sorry," he said as he brushed past Flynn.

Flynn spun back to face Donny's hasty retreat and shouted, "¡Párate! ¡No te muevas!"

Donny kept moving, though, picking up speed as he headed along the side of the house toward the front yard. Flynn instantly realized his mistake. "Stop!" he yelled again, this time in heavily accented English. "Hey, asshole! I'm talking to you!"

Donny's trot turned into a sprint and Flynn gave chase, his short muscular legs churning as fast as nature would allow, which wasn't all that fast. They bolted around the corner, past the kitchen window and the bright yellow marigolds. With one fluid motion, Flynn bent low, grabbed up the leaf blower left under the window, and pulled the cord. The machine roared to life as they raced to the front of the house and across the lawn. Flynn's legs churned faster, and he gained ground on the fleeing intruder, whose own physical limitations were also on display. Within a few feet of Donny, Flynn raised the blower, swinging it forward in an awkward attempt to connect with the back of his head. Just missing, he tried again. Donny, feeling the hot air blowing on his neck, ducked and swerved, like a child trying to avoid a bumblebee.

The two of them darted onto the sidewalk in a tornado of jumbled motion and whirring machinery. Unencumbered by a heavy piece of gardening equipment, Donny soon outpaced Flynn as he made his way toward Thacker's car, waiting a block away.

Octavio shut off the mower and looked at his partner standing in the driveway. Neither could make any sense of the deranged scene playing out before them, as the doughy-looking man put another fifteen yards between himself and the irate gardener before falling into the passenger seat of a waiting Mazda hatchback.

As the Mazda's tires squealed and the car sped off, Flynn stumbled along for a few more steps before coming to a stop in the center of the street, sweat and breath pouring from him in equal measure. He shut off the howling blower before raising it over his head like an angry gorilla shaking a stick. "You're not gonna get him, you son-of-a-bitch!" he shouted. "Because I'm not gonna let him out of my sight!"

A couple neighbors stepped outside to take in the surreal scene, listening to the gardener's angry shouts. But nobody had a clue what to make of it.

Flynn looked back at Andy's house, wondering what the hell Donny had been doing sneaking around inside. For the moment, he was reassured that no immediate harm had been done and—if he had any luck at all—perhaps his intervention had lowered his brother's Probability Index by a few percentage points. He'd take any amount he could get.

Flynn spent another two nights in the Porsche, terribly missing the king-sized bed at the Hotel Marigold, and when Andy left for work on Monday, he followed closely behind. Having fully plotted how he could keep control over the rapidly changing situation, it occurred to Flynn that when people talked of having guardian angles watching over them, they probably just had some poor graduate doing their damnedest to make things right. And for him to make things right, the safest place for his brother was at Bannon Imports, surrounded by as many familiar faces as possible.

And so when the muscle-bound UPS man came to drop off a package, he already knew where to find the boss without having to ask. "So, what do you have planned for the day?" Flynn asked as Andy signed for the overnight package that, when opened, would turn out to be empty.

"Just more of the same, I suppose."

The deliveryman pressed, "You going anywhere?"

"Why do you ask?" Andy reached over to take the package.

"I don't know," he said with a shrug. "I like it in here. If it were me, I'd stay in here all day."

"Yeah, I guess it's pretty nice. But with your job, at least you get some fresh air."

"You kidding? The air out there is disgusting. Smoggy. All those cars? It's nasty. It's much nicer in here. You should stay inside."

"Oh, okay," Andy said politely, unsure of the social graces needed to extricate himself from this increasingly bizarre conversation. He patted the package and took a half-step back. "Anyway, thanks for this."

"No problem. I can hang out if you have any packages going out later on."

"We're all set. Thanks again."

The deliveryman reached out for a handshake, which Andy reluctantly accepted. "You have a good day," Flynn said. "Be safe."

Andy forced a smile. "You, too."

Pulling his hand away, which took more effort than custom required, Andy moved up the stairs to the loft office and closed the door behind him. Standing at the large window overlooking the warehouse, he watched as the deliveryman lingered around for close to fifteen minutes. He must have told the truth about liking it there, Andy thought.

Despite the preference of the UPS worker, Andy left the warehouse at twelve thirty to run errands and eat lunch. As he made his exit, Flynn's strategy was put into full effect. It was no easy thing to do. But with careful planning (and Langhorne's help with the required leaping), the necessary defensive measures were precisely employed.

As Andy crossed the parking lot to his car, Flynn the phone technician, perched high up on a telephone pole, watched him with the intensity of a peregrine falcon following the meandering path of a grouse. And when Andy stopped at In-N-Out burger, the cashier who served him his Double-Double and fries made sure to ask, "Going back to the office?" Andy was at a loss as to why he'd been asked and grew even more confused when the cashier seemed irritated when he said he had a few errands. And when Andy stopped to make a deposit at the bank, the ripened bank teller at the adjacent window studied him with leaden eyes, while absently stamping a large stack of checks. "Shouldn't you be back at work by now?" she challenged him.

By the time Andy pulled his BMW into the gas station a

few blocks from the warehouse, he'd undoubtedly had his fill of service people for the day. But as Andy pumped gas, Flynn made sure he was not going to be left alone, even here.

Andy pretended not to notice the homeless man lingering like a smelly shadow behind him. The man's beard was matted, with bits of debris scattered throughout, and his clothes hung like oily rags. "Wash your windows?" the homeless man asked.

Andy turned. "No thanks."

The homeless man stepped closer, breaching the barrier of ocean breeze that held his fetid stench at bay.

Andy put the pump back in its cradle and twisted on the gas cap. As he waited for his receipt to print, he dug a five dollar bill out of his pocket. "Here you go, pal," he said. "Get yourself something to eat."

Flynn looked at the money but didn't take it. He wasn't surprised that the money was offered (though he had never given a dime himself when approached), but Andy's manner in giving it struck a chord. It wasn't merely a selfish attempt to buy off his advance, but rather an honest bid to help a less fortunate human being. Andy was still trying to take care of everyone. Flynn stared, realizing the terrible mistake he'd made in not seeing his older brother for who he truly was.

"It's okay," Andy said. "Take it."

Flynn hesitated, then took the bill. "Thank you."

"Good luck to you."

Flynn was distracted by the taxi pulling from the street into the station. The cab parked sideways, leaving no room for other cars to line up with the pumps. Not that it mattered. Nobody but Flynn would even realize it was there.

"This is a nice little trick you got going here," the taxi driver said, stepping out to greet him.

"Why don't you go haunt somebody else," said Flynn.

"Only stopped by to remind you that my offer still stands."

"Not interested."

The taxi driver laughed, spewing curdled breath that made Flynn's fetid aroma smell like a flower-mart in comparison.

"Not interested?" the driver said. "Bullshit."

Andy climbed into his car and glanced at the clearly disturbed homeless man having a conversation with himself.

Flynn stared after his departing brother, anxious to follow. "I've got it under control," he said, eyes tracking the BMW as it pulled into traffic and headed toward the warehouse.

The driver laughed harder. "You think so?"

Flynn's eyes darted back to the taxi driver.

The driver went on, growing more and more excited. "While you've been running all over town looking like Santa Crack, the situation you're so desperately trying to manage has already spiraled beyond your control. Just as I said it would!"

A twitch of anxiety registered in Flynn's stomach and lit up his eyes.

"There's the light of recognition!" the driver cackled. "Shall I continue? Or do you want to continue playing dress-up and run after your brother?"

"Go on," Flynn said.

The driver dangled a cigarette on his lower lip and crossed his arms over his chest, allowing the worry in Flynn's gut to fester a bit longer. "I warned you it was a shell game," he said, nodding toward the cab. The windshield slowly lit up like a movie screen, the image of Andy's craftsman house in Venice filling the space.

Blood beat in his ears as Flynn stepped closer. On the screen, a black Audi sedan pulled up the driveway and three men climbed out—Thacker, Covington, and the goateed thug from the King's Dragon Pub. Flynn swallowed, but his mouth was too dry to produce any saliva as he contemplated the horror of what was about to happen.

The three men knocked on the door and waited only a moment before Erin innocently greeted them with a polite smile. There was no sound accompanying the images, which lent a muted panic to the proceedings. A seemingly polite conversation passed between them, before Covington abruptly grabbed Erin at the throat, his massive hand fully encircling her neck, forcing her backward inside the house. Thacker and the goatee followed inside, and the front door slammed shut behind them.

The windshield then turned clear, reflecting only the homeless man's anguished face. He spun, looking wildly around, unsure what to do.

"In case you're wondering," said the taxi driver, "Langhorne's not coming. He's off orientating some idiot in Chicago whose inspiring last words were *Jump, I can catch you.*"

The driver's chalky laugh returned as Flynn pulled the rule book and glasses from his tattered pocket and furiously scanned the pages. His hands shook, making it difficult to read.

"Don't worry," mocked the taxi driver, enjoying himself. "You have plenty of time to figure out what to do. That book only has what, a *few billion* words in it?"

Flynn ripped the glasses from his face and took an aggressive step toward him.

"That your way of asking for a lift?" the driver asked, laughing. "Give me the word and I'll have you there in a blink."

The chest-rattling reverberation of a Harley-Davidson motorcycle stole Flynn's attention as it pulled up to the far pump. With little concern for the size of the buffalo-shaped rider or the denim vest he wore, stitched with bold red letters announcing his affiliation with a social group representing the celestial beings of Hades, Flynn ran across the hot asphalt and, using his shoulder like a battering ram, propelled the unsuspecting biker to the ground. The heavily tattooed man stared in shock at the crazed homeless man now straddling his Hog.

"What the fuck!" he roared.

Flynn looked down at him, gunning the engine. "Sorry," he yelled over the frenzied cacophony. "But I've seen real Hell's Angels, and you, pal, are no Hell's Angel."

The irate biker sprang to his feet, snapping a five-inch switchblade to attention. Using a shaky sidearm motion, he slashed at Flynn's chest. The blade cut through his raggedy clothes and sliced open a deep crevasse just below his collarbone. Warm blood spilled from the gash. Flynn cried out in pain as the stinging sensation momentarily overwhelmed him. The biker quickly reset himself and brought the blade back under control. With a grunting effort, he stabbed the knife forward, aiming directly for the heart. But the bold homeless man was half a step quicker. Flynn popped the clutch on the massive machine twitching beneath him and tore away. The biker let loose a string of threatening venality, but the words were lost to the earthquake of noise accompanying Flynn's escape.

Fighting the heat rising from the laceration on his chest, Flynn struggled to right the heavy bike as he rumbled diagonally across the gas station parking lot. With only tenuous control over the Harley and without consideration for the cross-traffic skidding to a halt around him, he cut into the flow of fast-moving cars on Sepulveda Boulevard. Horns blared as an unaware Honda Civic swerved and savagely collided with the driver's side door of a Volvo station wagon in an explosion of metal and glass. The sickening impact sent glass flying like hail onto an elderly couple walking along the far sidewalk. The man's knees buckled, and he collapsed to the sidewalk, his wife screaming out in shock.

Leaving the consequences behind him, Flynn turned south at the corner and rumbled off.

"Well done, Flynn!" the taxi driver called out, watching him speed away. He drew a long puff on his cigarette and smiled. "Well done, indeed."

CHAPTER EIGHTEEN

BETHANY WALKED THROUGH the gallery, making sure everything was in its proper place. The clicking sound of her three-inch black Louboutin heels echoed off the creamy white walls, the color of which almost perfectly matched her skirt and blouse. While not particularly fond of the featured paintings (too abstract for her classic tastes), she remained impressed by the understated class in which they were displayed, and she adjusted a few of the lights to better accent the drama of the exhibits. The space had been a café at one time, she understood, but had been reconfigured into one of the most sought-after gallery spaces on Canon Drive in Beverly Hills.

Bethany was relatively new to her job and was anxious for the owner's arrival, hoping she would be pleased with her attention to detail. "Ms. Bannon is due soon, isn't she?" she asked her assistant.

"We're trying to track her down," her assistant told her. "We thought she'd be here by now."

"What's the hold up?"

"We're not entirely sure," her assistant said, sounding a bit put out by the need for constant updates. "We're looking into it."

"Do you like this?" Bethany asked, pointing at an oil painting of what appeared to be some sort of bird taking flight, or perhaps an elephant waving its ears.

"Not bad," her assistant said. "Though it seems like a knock-off of de Kooning."

"I believe *homage* is preferred to knock-off." Bethany sighed. "All right, I have to run. I'm already late to greet a rather unfortunate ice fisherman in Finland. Please let me know as soon as Erin arrives."

"Of course," her assistant's voice sounded from wherever she was. "But she's just ticked down to ninety-four percent. Evidently this Flynn Barnes fellow is attempting to aid her."

"You're kidding me?" Bethany huffed. "I'd hate for her Happy Place to go to waste."

"At least your schedule might open up."

"I suppose," Bethany said, using a finger to check for dust on the white bench beside the de Kooning *homage*. "Perhaps I can get down to Chile and see off Mr. Jennat before returning. These changing schedules really are impossible to keep up with."

"I'll keep the Probability Indexes updated to see how we can make it all work," her assistant said, knowing that the newer Facilitators tended to be a bit jumpy about servicing the needs of their assigned graduates.

Bethany thanked her and disappeared, leaving the recreation of the brightly lit gallery on Canon Drive in Beverly Hills to wait alone for the woman who had never been happier than the day it finally opened. That was the day, Bethany had been told, that Erin Bannon's fiancé had finally proposed.

Covington's slap landed squarely, and blood rushed to Erin's swelling cheek like the bite of a thousand red ants. Mucous filled her nose and tears welled in her eyes, but she did not take her eyes from the tall Englishman glowering at her. It was unclear from his expression whether he had believed that she knew nothing about any missing gold masks. With short hiccups of breath constricting her chest, she steeled herself against the next act of violence undoubtedly coming. Another tear snaked down the side of her nose, fell over her lips and into her mouth. She tasted the salty discharge and wiped it away, sniffing through her clogged nostrils to keep from bawling like a child.

Following a destructive crashing of dishes and pans, the short man with the goatee left the kitchen, shaking his head.

A moment later Thacker returned. "Nothing," he said, playing out his role. Thacker had made a loud show of trashing the bedrooms, tossing drawers and knocking over lamps with improvised frustration, knowing all the while that he would come out empty-handed. "Maybe she's telling the truth," he said. "Probably has no idea what a bastard she's engaged to."

Erin shook her head. "I don't know what Flynn said or did to lead you to believe Andy would steal anything, but—"

"Goddammit!" roared Covington. Leaning close to Erin, his words hissed through his teeth. "Is it really worth dying for, you fucking bitch?"

"No, it isn't," she said, remaining defiant. "That's why I'd tell you if I knew anything."

"This is bullshit," said Thacker. "Whether she knows if Andy was involved or not doesn't matter. Flynn needed his brother's help to pull this job off. Trust me, I knew him better than anyone, and he wasn't smart enough to double-cross us alone. Who else could it be?"

Covington leaned back on his heels, straightened a bit, and spit on the hardwood floor. After years of beating the truth out of people, he had developed a keen sense for when he was being lied to. He grabbed Erin by the hair, pulling her face close to his. She let out a small yelp of shock but said nothing. Tears continued to drop down her cheek, carrying mascara with them. Covington's grip tightened, twisting her hair with such force that she thought he would pull it clean out. He stared at her, turning the situation over in his mind, finally deciding he believed her. And that he believed Thacker as well. "Keep looking," he said, letting go of the pretty woman whose face he would beat to a lumpy paste if he thought it would help. "We'll burn this place down if we have to."

A rush of anticipation jolted Thacker's heart when the goatee pointed down the hall. "What's in there?" he asked.

"Spare bedroom," said Erin, holding her emotions so tightly that her entire body shook.

"You people need to get a smaller house," the goatee snorted.

Making their way down the hall, Thacker placed his hand on Erin's back and pushed her forward. "You don't need to do that," she snapped, pressing her palm to her scalp to ease the pain. "I get the whole *keep it moving* thing."

They entered the room to find two overstuffed chairs, one made of brown leather, the other crushed green velvet, with an antique Spanish side table resting between them. Along the opposite wall stretched a floor to ceiling built-in bookcase filled to capacity. For now, the room was used as a quiet place to pay bills and read in peace, but someday it would be transformed into a nursery. Erin wasn't sure what would happen when the brutal Englishmen did not find what they were looking for there, but as they crowded in behind her, she could not ignore the possibility that whatever his reaction, it would be the end to every dream she'd ever had.

Flynn raced on the motorcycle, his chest aching from the knife wound that continued to seep blood down his torso. His tangled beard flapped on his sweaty neck and his clothes whipped in the wind like semaphore flags announcing a dire emergency. People stopped to stare with amusement at the homeless man speeding past on the Harley, unaware of the heinous truth behind the wailing pop-pop-pop of the two-cylinder engine. *Only in LA,* they joked.

Approaching a red light, Flynn charged onward, zooming past a long line of waiting cars to cut through the intersection. A distressed chorus of squealing tires and blaring horns rose into the air, but Flynn did not look back. Turning blindly up a one-way street, he played chicken with oncoming commuters for two full city blocks, not giving an inch. Cars banked wildly left and right to make room for the madman flying directly at them, a few bumping over the curb in a desperate maneuver to avoid impact.

One miscalculation and he would wake up back in his childhood bedroom, but he would not slow down, *could not,* knowing that somewhere, a Happy Place was being prepared for the woman his brother loved more than he did himself.

The goatee started at one end of the built-in bookshelf. He pulled books and knickknacks from the deep shelves, tossing them haphazardly to the floor. He dropped a framed picture of Erin and Andy atop the Ferris wheel at the Santa Monica pier, shattering the glass. Erin flinched at the sound; every nerve in her body stretched to its limit.

Thacker watched intently as the goatee moved along, achieving nothing but making a mess. Once the bottom of the bookcase was cleared, the goatee needed to stand on the cushion of the leather chair to reach the top. By then he must have believed it was a hopeless exercise because he started getting sloppy, missing sets of four or five books at a time as he went along. As he approached a large, colorful picture book of Basquiat art, positioned to face its cover outward, Thacker's eagerness grew to barely containable heights. The goatee absently knocked the picture book to the floor and Thacker's heart raced with rising anticipation. But the goatee continued on without a thorough investigation of the space behind, his short arms barely able to reach.

Thacker shifted his weight, trying to stay calm. But the fact remained: he couldn't be the one to find the mask. That one degree of separation between himself and the discovered mask was enough to keep him in the clear and could not be transgressed. It was a tiny detail, but Thacker had learned long ago that in any con, the tiny details were most important; they were the notes the entire endeavor danced to, and as with any song, the missed notes stuck out, bringing unwanted attention to the musician. He forced a laugh and said, "He looks like a fucking baby T-rex up there with those stubby little arms. Maybe we should give him a dictionary to stand on."

The goatee glared at Thacker, then continued on as he had been doing until Covington ordered him to go back and do it right. And there it was, the perfect note ringing out because Covington had been the one to play it. Thacker hid his pleasure behind a disgusted shake of his head as the short Englishman stepped up onto the arm of the chair to better the angle for the upper shelves. He swept his arm back along the passed-over areas, knocking over those books he'd skipped, rising up on the toe of his boot to feel more deeply behind them.

Arriving back to where the Basquiat book had been, the goatee suddenly stopped and looked at Covington with a sly smile. Covington's eyes flicked to Erin, who felt their piercing intensity as if they might turn her to dust. The goatee pulled something wrapped in a white cloth from the rear of the shelf. Erin looked on with considerable confusion as the goatee handed it to Covington, who in turn placed it on the antique side table.

The three men crowded close around the mystery object, blocking Erin's view. She inched closer but could not see what they'd found. Nor could she see the expression on Covington's face when he lifted the cloth to reveal their prize. She could only hear Thacker's raspy voice as it sounded out in victory.

"I told you it was him," he said.

Erin's chest constricted around the thump, thump, thump of her heart. It banged in her ears like gunfire. Covington lifted the five-hundred-year-old solid-gold burial mask he'd arranged to be stolen from the Museo de Arte in Cusco, Peru, and turned to her as if he, too, could hear the sound of her telltale heart. "Either your husband's been lying to you," he said, "or you've been lying to me."

Covington sat in the front seat of the Audi outside of the house in Venice, caressing the edges of the gold Incan face staring back at him, not looking up as the goatee opened the rear door of the car and pushed Erin inside. She lay face down on the sun-heated leather of the back seat and buried her face in her arms. It felt as though a ball of glass was lodged in her windpipe and with each gulp of air another shard broke off, slicing her throat as she swallowed silent sobs. The goatee irritably kicked at her foot, which still dangled out of the car. She bent her legs up toward her chest and he leaned inside. "You keep your goddamn head below that window or I'll put a bullet in it," the goatee said. "You got that?" The door slammed closed before she could answer.

The goatee anxiously glanced around. The street was empty, so he crossed to the driver's side and climbed behind the wheel. Starting up the engine, he gave an impatient honk of the horn for Thacker.

"Knock that shit off, dumbass," Covington snapped, never once taking his eyes off the mask lying across his lap.

"We gotta get the hell out of here," the goatee grumbled.

"You worry too much," Covington said.

Listening to the men in the front seat, Erin surmised that if Andy had been home, they'd both be dead. Or at least she would be. It was Andy they'd accused. What use would they have with her? They wouldn't hesitate to take her life, or to do with her as they wished before snuffing out her light. The thought was like an icepick stabbing at her. There would be nothing she could say to convince them otherwise, nothing she could offer to save herself. To men like these, she held no value beyond being a way to force Andy to admit to some crime he knew nothing about. Whatever they had planned, they hadn't even bothered hiding their faces. She understood what that meant.

None of it made sense. Andy wouldn't have involved himself with Flynn and men like them. But the mask *was* in their house. Had Flynn hidden it there? No. He hadn't so much as come over for a visit after his parole. Tears gathered with greater urgency as Erin considered the possibility that Andy, with his damned inability to turn his back on his brother, had agreed to hide the mask. If Flynn had gotten in over his head, it was easy to imagine Andy saying, "Give it to me. I'll keep it safe until we figure out the best way to get you out of this." Yes, somehow that bastard Flynn had sucked them into his despicable little world of personal destruction. She cried out, her sobs unexpectedly bubbling up.

The goatee turned and glowered at her. "Shut the fuck up."

And she did. It physically hurt to stifle her despair, but somehow, she stayed silent. Her thoughts, though, continued to scream: *Fuck you, Flynn Barnes. I fucking hate you.*

Thacker finally exited the home and climbed into the seat next to Erin. She curled herself against the opposite door, and the bastard Englishman sharing the seat patted her gently on the ass. She kicked out, landing a solid heel on his thigh. Thacker laughed and pushed her foot away, but he left her alone after that. He looked out the window and her silent tears flowed.

The Audi backed into the street and casually drove off. Only Thacker noticed the Harley-Davidson motorcycle parked by the curb, just past the apron of the driveway, but he didn't give it any thought.

CHAPTER NINETEEN

THEY MUST HAVE gone at least ten miles by now. Maybe fifteen.

Even if Flynn had a watch, he wouldn't be able to see well enough to read it in the cramped darkness of the Audi's trunk. He lay on his side, arms folded across each other. The awkward position sent shockwaves of pain from the epicenter of shredded skin and bleeding tissue on his chest. The stinging knife wound pulsed, radiating heat, and he imagined the awful infection that would ensue if he were to keep ownership of the body he currently inhabited. The smell of sweat and blood in the cramped space made the whole ordeal that much more unpleasant.

Erin had been taken alive; at least there was that. Ransom, Flynn figured. Her life for the remaining masks. But Andy didn't have the remaining masks and they wouldn't hold up their end of the deal even if he did. But where were they taking her? *Someplace they can control the situation,* Flynn thought, someplace isolated. And what, exactly, was he to do once they got there? He inhabited the body of a dilapidated homeless man, not a warrior primed for battle. Without the rule book, there was no way he could recall the necessary steps to change bodies now. Could he somehow overwhelm the three men without a weapon? That winning scenario was highly unlikely, if not impossible. He'd witnessed in the King's Dragon what Covington and the goatee could do in a fight, and Thacker alone was one of the toughest men he'd ever met.

Flynn began to regret his hasty decision to climb into the trunk. Would it have been better to wait for Langhorne's guidance? At the very least, Langhorne could have told him where they took Erin, as he had told him that Thacker was in Saint John's Hospital, so he could be better prepared. Hell, for that matter, did his presence in the trunk *lessen* the odds of Erin's graduation, or *increase* them? The car braked and Flynn rolled slightly, eliciting another sharp jolt of pain from the gash on his chest. At this rate, he might bleed out before having to make any more decisions.

After another twenty minutes of stop-and-go traffic, a consistent rush of wind made its way into the trunk. They were traveling at higher speeds. The hum of other cars came less frequently, until he could not hear any at all. Then, the car weaved. A winding road, he realized. A forgotten golf ball bounced from the corner of the trunk, settling next to the tight curl of his feet. They were on an incline. Flynn's every sense heightened, all working in unison to solve the riddle of where they were headed.

The car eventually slowed to a stop, and Flynn heard what he determined to be the scattered popping of gravel crushed under the tires. His breath shortened with anticipation—wherever it was they were going, they had arrived. The change in position was not easy, but he curled onto his back, legs bent like coiled springs waiting to be released. The move painfully stretched the skin around his knife wound, but he remained silent. It wouldn't be long before he could discard the wretched body he was temporarily stuck with.

He envisioned the startled face of the goatee or Thacker opening the trunk to discover him, a crazed homeless man trapped like a rabid dog in a rattling cage. He could not explain his presence, of course, and he could only act the role of disoriented fool for so long before one of them would fire a bullet into his head. Men like Covington didn't allow loose ends. If the trunk opened, Flynn would have only a moment to strike, to push his feet forward like a battering ram. Sweat slipped from his pores like water squeezed from a sponge, soaking his gnarled beard.

The doors of the sedan were opened and slammed shut, vibrating the car with a hum of foreboding. His back ached as his muscles twitched with anticipation. He strained to decipher the muffled voices but couldn't make out the words as the men drifted away from the car. The only sound he heard now were the shallow pants of his own breathing. A few more moments passed, and he thought the heat in the inky black trunk would smother him. It felt, appropriately enough, like a coffin.

Slowly, his muscles relaxed. Confidence rising that he had been left alone and it was safe to investigate, he searched blindly for the safety latch. Gripping it tightly with exhausted effort, he popped the trunk. His opposite hand darted up and caught the rising trunk, allowing it to open only a few inches.

Light streaked inside through the narrow opening, his pupils instantly dilating to pinpoints. The cool breeze tickled his clammy skin. Once his eyes adjusted, he peered out at a thick collection of eucalyptus and oak trees, dappled by late afternoon sun. He remembered the night he graduated, when he was to go with Thacker to Covington's rented home in Topanga, nestled in solitude high in the Santa Monica Mountains.

Slowly, he pushed the trunk open enough to climb out and fall to the ground. From the rear fender of the car, he craned his neck toward the ramshackle two-story house but saw no activity. Standing, he stretched the muscles in his reedy thighs. A screeching blue jay, crown of feathers raised in agitation, flushed out of the trees behind him, but Flynn gave it no thought, concentrating on his next move.

As he gently shut the trunk, gravel shuffled behind him. All deliberate thought retreated at once, leaving him with nothing but an uneasy spasm of fear. Turning, he immediately understood the reason for the blue jay's hasty exit. And it became instantly clear that his next move was no longer up to him.

Three massively proportioned bullmastiffs, their bared teeth extending from squared-off snouts, formed a tight semicircle a few inescapable feet away. Flynn's stomach slipped dramatically, as if it might fall out of his ass. The body he inhabited could barely remain upright. With a constricted throat, he whispered, "Langhorne!" There was no response. He stumbled a half-step backward before coming up against the bumper of the sedan. The mastiffs, saliva dripping with anticipation, grew ever more agitated with his rising fear, smelling the wafting pheromones like flames rising from a grilling steak. The dogs inched forward. The guttural snarls grew louder, more intense. "Langhorne!" Flynn said again, louder this time, with increased urgency.

With mounting ferocity, the dogs began barking. The saliva around their muzzles now foamed milky white; their thick muscles twitched with anticipation. There was nothing to do, no defense Flynn could effectively employ. So he ran. He jutted past the dog to his right as quickly as he could. The dogs gave chase, toying with him as they nipped at his heels. He made it halfway down the gravel road toward the main street before he tripped and fell.

Sprawled on the ground, he looked up as the dogs pounced, their jaws snapping.

He didn't bother to scream.

Langhorne stood before Flynn, trying to affect a sympathetic tone. "It's somewhat curious, isn't it?" he asked. "You'd think the three of them working together would have been able to finish you off faster than that."

Flynn, back in his bedroom, wearing his pajamas, stood from the edge of the bed with a yelp of frustration. He slammed his hands together. "Nothing's working!"

"I appreciate that things aren't going well," Langhorne tried. "But it's not over yet."

Flynn was in no mood for platitudes. "What kind of help is that?" he bellowed. "It's useless! If it weren't for the taxi driver, I wouldn't even have known they took Erin."

"You're not my only assignment," Langhorne said.

Flynn looked seriously at him. "That's right, people graduate all the time. But you Facilitators only start preparing for their arrival when the Probability Index reaches a certain number." His eyes bored into Langhorne. "What's Erin's Index number now?"

"I'm not her Facilitator, so there's—"

"What's her damn number?"

Langhorne hesitated. "Ms. Bannon is currently at ninety-five percent," he said finally.

Flynn shut his eyes. "And Andy?"

"Ninety-four." He listened to some other voice. "I'm sorry, it's now ninety-six."

Flynn sat back down on his bed. "God, Langhorne," he said, the fight slipping away from him. "The taxi driver is the only one helping me at all."

"Is that what he's doing?"

"Over ninety percent! Both of them!" Flynn said. "The driver was right. I can't do this. Not alone. I might as well go with him."

Langhorne remained stoic. His expression was as dispassionate as ever. "As I've said, many people make that choice."

The words caught Flynn off guard. He stared at Langhorne, unsure if the acknowledgment was merely another challenge to stare down, another moral deficiency to rise above, or an actual *suggestion*. Langhorne went on in a neutral tone, "Remember that you're in charge here, Flynn. As long as you understand the consequences, you're free to do whatever you want."

Flynn's agitation doubled. "*That's* the problem! I'm *not* free to do whatever I want!" Grabbing the rule book and glasses from the side table, he flung them against the wall. "You've got me so restrained, I can't get anything done!"

Langhorne didn't argue the point. He pressed on with a quiet consideration customarily reserved for a therapist's office. No judgments, only simple questions in the Socratic tradition, to help his subject arrive at a self-evident truth.

"Would you prefer to live in a world where there are no rules?" he asked. "A world where you can do whatever you want with no repercussions? Is that really who you are?"

Flynn answered as truthfully as he could. "Yes, I think it is."

Langhorne didn't know whether the admission was borne of frustration or was an epiphany brought forth in a moment of unguarded honesty. If it were indeed the latter, then Langhorne considered his work finished. He studied Flynn for a moment, then simply acknowledged, "Well, then, that's a decision only you can make."

CHAPTER TWENTY

ERIN'S MOTHER, JANE, sat in the living room of the craftsman home in Venice, staring out the window. Between her thumb and first finger, she gently rubbed the silver locket Erin had given her for her fiftieth birthday. "Do not fear," she silently prayed, reciting the biblical verse her own mother had her memorize when she was seven years old and so worried about the monster hiding under her bed. "I am with you; do not be dismayed, for I am your God." She closed her eyes. "Please protect my little girl. Bring her home to me." Her prayers were so loud in her head and heart, so intensely offered, that she no longer heard the argument swirling around her like a sandstorm.

"The police would know how to handle this," Jimmy was yelling. "They could send a—"

"Forget it, Jimmy!" Andy yelled across the room at him, still clutching the note he'd found upon returning home to find his fiancé gone. *Call the police*, it warned, *and there's going to be a funeral instead of a wedding. If you want to see Erin again, give us the rest of our masks.*

"I'm not going to take that risk, not yet. We have to—"

"We have to what?" Hoyt countered, his voice a painful

rasp as it sprang from his throat. "You don't have any god-damned idea."

"No, I don't," Andy said. "But until we talk to them, until we know what's going on, calling the police will only make things worse."

"And then what?" Jimmy asked, almost crying.

"Then I'll do whatever they want, if it's going to get Erin home safely."

"They want their fucking masks!" Hoyt yelled at him. "And every goddamn time you deny knowing anything about it, I'm finding it more and more difficult to believe you."

It was just as difficult for Andy to continue defending himself. His own spirit was so injured by all that had happened since finding the note in his entryway, he felt it bleeding from him like an open wound. "I don't know how many times or in how many different ways you want me to say this," he said. "I don't know who these people are, and I don't know *anything* about any fucking masks! Flynn must have been…" His voice crackled with emotion as he struggled to make sense of every-thing. "He must have been in business with them or stolen these masks or…he must have…"

"Andy," Hoyt said, his tone calming, though his face con-tinued to redden. "Sometimes people get in over their heads and before they know it, they can't see a way out. They get desperate and make bad decisions. I understand that, I do. If you've done something, I don't care, I only want you to undo it so we can get our daughter back. Whatever they want, however much money it takes, we'll pay it."

Andy looked to young Jimmy, who had moved to sit with his mother near the window, and back to Hoyt, whose expres-sion had taken on a pleading resolve. "I haven't done anything wrong," he said, his ruined voice now barely audible. "I would give up my life to bring Erin home safely."

Jane broke from her trance and walked toward Andy. Her face was set in stone. Andy expected a slap across the face—surely, she *needed* to lash out—but he didn't flinch as she stepped close. If that's what she needed to do, then he was going to let her do it. His chest rose and fell in anticipation, but Jane reached out and wrapped her arms around him, hugging him tightly, her touch a life preserver tossed to a drowning man. And they both cried.

The phone rang like a bomb going off. The walls of the room seemed to tumble down on them, and everyone's focus melded into one as Andy reached for the cell phone resting on the rounded arm of the sofa. Fighting through the rubble of emotion, he pushed the talk button. "Who is this?"

The voice on the other end was thick and heavily accented. "Do you have the masks?"

"I want to talk to Erin."

The gruff Brit on the other end of the line ignored the request. "A car will be in front of the house in one minute."

The line went dead, and Andy looked to the expectant faces surrounding him. "They're coming," he said.

Jane's tears streamed down her cheeks. "We should have called the police."

"No," Andy said, although now that the moment was upon him, he had his doubts. He quickly texted Hoyt, and his future father-in-law's phone dinged in his pocket. "If you don't hear from me in an hour, call the cops and give them the number these assholes called from. Maybe they can trace it or something."

Hoyt pulled the phone from his pocket and stared at the

number of the man who took his daughter. "Any amount of money, you hear me, Son? I'll pay it."

Andy nodded. He walked to the door and stepped onto the porch. In the fading light of evening, he saw a pair of headlights making their way up the street toward the house. He moved to the bottom porch step as Hoyt and Jane stepped into the doorway behind him.

"I believe you, Andy," Hoyt said. "And I trust you'll do the right thing."

Andy looked at him, then walked across the lawn to the sidewalk. The black sedan pulled to the curb and sat like a demon idling, its exhaust fouling the crisp air of dusk. The passenger side window lowered, and Andy looked inside to see a thug with heavy jowls sitting behind the wheel. "Get in," the thug ordered, his deep-set eyes unblinking. It was the voice he'd spoken to on the phone.

Andy reached for the car door, stopping short at the sounds of commotion behind him. He turned back to see Jimmy struggling to get between his parents.

"No!" Jane cried, her voice like a whip cracking. "No!"

Jimmy broke free, then jumped off the porch and ran to the waiting car.

"Jimmy, get back here now!" yelled Hoyt.

Ignoring his parents' desperate pleas, he pushed past Andy to open the rear door of the sedan.

"What the hell are you doing?" Andy asked.

"I'm going with you."

"No," Andy said, grabbing his arm. "Get back in the house."

Jimmy pulled himself free. "She's my sister and I'm going," he stated firmly, climbing into the back seat and pulling the door closed behind him.

"I don't give a shit who's coming, just get in the damn car," the thug snapped. "I don't have time to fuck around."

There was nothing Andy could do but follow orders, so he climbed into the front seat and shut the door. As the car pulled away, Jimmy looked through the window at the terrified faces of his parents, both crying now, struggling with the unspeakable fear that they would lose both their children in one night. Jane collapsed to her knees as the sedan disappeared around the corner.

Inside the house, the phone rang again.

Donny, who had been waiting at the curb for the sedan to pass, started up his SUV and began to follow. His phone rang. "Yeah?" he answered.

"What the hell's going on?" came Thacker's voice.

"Everything's fine. That dumb-shit little brother of hers decided to come along, but I've been watching for the past two hours, and no police have been here."

"I don't know what the fuck you're talking about. I just called over there and they said someone picked him up."

"Yeah, no shit!" said Donny, looking into the glow of his headlights at the sedan in front of him, "Isn't that Covington's guy?"

Inside the sedan, Andy and Jimmy waited for the intense English thug behind the wheel to speak. But the thug drove silently, intently.

"I don't know how this got so twisted," Andy said. "But we're prepared to pay any amount of money to end it."

The thug shot him a sideways glance. "It's not about

money," he said. "They had something taken from them. They take that shit very personally."

"We didn't take anything," Jimmy said from the backseat.

Andy glanced back, giving Jimmy a look to shut the hell up. "These masks," he said to the driver. "Whatever they are, we don't know anything about them. I think it must have been my brother. It's the only thing that makes any sense. And if that's what happened, I'll help you find them, no cops. But you gotta let Erin go. You can keep me instead."

"Let me think a second," the driver said.

"What do you have to think about?" Jimmy asked.

Andy again glanced into the back seat. Jimmy's face was dappled with sweat. Andy nodded his encouragement and Jimmy let out a series of exhales and inhales as if to keep from hyperventilating. "Relax," Andy said, gently.

But Jimmy wasn't panicking; he was hyping himself up. His eyes widened with expectation as he raised his shirt to reveal a handgun tucked into his waistband.

"But I'm following them right now!" insisted Donny.

The headlights of his car framed the sedan ten car lengths in front of him. "It's gotta be one of Covington's men."

Thacker stood outside the Topanga house, shivering in the evening air. "Covington's man never made it. His car broke down before he reached the bottom of the goddamn road here."

"Then who the hell picked up Andy?"

"How the bloody hell should I know, ya fuckin' Nellie. Just get rid of whoever it is and bring Andy here *now*."

Andy studied the profile of the thug driving them through the darkening city. He needed information before Jimmy tried anything stupid. "Was Flynn working with you?" he asked.

The thug remained silent.

"My brother was a thief," Andy went on. "This wouldn't be the first time he took something that wasn't his. But I swear I knew nothing about it."

The thug wanted to tell him that he knew all that already. He wanted to say that he knew because they'd shared a bathroom as kids and that their father was named Harry, and that the face he was looking at was not his own. But all Flynn could say was, "I'm sorry for all of this."

"You're sorry? I don't understand."

"Yeah, I know."

"What's going on here?" Andy pressed.

Flynn hesitated. "I can't tell you."

"Why not?"

"You don't understand. I mean, it's not physically possible for me to tell you anything. Just know that the men you're dealing with aren't the type to believe anyone can be innocent of anything, so pleading your case will do no good."

"Then what are you suggesting I do?"

"Let me take care of it. We'll have to make up a lie, something to buy us time. I'll tell them I'm your partner and I'll work something out with them to—"

There was a kinetic crunch of metal as the sedan lurched from the impact of Donny's SUV slamming into its rear bumper. Flynn accelerated, but the heavier SUV was immediately upon them again, clipping the rear bumper. The sedan spun sideways, tossing Jimmy to the floor and knocking Andy against the side window. A welt appeared on his right cheek.

The car came to a sudden stop, stalled dead. Flynn turned the ignition furiously, his foot working the gas pedal. The ignition screeched and wailed, but no sparks were thrown. He looked through the windshield to see the SUV pulling in front of them. Before he could formulate a defense, Donny jumped out and ran to the driver's side window, pointing his forty-five caliber, semi-automatic Glock 30 directly at Flynn's left temple.

"Get out!" he said.

"I'm doing it," Flynn said, pushing open the door and raising his hands.

He set his face with his best hard-core gangster expression, hoping to buy enough time for a miracle. *If you're out there, God*, he prayed, *now would be a good time.*

Donny patted him down for a weapon.

"You're making a big mistake," Flynn said, using his new-found baritone to its fullest effect.

"Don't worry about it," said Donny. "I've got collision insurance. Now you," he ordered, flicking his gun toward Andy.

Andy steadied himself, feeling dizzy as he moved from the wrecked sedan. Donny rushed around the front of the car, with a darting glance for any unwanted Good Samaritans he might have to shoot, and grabbed Andy by the back of the neck. "Let's go," he snapped, wasting no time.

Andy flinched like a spooked horse at the sensation of Donny's fingers clamping down and broke free. Taken by surprise, Donny wildly shuttled his gun back and forth between the men. "Don't fucking run, asshole," he warned. "Get in my car."

"Don't do it," Flynn said to Andy. "They'll kill you if you go with him. You have to trust me."

"I don't even know you," said Andy.

Flynn took a step closer. "Yes, you do," he said, still hoping for his miracle. "You *do* know me. Look in my eyes and really see me. *Try*. Or it's gonna be too late."

"This is all very romantic," Donny said. "But I'm gonna have to break you two up."

Flynn inched closer still and his eyes bore more deeply into his brother's. "It's me," he said. "Ffff, Ffff, Ffff—" he struggled to get past the first sound of his name, willing himself to say it. "Ffff, Ffff, Ffff—"

Andy strained to comprehend but only grew more puzzled by the thug's sudden difficulty.

Donny had heard enough. "Whoever the fuck you are, you stuttering piece of shit, you shouldn't have stuck your nose where it doesn't belong."

Flynn stared down the barrel of Donny's gun. He knew he'd failed. He was seconds away from waking up once again in his pajamas. And Andy would be whisked away to his death.

"Don't move, asshole!" Jimmy's screeching voice came from behind them. All eyes flicked over to the sweaty young hero pointing his double-action nine millimeter in the vicinity of— if not directly at—Donny's head.

It was unclear if Jimmy had the balls to actually pull the trigger, but it was apparent that at any moment his nervous trigger finger might take matters onto itself.

"Take it easy," Donny said.

"No, *you* take it easy!" Braces glistening, Jimmy swallowed hard and said to no one in particular, "What am I supposed to do now?"

Before anyone had the chance to respond, the magazine clip slipped out from the bottom of Jimmy's gun and clanked harmlessly to the ground. He stared at it in anguished disbelief. "Oh, shit," he whimpered. (Unbeknownst to him, at that moment, his Probability Index rose to ninety-nine percent.)

Donny smirked. "Looks like you need a little more practice, kid."

He trained his gun and Jimmy shuddered with the onerous realization that he was about to die. He looked to his future brother-in-law, helpless, tears welling in his eyes. "Andy?" he cried.

But there was nothing Andy could do.

Donny pulled the trigger and, instinctively, Flynn jumped to his left. "No!" he yelled, but the plea got no further than the top of his throat as the bullet struck him in the chest, dropping him to the ground like a marionette whose strings had been cut. He was gone before the body hit the ground. His arms folded awkwardly under his torso, his face expressionless as blood stained his white shirt a deep crimson in the misty light from the streetlights.

Jimmy leapt behind the crumpled sedan as Donny squeezed off another round. The second shot pinged into the fender, just missing its intended target. Jimmy screamed, squeezing his eyes shut and burying his face between his knees.

Distant shouts came from somewhere down the street. Agitated, Donny lurched forward, dragging Andy along before pushing him into the SUV. Jimmy continued to huddle behind the car, too scared to move. The tires of the SUV screamed as it peeled out and roared off, leaving an eerie stillness in its wake.

Jimmy's breath exploded from his chest as he peered around the bullet-scarred fender. Ears still ringing from the gunshots, he scanned the debris of crumpled steel and broken taillights scattered on the road. The fallen gun clip lay coldly where it had fallen, but the thug's body was gone.

Flynn awoke in his bedroom, panicked by the notion that Jimmy was just then waking up in his own Happy Place, which he imagined involved some sort of inflatable bounce house. "Damn it!" he shouted, climbing from the bed. By now Andy, too, had probably been killed. And Erin. "Where the hell are you, Langhorne!" he yelled out. A note taped to the back of the bedroom door caught his eye. He pulled it off and read: *Beekeeper's apprentice in Alabama just found out he's allergic. I'll be back as soon as I can.*

Flynn crumpled the note and threw it to the floor. He was trapped. He scuttled across the bed to scoop up the rule book and glasses, where they had settled after he'd thrown them against the wall the last time he was there. His eyes strained behind the glasses as they traced the incessant paragraphs and footnotes filling page after unending page. But he found nothing to indicate how he could escape the confines of his bedroom without the help of his Facilitator, only a section entitled, "When Your Happy Place Makes You Sad. How To Turn Your Frown Upside Down," which mainly included tips on forgiving others and information about the proper positioning of decorative rugs and throw pillows.

From somewhere outside, a barely perceptible melody trailed into the room. Flynn raised his eyes from the book and listened, trying to make out the tune as the volume increased. Lowering his glasses, his ears finally caught hold of it. It was a Muzak version of "Feelings." There was no doubt about it; Hell was definitely close at hand.

Flynn folded open the yellow blinds and slid open the window. The music played louder as the glowing headlights of the taxi cut through the soupy atmosphere, illuminating the cobblestone path leading to the room. Flynn's mouth went dry as the music cut off and the cab turned parallel to the window, idling expectantly a mere twenty feet away.

Flynn looked back to the bedroom door, hoping against all current evidence that Langhorne was about to step into the room, prepared to help him continue the fight. The door, however, remained closed. He turned to the open window and was greeted by the rotted smile of the taxi driver, who was now directly in front of him, leaning on the window frame. "Hey there, Flynn," he said, blowing cigarette smoke into his face.

Flynn recoiled, coughing out the unwanted smoke and the putrefied odor of the driver's breath. An odd metallic taste flooded his mouth and he spit on the floor. "Careful," the driver laughed, "You don't want to get any of that on Mr. Foo-Foo."

Flynn looked at the stuffed teddy bear sitting on the tiny chair and felt the sting of an innocence lost long ago. He had never felt so utterly alone. "I failed, didn't I?" he said, more as a statement than a question. His stomach knotted as if his body was preparing him for the impact of what he was about to hear. "That's why you're here, waiting for me. Because they killed my brother."

The driver straightened up and flicked his cigarette away, its orange-tipped glow floating into the ether like a firefly. "Yes," he said, simply. "And Erin too. They shot them while you were sleeping. Jimmy survived though. Donny missed him after taking you out. So at least you've got that going for you. Can't say I didn't warn you this would happen. Right now, Andy and Erin are waking up in their Happy Places, preparing to move on. Just as you should be doing. There's nothing left to be done. It's over."

Flynn imagined Erin's eyes slowly focusing on some treasured sight she had long ago cherished. But where she was, he had no idea. He felt ashamed for never having bothered to learn much about her, for having no idea what made her the happiest. Except being with his brother. He pictured Andy standing in their childhood yard, wearing his cowboy hat, his silver-star sheriff's badge pinned to his shirt, having the universe explained to him by a harried Facilitator in a peach-colored suit.

Flynn understood why Langhorne was in no rush to return to this particular re-creation of a remembered happiness. There was nobody to return to, just a lost soul on his way to Hell.

A strange calmness washed over him, as if he'd come to the finish line of a long, grueling race. The desire to push forward finally drained, replaced with the tranquil acceptance of his final ranking.

The driver chortled. "I'm just messing with you, man!"

Flynn stared at him, no longer sure what to believe.

"Oh, don't give me those wounded puppy dog eyes," the driver said. "I only said all that so you could feel what it would be like to have this thing finally over. It felt good didn't it? Admit it! I've seen it a million times. Don't feel bad for feeling that way. I mean it was *Boom! I'm going to Hell, fine, let's get the party started.* Right? My point is none of this is about anyone but *you*. It's *always* been about you—what's best for you."

"You don't give a crap about what's best for me," Flynn said. "All I am to you is a *fare*. You're only thinking about yourself."

"Of course I am! That's life," the driver said, his tone dropping to a whisper. "If I don't book my fares, I get fired. And I mean that in the literal sense. It's not fun. How many fares I book is all they care about, so it's all *I* care about. Forget all that touchy-feely crap you've been spoon-fed since you were a baby and grow up! It's all a numbers game. And I gotta take care of number one."

Flynn knew he was right. He knew it as well as any graduate had ever known it; after all, he'd been taking care of number one his entire existence. In an instant, the path before him crystallized. And in that moment of absolute clarity, Flynn accepted that only one option remained. There was no time to conference with Langhorne about it, and even if there had been, there would be no reason. Only one outcome mattered: the responsibility to ensure his family's safe delivery was his, and his alone. Where he ended up was no longer important.

"What's it gonna be?" the driver asked. "I got appointments to keep. You gonna come with me or not?"

"If I do, how can I be sure you'll do everything you say you will?"

The driver put his hand out, palm up. "May I?" he said, nodding to the rulebook.

Flynn handed him the book, then the glasses.

"I don't need the glasses," the driver said, mocking the offer.

Flipping through the pages, the driver quickly found the page he was looking for and pointed his shiny, buffed nail at the pertinent passage. Putting the glasses on, Flynn read: *Any and all accepted offers of help, no matter how small or seemingly inconsequential, made between a Graduate and Taxi Driver, regardless of any attendant physical, intellectual, or emotional duress on said Graduate's part, will be honored by said Taxi Driver without equivocation or exception, or said Taxi Driver will be remanded to Limbo for a sentence lasting in accordance to the schedule laid out in Chapter Fifty-Six, section two thousand six hundred forty-one, subsection five hundred eleven.*

Flynn closed the book and felt the rush of adrenaline he'd been addicted to since he was a child. That feeling had invariably led to trouble, but he would let it carry him forward once more.

It was his nature, after all.

Flynn took off the bulky reading glasses. "All right," he said.

The driver's eyes narrowed. "All right, what?"

Flynn flashed the sly grin that could get him into, or out of, all sorts of trouble. "There's no rule against making a deal with the Devil," he said, tossing the rulebook and glasses on the Lone Ranger bedspread. "I checked."

The driver nodded, offering his hand. "If free will had limits, it would no longer be free."

Flynn took his hand, and they shook. "Amen," he said.

With the physical contact, Flynn immediately relaxed; suddenly, it seemed so easy. The rancor was gone, replaced by a sort of calm acceptance. Flynn was at peace.

"So, tell me," the driver said. "You have a plan?"

"Oh yeah." Flynn took one last look at his childhood bedroom, feeling truly free for the first time since graduation day. "I know exactly how I want to go out."

He then turned toward the waiting taxi and climbed out the window.

CHAPTER TWENTY-ONE

DONNY DIDN'T SAY a word about where they were going. Andy hadn't expected conversation, but he did want a few answers—answers about Erin and about the men who had taken her. When it became clear his questions would be ignored, he remained as silent as the driver. They made their way north from Venice, up the Pacific Coast Highway, beside an ocean as black and deep as the pit of worry in Andy's stomach. Turning east, they made their way up Topanga Canyon Road. There were no streetlights here, and the darkness was like a mouth swallowing them whole. Andy's fear rose with the winding elevation, each twist of the road like the tightening of a noose.

By the time the dented SUV turned off the main street and up the gravel road, the adrenaline in Andy's veins had turned to poison, making him want to throw up. At last, they stopped in a clearing of trees; the SUV's headlights illuminated a man standing in front of a two-story house. Andy silently prayed Erin was inside, alive and unharmed. The barrel of Donny's gun pushed cold against the side of his neck. "Get out," Donny ordered, and Andy opened the car door. He had never been so scared.

They approached the waiting man and Andy recognized the face, though he couldn't immediately place it.

"Nice to see you again," the man said.

Hearing the accented voice sparked Andy's memory. "You were at Flynn's funeral," he said. "I saw you talking to that strange man who went on and on about how great Flynn was."

"That's right," Thacker said. "And Flynn was great, wasn't he? I'm not lying when I tell you, I'm sorry things had to work out the way they did. He was the best partner I ever had."

"Partner in what?" asked Andy, still searching for answers— for something that would make sense of everything.

Thacker ignored the question, just as Donny had ignored them during the drive. "Who picked you up?" Thacker asked.

"I don't know," Andy told him.

"Was it the man from the funeral?"

"No. I'd never seen him before."

"I didn't recognize him either," Donny said. "He was a Brit though."

Thacker nodded, turning over all the evidence. "Someone's been talking out of turn."

"If that's directed at me," Donny said, "you can kiss my ass."

Thacker was intent on questioning Andy further, to try to solve the mystery of who was gumming up the works, but his ruminations were cut short by Covington's harsh voice from the porch behind them.

"Is that him?"

They turned to see his tall silhouette towering over three dark, motionless shapes at his side. Andy could not make out any features on the man, but he was, without question, imposing as hell. After a moment, Andy could make out that the shapes beside the man were dogs, sitting on their haunches, staring forward like cast-iron statues.

"Yes sir," Thacker called back. "I had another man staking out his place and he brought him along. Just a little mix-up. Sorry for the confusion, but there's no problem."

Andy took a breath, wanting to call out to the man on the porch; his instinct to find and protect Erin was almost uncontainable. But there was something so completely sinister about the man's voice, and the way it had caused Thacker to grovel, that Andy held his tongue.

"Get him inside," Covington ordered, and turned back toward the house.

Thacker said to Donny, "Wait here and keep your eyes open. We've had enough trouble, and I don't want any more. I want this fucking thing finished so we can get the hell out of here."

"Hold up," Donny said. "You sent another man?"

"Lower your goddam voice, ya tosser," Thacker snapped. "You want me to tell Covington some other player is out there trying to fuck him over? You think that will help the damn situation? Whoever the hell it was, there's nothing we can do about it right now. Let's just get through tonight and we're out of this shit once and for all." He grabbed Andy's arm and led him toward the house, stopping short to turn back. "And keep your fucking eyes open!"

He yanked again on Andy's arm and they made their way up the stone steps of the porch. The three mastiffs faced forward, muzzles rising slightly to reveal a warning flash of teeth as the men passed.

Once inside the living room, Thacker let go of Andy. He nodded at the short black man with the goatee and the taller, redheaded thug standing at the base of the stairs, but nobody spoke. It was clear they all knew their ranking in the pack, and as none of them were the alpha, they did not break the silence.

Andy's eyes darted around the room. He'd imagined a flop house or a back alley, possibly a cold pit, but this place had vaulted ceilings, a stone fireplace fronted by dark leather couches lain with knitted afghans, and expensive artwork on the walls. These men, whoever they were, were not the amateurs he had suspected.

"Where's Erin?" he asked, breaking the silence.

Nobody answered. At the sound of heavy footsteps behind them, Thacker stepped away. Andy remained still, eyes forward, as the steps grew nearer. They finally stopped behind him and Andy felt the presence of the alpha. He shook as Billy Covington stepped around him, staring with an imposing cool. The large man said nothing. He only stared, much in the same manner as an artist stands back after unveiling a long-anticipated work of art. Andy, very much on display, said, "I'd like to see Erin."

"Of course you would," Covington said, his voice a soft murmur before he slammed the crown of his head squarely on Andy's nose, dropping him in stunned agony to the creaking hardwood floor. A torrent of blood flowed over Andy's mouth and covered his chin, his legs twitching with spasms of pain. Thacker and the two thugs looked on, impressed at Covington's ability to remain utterly calm even as he exploded with violence.

Covington's booted foot swung forward into Andy's stomach. He then raised his foot and dropped it like a sledgehammer onto Andy's spine. Andy screamed and his back arched in spastic response. He nearly vomited. Before he could pull his flailing limbs close to protect himself, Covington landed another kick to his chest. Covington's expression remained fixed, vacant, as the savage beating went on unabated.

An ocean breeze blew in, and Donny zipped his jacket to cover his chest. He didn't like being told what to do by Thacker, and standing guard was like being told to play right field in Little League. They were supposed to be even partners and he believed, perhaps rightfully, that he had somehow been demoted even though he had done all the dirty work. While Thacker had been off kissing Covington's ass and convincing Flynn to behave himself at Bannon Imports, he had been out there running Flynn down on Mulholland Drive and planting the mask on the shelf in Andy's house. Why was he always the one taking the bigger risk? Thacker hadn't been the one almost caught and beaten by the maniacal gardener with the leaf blower, or the one who barely survived almost being shot by Jimmy Bannon. That bastard Thacker, despite his denials, probably did send somebody else to pick up Andy, too. *Fuck him*, Donny thought.

The bounty he and Thacker would split once they sold the remaining masks was the only thing that kept Donny focused, as did the notion of shooting Thacker in the stomach and taking all the loot for himself. He warmed with anticipation at the thought of his partner's slow death, blood draining out of him like rusted water from a crippled spigot. There was no other way to end their relationship. Ever since they'd pulled off their first score—an embezzlement scheme involving an accountant with heavy gambling losses—Donny had had a janky feeling about Thacker. He was tired of constantly having to acquiesce to the tougher—though, in his opinion, dumber—man.

He had intended to end things years ago, but then Thacker had been pinched after serving as the middleman in some bullshit stolen car deal Donny had wanted nothing to do with. The three years Thacker spent inside prison would have ended the shaky partnership, but it was there that he'd met Flynn and the opportunity for their next (and final) scheme had proven too enticing to pass up.

Someday, Donny believed, Thacker would get caught again for some other impulsive theft and his name would pop up as a known associate. But if Thacker were to simply disappear, he could as well. Tahiti seemed an acceptable destination, or some other island with warm sand and warm women. He glanced at the windows of the isolated house set back in the trees, their pleasing glow betraying the brutality taking place inside, and pulled his jacket collar up to cover his neck.

Donny heard a rustling of leaves and stood straight, peering into the darkness behind him. The moonlight offered only enough illumination to see about twenty feet in any direction. He walked a short way down the gravel road and stared into the woods, listening intently. Maybe it was nothing, but maybe that asshole Thacker had denied sending was back. Maybe Thacker had the same plan as he did to break free of the partnership. Donny unzipped his jacket and reached inside for the Glock resting in his shoulder holster.

He walked to the edge of the road and peered into the woods. The sound of crushing leaves grew faster, louder. The sound was irregular and without the shuffling quality of human feet. No, it was clearly some sort of animal. For a moment, he relaxed. But then he saw it.

"What the hell?" he gasped as a shaft of moonlight illuminated the glistening white coat of the charging horse.

The stallion was quickly upon him, and in that instant, Donny could clearly make out the rider sitting tall in the saddle. A white cowboy hat sat squarely on his head and a red bandanna hung loosely around his neck. But Donny could not see the rider's eyes because they were hidden behind a black mask.

"Howdy, asshole," said Flynn, with a smile.

Donny faltered before regaining his composure. He raised his gun, but not quickly enough. Flynn's lasso whipped through the air, its perfect loop dropping over Donny's head, pinning his arms to his sides, the gun dropping from his useless hand.

With blazing speed, Flynn wrapped the opposite end of the lasso to the horn of his saddle, as his mount reared onto its hindquarters and kicked its front hooves, yanking Donny to the damp ground. In a flash, the horse turned and bolted into the woods away from the house, dragging Donny behind. Donny cried out, howling in agony as they sliced through the rugged terrain, across sharp twigs that stabbed like knives and over felled logs that gave no ground to the limp body smashing against them with bone-crushing indifference. The stallion leapt over a shallow creek, pulling the helpless, mangled body through the frigid water. Once across, the horse came to a sudden stop, its hot breath coursing like mist from its flared nostrils. Donny lay still on the shore of the creek, an exhausted fish at the end of a long line, pathetically gasping for air.

Flynn jumped from the saddle and, pulling hand over hand, dragged Donny toward him. Mud and leaves stuck to Donny's battered face as he was helped to his feet. He moaned, blood trickling from his nose and busted lip as his knees buckled.

"I can help you with that," said Flynn, propping him against the trunk of a massive oak tree. He leaned into Donny's chest and wrapped the end of the lasso around the trunk of the tree, pulling it tight. "Better?" he asked, enjoying the grimace the taut lasso evinced. He stared into the strained, puffy face of his killer, feeling no remorse for the blood he, too, would have on his hands, knowing it must be done to save his brother and Erin.

Donny struggled to focus on the unwavering eyes behind the mask. "I can pay you," he said, wheezing.

"How much?" Flynn asked, toying with him.

"Whatever it would take," Donny said.

Flynn shook his head, enjoying the newfound freedom to do as he pleased, with no rules in place to stop him. "I'm not going to kill you," he said.

Donny's eyes widened in their bruised sockets. "You're not?"

"No," Flynn said, stepping aside. "They are."

The rough bark of the tree dug into the back of Donny's head as he stared into the darkness, dread encasing him like a tomb. It took a moment for the manner of his impending death to be fully realized. A pathetic cry escaped from his mouth. He turned his head from side to side as if to find a means of escape, but it was merely a grotesque display of utter helplessness in the face of certain doom. He kicked his legs out, the muscles in his arms struggling in vain against the strength of rope around him as the three bullmastiffs streaked forward through the woods, saliva dripping from their black mouths.

"Get comfortable," said Flynn, stepping into the stirrup and backing the horse away to make room for the approach of the canine executioners. "It takes them a lot longer to finish you off than you might think." Flynn turned the horse and trotted back toward the house.

Like darting shadows in the moonlight, the snarling dogs

cut past him, their furious barks mingling with Donny's terrified screams.

"Happy graduation," said Flynn, without looking back.

Covington stood over Andy like a grizzly bear sniffing to see
if its prey was still alive. Using his foot like a heavy paw, he
pushed against Andy's shoulder. Andy rolled onto his back, his
eyes showing all white before his focus returned. "Why are you
doing this?" he asked weakly.

"I'm not doing anything," said Covington. "You're doing
it to yourself. Where are the rest of my goddamn masks?"

Andy again shut his eyes, and when he opened them, Covington was no longer hovering above him. He had stepped back
to take a sip of Guinness from a bottle handed to him by the
goatee. With considerable effort, Andy pushed himself to his
knees, his elbows almost giving out. "I don't know what you're
talking about," he said, wiping blood from his mouth.

Covington exploded, "You chose the wrong fucking man
to cut out of the deal."

Andy spit a mixture of mucous and blood onto the floor
and realized a tooth came out with it. He winced as he poked
a shaky finger into his mouth to find the empty space along
his gum line. "Where's Erin?" he asked. His mind was lost in
a haze, unable to fully focus. "Don't hurt her."

"This fucking guy!" Covington squatted beside Andy.
"You should have shown this much concern for her before
you decided to go into the smuggling business."

Andy turned his face upward toward him, a sticky string of
bloody saliva hanging off his lower lip. "I'm not a smuggler…"

"Bullshit!" Thacker threw up his hands irritably, stealing
Covington's attention. "You had the fucking mask in your house!"

"I don't know how it got there," Andy wheezed.

"Flynn gave it to you!" Thacker screamed.

Andy shook his head weakly.

"He's obviously trying to protect someone," Thacker said. "Probably that bitch upstairs."

"Erin," Andy said, lungs heaving as he deliriously crawled forward on all fours.

The goatee laughed. "Where the fuck does he think he's going?"

Covington considered the battered man inching his way toward the staircase and then nodded to the redheaded hooligan. "Go get the woman," he ordered, kicking Andy over like a wobbly table. "We'll see how far he wants to take this."

Thacker nodded his pleasure. His performance had clearly convinced Covington of Andy's guilt, and once Covington believed something, no amount of pleading would change his mind. Thacker was now above suspicion and would soon complete the biggest score of his pathetic life. The remaining masks, safely tucked away in the storage unit, would be sold and he would be rich. There was nothing that could stop him now.

Erin sat on the bed, staring out the window as incandescent clouds floated by in the moonlight. She had heard every agonized cry of the man with whom she planned to spend the rest of her life, every animalistic grunt he involuntarily released with each assault. It was the sound of every hope she'd ever had—every good thought and feeling—being annihilated, like a nightmare from which she could not wake. Downstairs now, the silence was the sort that cut loudly, and she strained to hear any evidence that her beloved Andy was still alive. Her head fell forward in silent prayer: *God, please don't let him die.*

The door creaked open and the redheaded hooligan stepped into the room. "Let's go."

Erin remained still, with her head bowed. She was afraid to look up, as if doing so would lift the invisible quilt of protection she had draped over herself.

"What the hell, woman," the thug snapped. "Stand the fuck up!"

Still, her bowed head did not lift, even as tears dripped off the end of her nose. *Stay with me, God*, she prayed. *Please, God. Please.*

The redheaded thug stepped aggressively toward her as the window opposite the bed shattered, glass exploding into the room like fireworks as the blur of a figure swung through. Erin recoiled, slipping from the edge of the bed onto the floor. She ducked away from the splintering hail of glass, eyes slamming closed, her face shielded by a raised arm. And then nothing. Nothing but the sound of her own panicked breath.

When she opened her eyes, two black cowboy boots were planted firmly on the floor in front of her. Her stunned gaze moved up the sturdy legs inside the boots, past the low-slung silver-studded holster with a pearl-handled six-shooter full of promise on one side, the other holster empty. Her eyes continued their steady ascent up the crisp button-down shirt and red bandanna, to the squared jaw and the serenely confident eyes hidden behind a black mask under a white Stetson hat. The cowboy's right arm was outstretched, holding another six-shooter. The rounded barrel of the glistening revolver rested squarely on the forehead of the trembling, redheaded hooligan.

"What the fuck's going on up there?" asked Covington, his calm exterior losing its icy luster. No one had an answer for the commotion upstairs, though a clue was supplied when the redheaded hooligan's unconscious body dropped past the downstairs window and landed with a sickening thud on the front porch. Covington crossed to the window and peered outside at the mangled lump lying there. He turned and growled at the goatee, "Get up there, now!"

The goatee balked and pointed at Thacker. "Why doesn't he have to go?"

Flynn pulled Erin to the window. The chaos of the last few moments had left her unsure how to process the extent to which the situation had changed; her thinking was rattled, and she wiggled free from Flynn's grasp.

"I'm not gonna hurt you!" he said, grabbing her again as she continued to resist. "Listen to me! You have to go now. I'll take care of Andy."

Hearing the name instantly calmed her. "You know Andy?" She searched the blue eyes hidden beneath the mask. "Who are you?"

"It's impossible to explain," he told her. "But you need to do exactly as I say, or this can still go very badly for all of us."

"I don't understand."

"Yes, I know!" Flynn said, his tone sharpening. "That's because it's impossible to explain. I just said that!" He took a breath. "Just get to one of the neighbors down the road as fast as you can and call the police."

Cool air through the blown-out window slapped at her face, sharpening her focus. She leaned out and eyed the unconscious redhead almost twenty feet below. "I can't make that jump," she said.

"I'm gonna help you." Flynn then leaned through the

window and whistled, drawing the majestic white horse from the surrounding trees.

"This is insane," Erin noted as the horse settled itself directly below, straddling the redhead.

"He'll take you down the road," Flynn said, not arguing against her assessment. "You have to go. Now!"

Still, she hesitated. Flynn swiftly brought one arm under her legs, the other bracing her back, and lifted her over the ledge of the window. "Oh shit," she said, tensing in his arms. "Wait, let me try to—"

But there was no time for discussion, as the men downstairs had to be wondering by then what the hell a goddamned *horse* was doing outside their house. Flynn let go and Erin dropped through the air, landing perfectly, if not comfortably, onto the wide seat of the silver-studded saddle. A throaty grunt, married to a sharp squeal of pain, escaped her mouth as she grabbed at her aching hips.

Flynn thought for a moment that she wouldn't be able to hold on, fully understanding why actors always step aside for stunt doubles. But when the horse lurched forward, Erin grabbed hold of its neck and gained enough balance to stay in the saddle as they bounded off the porch. From his vantage point, Flynn watched Thacker run out the front door of the house, giving a futile few strides of disbelieving chase as the stallion tore off into the night with its precious cargo intact.

"Don't fucking move," the goatee shouted behind him, drawing Flynn's focus.

The goatee stood at the door, pointing his Sig Sauer pistol.

"Howdy," Flynn said, hands raised.

"What the hell is this?" He stared incredulously at the masked cowboy.

"Is the outfit too much?" Flynn asked, inching forward. "I was worried it would look silly."

"Stay where you are," the goatee ordered, extending the gun. "Covington! Thacker!" he called out. "Get up here!"

"Why don't we go down and see them instead?" Flynn suggested.

"Shut up! Or I'm gonna put a bullet in your—"

Before the goatee could finish explaining where exactly he would like to put his bullet, Flynn drew his pearl-handled six-shooter from its holster and delivered one of his own. The goatee's gun fell to the hardwood floor as Flynn's bullet convulsed through his hand. The goatee fell to his knees, his hand now a gruesome lump of distended flesh and shattered bones. Blood coursed from the wound, dripping down his wrist, as the goatee tucked it between his opposite arm and his chest, grimacing with pain.

"You saw how I'm dressed," Flynn scolded him. "Did you really think you'd be faster on the trigger?"

Hearing the single shot fired above, Covington lurched forward and pulled Andy to his feet, using him as a shield. Andy was in no shape to resist, let alone fight back, and his knees buckled. Covington gripped tighter, needing all of his considerable strength to hold Andy up.

Thacker ran back into the house. "That bitch got away," he said. "She just rode off on a goddamn horse!"

Covington's expression leapt right past confusion and landed on delirium. "What the hell are you talking about?"

Thacker retrieved the Glock from the table next to the couch. He checked the magazine. All ten rounds remained. Covington indicated with a sharp nod that he wanted him to take position at the bottom of the stairs. But Thacker was in survival mode now; he crossed behind the couch, holding his weapon straight out in front of him, ready to fire like hell at whomever came down the stairs.

His mind raced. Was it Donny causing all this mayhem? Had he decided to take everyone out? Would he be so bold, so crazy to try something like that? Or was it someone else? The man who'd picked up Andy? It occurred to Thacker he might have unwittingly stuck himself in some unknown war between Covington and some other crime lord. The tension grew and crept up his spine into his brain. The pain throbbed and expanded until his head felt like an over inflated balloon about to pop. Fuck it, he thought. He was done with this shit. He certainly wasn't going to wait to discuss it with any of these assholes.

Feet shuffled on the landing above as Thacker aimed, and the goatee stumbled down the risers, thanks to a gentle push from the nameless cowboy behind him. He was halfway to freedom when Thacker's bullet entered his right temple, killing him instantly. His lifeless body continued its awkward descent, coming to rest in a wretched ball at the bottom landing.

"Dammit!" Covington yelled at the sight of his friend lying dead. "What the fuck is wrong with you?" he yelled at Thacker.

Thacker swallowed hard and continued pointing his weapon, unsure where he should be aiming it. With everything going to shit, one dead and the other presumably on his way, he considered the option of turning the gun on Covington, the man he had once revered and feared in equal measure. Measuring the odds of escape if he shot Covington and ran, he decided to stand pat. Like any gambler, he wasn't willing to place a bet without assurances it would pay out.

A jangling of spurs in the darkness at the top of the stairs refocused his attention. Slowly, footsteps made their way down, each thudding step announcing a coming specter of destruction.

Thacker and Covington shared a nervous look as the footsteps stopped, just as the phantom responsible was to make an appearance. Covington, still clinging to Andy, moved back. Thacker trained his gun at the top step visible to him from his vantage. His finger rested on the trigger, waiting. Anticipating.

From his position on the stairs, Flynn gathered himself. This was the moment. If the taxi driver had told the truth, he would not once again wake up in his childhood bedroom, learning of his brother's demise. He took a breath. Putting all of his weight on the heels of his black boots, he bent his knees and leapt forward, as if sprung loose from a tight spring. Thacker's finger twitched on the trigger of his Glock, and the magazine spit out a fountain of bullets with a deafening cacophony. The iron guard rail of the stairs sparked and rattled with their chaotic impact, the bullets ricocheting off, pockmarking the walls.

Flynn's torso stretched out in front of his falling body. In mid-air, he turned sideways to the room below, his pearl-handled six-shooter finding a steady horizontal plane as it sounded out its presence with a deafening report, finding its target. With the impact of Flynn's bullet shredding his shoulder, Thacker dropped his gun and stumbled away from the lost protection of the couch, yelping and cursing.

Flynn rolled forward as he landed at the bottom of the stairs, using the lifeless body of the goatee to soften the landing. With one fluid motion, he sprang to his feet and trained his gun directly at Covington.

Covington, in all of his years facing both criminals and

cops, had never been so shaken. "Drop your fucking gun!" he yelled. His muscular arm was wrapped around Andy's throat, his opposite hand in position to twist Andy's head like bottle cap. "I'll break his goddamn neck."

Andy's swollen face sagged under the pressure of the larger man's lethal pressure. His eyes, blood red, filled with tears.

"I'm not here for you," Flynn said to Covington.

"Then what the fuck do you want?" Covington asked.

Flynn considered his answer. What he wanted was something he couldn't have: a life that had once been possible, which he had rejected without regard. It was a notion, however, that Covington was not equipped to understand. Besides, the time was not at hand to explain anything. There were still sacrifices that needed to be made.

He turned the six-shooter on Thacker. "Why don't you tell him?"

"I have no bloody idea," Thacker raged, spit flying from his mouth as he grabbed at his wound. Blood seeped through his shirt, staining his fingers.

Flynn stepped closer. "Sure you do," he baited him. "Tell him who was really behind the double-cross."

"We already know who was behind it," Thacker yelled, as much for Covington's sake as his inquisitor's.

"Do we?" Flynn asked.

"What the fuck is he talking about?" Covington asked, loosening his grip on Andy. It was becoming clearer that the cowboy's presence—as strange as it was—indeed had more to do with Thacker than him. "What have you done?"

"I haven't done anything, goddamnit!" Thacker insisted.

The massive Englishman's hand slid free from Andy and he took a small step forward.

Flynn glanced his way and Covington hesitated, but Flynn had no intention of stopping his approach. In fact, he wanted him to have a front row seat for the show. He turned back to Thacker and raised his six-shooter once again. Thacker sucked in his breath, shaking with anticipation of the next bullet.

Flynn, though, had other plans for his one-time best friend. He swung his arm wide and fired at a wrought iron crate next to the stone fireplace. The solid silver bullet shattered the rusty hinges of the ancient crate and they flew loose. Onto the floor spilled the five remaining burial masks, their bewildered gold faces staring back through history at the equally bewildered faces staring down at them.

Covington took another step toward the masks. "Son-of-a-bitch."

Surprise, pain, and confusion flushed Thacker's face. "Donny," he said, all other suspects falling away. "He fucking turned on me, didn't he?"

Flynn shrugged. "Sorry," he said. "Dead men tell no tales." He leveled the gun at Thacker's head.

"No!" Thacker screamed.

"Go ahead," Covington said to Flynn. "Kill the bastard."

With Covington's directive ringing in his ears and nowhere to hide, Thacker panicked and stumbled onto his backside, recoiling in the panicked retreat of a trapped animal. But there was nowhere to go, no rat-hole to crawl into. It was not the first time Thacker had stared down the barrel of a gun, but it looked to be his last. He cried out for mercy like the coward he was, while Covington watched with the calm detachment of a true killer.

Andy lowered his eyes and waited for the gruesome death to play out, not wanting to witness the fate he still wasn't sure wouldn't be his own. There was a slight hesitation in the room, a palpable break in the hostility, but instead of a sickening gunshot filling the void, Andy heard the cowboy's voice.

"Andy," Flynn said.

Andy looked up to see the cowboy staring at him beneath the mask, his back now turned to Thacker, his pearl-handled six-shooter lowered to his side.

"You're gonna be okay," Flynn said, softly. "I made sure of it. It's my payment for everything I took from you."

A shot rang out. Flynn's eyes flinched and a small gasp escaped his mouth. Andy did not fully comprehend what had happened until the cowboy fell to his knees, his body folding inward like a collapsing tent. Andy looked past him and saw Thacker holding the nine millimeter Glock he had retrieved from the floor.

Thacker struggled to his unstable feet, sweat pooling at his temples, his bloody shoulder sagging. He swung the gun toward Covington. "I'm just a thief," he said, steadying himself. "I never intended to kill you, but now I have no choice."

Covington worked through the situation before erupting. "Then you'd better shoot right, you bastard, or you're a dead man!"

The ferocity of the threat startled Andy and he looked up from the dying cowboy before him.

Thacker, however, was not startled. He was back in control. Now his voice was solid ice and Covington's trembled with emotion. Thacker allowed the moment to linger, enjoying the role reversal. "It was you I always wanted to be like," he said. "And now, here I am. I guess there's a certain poetry to all of this. As if there was no other way it could end."

Flynn, moments away from his final collapse, knew that

was not exactly true. He extended his pearl-handled six-shooter to Covington. Covington grabbed the gun but was too slow by half. Before his fingers could grip the smooth pearl handle, Thacker blew a hole in his sternum just below his neck. Covington collapsed, gurgling as his chest filled with blood. He died with his eyes wide open, staring out at the world with the same numb detachment as when he was still an undergrad. Thacker inched forward and stared down at the lifeless body of his one-time mentor.

Andy, unaccustomed to such violence, vibrated with emotion as the cowboy stared at him, seemingly transfixed in his own moment of death.

"You were right when you said I only cared about myself," said Flynn, lowering the mask covering his teary eyes. "But you were wrong about losing me. It was me who lost you."

The conversation with his father only days before washed through Andy's reeling mind as he struggled to recognize the man staring back at him.

Flynn's expression lightened and his body warmed as if a blanket had been laid across his back. "I finally got to be the good guy."

A spark of realization lit in Andy's mind. "Flynn?" he asked, knowing the question was lunacy but unable to restrain himself. Flynn's eyes closed and his head lolled at the end of his limp neck. Andy reached out, as the weight of his little brother's body fell against him.

"You're both fucking daft," Thacker laughed. "And I've had enough of it."

Andy straightened to see Thacker's gun pointed at him. He had no time to react before Thacker fired, the deafening blast of the gunshot jolting the air.

In that very instant, Flynn cried out, "Taxi!"

At once the room stuttered like a reel of film stuck in its projector. The bullet from Thacker's gun lurched forward by inches, as if struggling through molasses before stopping in mid-air, hanging unsupported halfway to its target. Andy's right hand moved upward in a defensive movement and then froze in place, part of the rigid statue that he had suddenly become. Thacker, too, remained fixed in time, his eyes caught in the half-mast of a blink, a drop of blood from his bullet wound hovering in space, halfway to the floor.

It was more than silence that swallowed them whole—it was the total absence of all *resonance,* a void in which not even a vibration of existence could be heard or felt. The condition that is, quite simply, the opposite of life.

While undergrads often assume death is the opposite of life, that's only because they're not very bright and don't real-ize death is nothing but a confusing concept thought up by a fellow undergrad during the Lower Paleolithic Period of human existence. Evidently, the responsible undergrad was upset he wasn't the one to master control over fire and was sulking as his friends warmed themselves around what had previously been an uninspiring pile of dried sticks. So he made up the entire concept of eternal death in order to scare them. Death, then, was merely the world's first really good campfire story.

And now the only thing moving inside the house in Topanga (though not at all willfully, as it was actually a state of non-existence) was Flynn. To be exact, it was Flynn's head that was rolling forward, though he had no way of knowing if it was still attached to his neck, as he could not *feel* anything. His eyes stared down at what he had once considered to be the floor, but he could no longer discern what it was, exactly, or for that matter if he was floating above it or resting on top of it.

In truth, there was no longer any meaningful difference between him and the floor. It was all one thing. There was no pain or pleasure in this awareness, or more specifically, this lack of awareness. He felt neither sad, nor concerned, nor afraid, nor happy. He just *was*. And where he *was,* in fact, was *Limbo,* a sort of clearance house, a place where souls are stored as their fate is worked out and their shipping destination determined.

Flynn had no concept of how long he had been in this state, or how long he was to remain, which is the one and only blessing afforded anyone unlucky enough to be stuck in Limbo. If even the slightest drop of consciousness were to find its way inside, the anguish would be horrifically searing, enough to cause a soul to tear from the fabric of existence and implode into itself. It is such a terribly painful fate, it is reserved only for a select few that even Hell doesn't want. Hitler, for example, had his ticket punched there. Six million times.

Only once Flynn's decision to accept the taxi driver's help had been fully dissected by the powers that be did Flynn come to realize it was indeed a floor beneath him and that he was not floating above it but kneeling on it. The fact that he could realize *anything* meant he was not destined to stay, and was, in fact, leaving Limbo. Or *separating* from Limbo, as it is called by those in the know.

He presently felt the wood floor once again creaking beneath his knees and heard the familiar strains of "Feelings" drift into the room. A moment later the yellow taxi arrived like a phantom through the wall.

The driver leaned out of the window. "Are we having fun?" he asked, smiling.

Flynn had no time to respond. Like a branding iron pressed into his back, he felt the searing burn of Thacker's bullet fully return. The last bit of breath inside of him unceremoniously floated out of his mouth, and he collapsed to the floor.

CHAPTER TWENTY-TWO

FOR THE FIRST time since graduating, Flynn awoke someplace other than his childhood bedroom. He stood on an expanse of impossibly green grass at the very center of a massive stadium, surrounded by sixty-eight thousand empty red seats. Curious, he thought. But he hadn't the energy to figure it out. For now he was simply happy that the taxi driver hadn't lied to him after all, and he wasn't waking up tied to a lake of fire or some such other fate that fearful and imaginative undergrads believe Hell to be. Though he considered the possibility of the surrounding seats suddenly filling with bloodthirsty succubi with stubby horns on their heads, waving pitchforks and calling for the show to begin, he took solace in the fact that he was, at least momentarily, safe.

It took Flynn a moment more to notice that he was no longer dressed as a cowboy, nor was he wearing pajamas, but rather a powder blue smock, like a doctor's scrubs. He had no shoes on and the grass under his feet tickled between his toes.

My toes, he thought. Even though he was no longer confined to his Happy Place, they were actually his toes, not some foreign digits of a foot he didn't recognize. He held his hands up for examination and found them to be his as well. He ran his fingers over the contours of his face, tracing his nose, cheeks, jaw, and lips like a blind man trying to make a positive identification. He pulled the waistband away from his hips and looked down at his penis. "I'm free!" he shouted, his voice reverberating in the cavernous space.

Behind him came the rumble of a car, and he turned to see the taxi slowly approaching. His excitement receded. The car pulled close and the driver got out without so much as a glance toward him. It was as if he didn't even see him standing there.

"Where are we?" Flynn asked.

But the driver said nothing, still not bothering to look Flynn's way. He moved with purpose to the passenger door of his cab. Unsure what to expect, Flynn felt exactly like he had the first time he awoke in his childhood bedroom and Langhorne came through the door to greet him. He wondered when Langhorne would learn of his deal with the taxi driver. Would the decision bother him? He imagined his Facilitator taking it all in with a shrug. Langhorne never had been much for sentimentality, now that he thought about it. Perhaps he would never even see him again. The notion saddened him. He accepted, though, that even if Langhorne didn't share his feelings, even if he had read too much into their relationship and was merely another assignment to be logged into some cosmic ledger, Flynn would miss his one-time Facilitator.

Langhorne's reaction to all of this would, however, be discovered much sooner than Flynn could ever have expected. He watched the driver dutifully open the back door to his rusty bucket of a taxi and Langhorne himself stepped out. He straightened his perfectly tailored peach-colored suit and, with a gentle finger, returned a stray hair to its proper place upon his head.

Flynn shuffled his feet and tilted his head slightly to the

side, as if not believing his own eyes. But they *were* his own eyes, and they were not failing him.

Langhorne advanced toward Flynn with his customary casual gait, the driver lingering a few unassuming paces behind. "Sorry we're late," he said, stepping close.

Flynn's confusion mounted. "What do you mean sorry *we're* late?"

"Just that," Langhorne answered with his familiar, easy grin. "Meaning we would have been here waiting for you when you arrived, but my driver had to stop off and see a congressman he's been consulting with."

"Your driver?" he stammered. "I don't understand, what are you doing riding with him at all?"

Langhorne studied Flynn with a glint of mischief in his eye. He had something up his sleeve, *but what?* Flynn's sharp mind turned it over, but he couldn't figure it out. Langhorne gave no answers as he casually removed a pack of Chesterfield cigarettes from his coat pocket and shook one into his hand. The driver dutifully leaned between them to light it for him.

"And since when do you smoke?" Flynn asked, his jaw aching from the diffuse stress circulating in his body like a discharge of electricity.

Langhorne blew a perfectly executed smoke ring into the air and laughed. It was the sort of laugh one gives not when they *hear* a joke, but when they've already *told* one and the audience is on the verge of getting it. As Langhorne's merriment grew louder, more biting, the colors of his suit began to bleed and darken, the peach turning to a muted pink, then crimson and finally to a deep blood red.

"This is much better, don't you think?" Langhorne asked,

taking another puff. "Be honest, the peach made my thighs look fat, didn't it?"

Flynn's body quaked under the blue smock. He tried to focus but found it difficult to maintain balance. His blood flowed hotter in his veins, struggling to make it up to his overwhelmed brain, fighting all the way against the gravity of the moment.

"You see, Flynn," Langhorne said. "God's not the only one who works in mysterious ways."

When the taxi driver reached over to pick a piece of white lint from the arm of Langhorne's suit, the panicked suspicion coursing like hot oil through Flynn's veins was instantly solidified, immobilizing his limbs and setting his expression like stone. "Jesus," he gasped.

"Not quite," said Langhorne with a slight shrug.

Flynn's senses were so scrambled, so muddled with confusion, that he found it difficult to choose which one to engage. "You're the Devil?" he managed to spit out.

"Of course not!" retorted Langhorne as if the question were the dumbest thing he'd ever been asked. "After all we've been through and you're still thinking like an undergrad. The Devil's not a *person*."

"Then who, or *what* are you?"

"I've told you what I am. I'm a Facilitator."

"Yes, that's what you *told* me," Flynn said, his innards slowly rearranging themselves into a semblance of useful productivity. "You told me lots of things. But it's all been a lie, hasn't it? This whole thing's been a lie."

Langhorne twirled the cigarette in his long, delicate fingers and shook his head. "I'm hurt you would think that," he said.

"I really am. I've never once lied to you. Everything I've told you has been the absolute truth."

"How can that be if—"

"Your actions did put Andy and the others in jeopardy, didn't they?" Langhorne interrupted, as though leading a four-year-old to the simple conclusion that one plus one equals two.

Flynn took the question at face value and nodded his assent. "Okay, that part might have been true, but—"

"But nothing, Flynn." His chin gave a slight hitch downward and his eyes widened underneath a modest arch of his brow. "It's really quite simple. I have been doing everything I can to help you. But I never said I was trying to help you get to *Heaven*."

It all instantly clicked, the shimmering mirage in Flynn's mind taking on a fixed and steady disposition. "You're a Facilitator for *Hell*," he said.

"You see," Langhorne explained, "the problem was that you weren't quite deserving enough to be let right in without debate, so we needed to see how things played out—to see which path you would choose. That's how it works for graduates such as you. *The Pales*, as you're colloquially known, a name a bit too poetic for my taste. But be that as it may, we're afforded the final crack at collecting your soul. It would help to think of us as the prosecution."

"I've been on trial this whole time?" Flynn asked.

"Yes. To determine whether you could achieve an FRR."

"An FRR?"

"A fully realized redemption," explained Langhorne. "The one thing we fear most."

Flynn's mind continued to roil. "All those times you disappeared when I needed you, when you let me stumble down the wrong path. You wanted me to fail all along."

"I didn't care one way or the other," Langhorne told him. "If you had failed to save your brother, or your father, or Erin, or whoever it turned out to be, we'd still get you for a quarter of an eternity. That's not bad. The real point of the trial was your personal redemption—which disparate bits of your nature would win out."

For Flynn, it was all slowly sinking in. "You wanted me to *choose* Hell," he said. "That way, you'd get me forever."

Langhorne nodded. "If you think about it in those terms, you should feel complimented."

Flynn felt many things, but complimented wasn't one of them. "You tricked me into accepting the driver's help!"

"I did no such thing. You made that decision all on your own."

Flynn shivered, even though he wasn't cold. "What happens to me now?"

"You're gonna burn!" the taxi driver cackled.

Flynn backed away. For a moment he thought to run, but to where? He was as trapped here as he had been in his childhood room.

"Look at his face!" the driver said. "He's so scared!"

"Yes," Langhorne said. "It never gets old."

The driver's laughter abated as he composed himself. "I love it when they fall for that. They're so stupid."

"Fall for what?" asked Flynn, unable to shake the quiver of trepidation from his voice.

Langhorne took a deep breath and tried to explain. "During your suspension in Limbo, your trial was fully adjudicated, all your behaviors, your actions and reactions, all of your motives and intentions. Everything was poured over, including every effect on the undergrads in your sphere of influence. Nothing was left unweighed. We really made a milkshake of it all. Of course, when discussing any exercised cooperation between the Taxi Drivers and the the Pales, that sort of debate isn't uncommon between the opposing sides of the eternal divide. It's imperative, after all, that any and all agreements fall strictly within the well-defined parameters of free will, without any undue coercion from either the Taxi Drivers or the Facilitators. You didn't feel coerced into going with him, did you?"

Flynn shook his head.

"Of course you didn't," Langhorne said, proudly. "We're sticklers for never losing a soul on a technicality like that! But, even under the best of circumstances, it's always a grey area." Langhorne sighed. "Unfortunately, despite our best effort, in the end it was ruled that, even though I won the battle to get you into the taxi, I lost the war for your soul."

Flynn raced to catch up to the implication. "You mean…"

"Yes," Langhorne said, looking like saying the words made him sick to his stomach. "You've been granted your precious little redemption."

"It's too bad," the taxi driver said. "I tried my best to strike a deal with you before your FRR. I almost had you, too, with that move into the Hotel Marigold." He shook his head. "But I couldn't close the deal."

"But if I was already redeemed," Flynn said, still trying to piece it all together, "then why help me save Andy in the end?"

The taxi driver rolled his eyes with disgust.

"You really don't pay attention, do you?" said Langhorne. "How many times do you need to be told that the drivers only care about the number of fares they book?"

The taxi driver said, "I figured even if I lost your fare, I might as well book as many others as I could before they also had a shot at redemption."

"The drivers do it all the time," Langhorne added. "In fact, their behavior with Pales such as yourself is the basis of most ghost stories." He chuckled. "Undergrads are so simple that way. I told you from the very beginning how oblivious they are." He stepped close and patted Flynn kindly on the arm, and once again Flynn felt its unmistakable warmth. "Now, despite the ruling against us, it's not too late for you to come along. It's a better reality for you, I promise. All that struggling with the rule book did you a favor by demonstrating the horrendous amount of rules they have in Heaven," he said. "I mean, come on! Here's a fruit tree for you, but you're not allowed to eat any of it! What's *that* about? Yes, it's merely an allegory, but still, my point holds. That's not the way you spent your undergrad life and I know that's not the way you want to spend eternity." Langhorne paused, looking down on him like a favorite uncle. "I really do like you, Flynn. And I don't say that to very many graduates." He looked back to the taxi driver. "Do I?"

"Not many," the taxi driver echoed.

Langhorne turned back to Flynn. "You see? I had a lot of fun hanging out with you. And I'm pretty sure you feel the same." He started to chuckle. "Remember when you kissed me in the hotel room in Santa Monica, thinking I was that girl from the bar?"

Flynn pulled away from him, "What about it?"

"What do you mean, *what about it?*" Langhorne said. "That was hilarious! And that's the great thing about all this, the fun doesn't have to end. Come with me and you can kiss anyone you like, whenever you feel like it! What do you say? Let's let bygones be bygones and keep the party going."

Before Flynn could respond, a dazzling display of bikini models at once surrounded them. Curiously though, the blondes, brunettes and redheads were all of one identical shape and size, all in exactly matched skimpy yellow bathing suits. The identical beauties danced to the swing-music strains of Benny Goodman's "Sing, Sing, Sing," while barbecuing thick T-bone steaks and tapping kegs of beer that rested atop massive tubs of ice.

Flynn took in the surreal collection of lusty flesh as Langhorne raised a frosty mug of beer under his nose. The redolent aroma served as a welcome sense memory of a past life he had so often longed for. "Now, how did it go?" said Langhorne. "Oh, yes. To the fools of the world…"

Flynn closed his eyes. *Without them, the rest of us cannot succeed.* His eyes sprang open as the sweet smell of beer vanished, along with the mug, and the dancing women; the once blaring music was replaced by the confused wail of Billy Covington.

"Where the fuck am I?" Covington demanded to know.

Langhorne stepped away from Flynn, turning to smile at the pissed-off Brit standing in the center of the grassy field. "O and F," he said as if the letters meant something. He went on to clarify, "Orientation and Facilitation for the recently graduated."

Covington blinked stupidly at him.

"This is your Happy Place," Langhorne said, sweeping his hand across the expansive grounds.

"My Happy Place?" Covington scowled. "What the fuck are you talking about?"

"This is where you were the happiest as an undergrad," Langhorne explained. "Old Trafford football stadium. All those years you spent beating up opposing fans." He turned to Flynn. "It's really quite fun once you get into it."

"How did I get here?" Covington asked.

"I already explained that," insisted Langhorne. "You graduated."

Covington's shaky mind was clearly struggling to catch up to the conversation. "I don't get it. What's that mean?"

"It means you're *dead*, asshole," Flynn interjected.

Langhorne offered Flynn an encouraging thumbs up. "I appreciate the help," he said. "Unfortunately, you're not part of his Happy Place, so he can neither see nor hear you."

"Who're you talking to?" Covington asked. "And while I'm at it, who the hell are you, anyway?"

"The name's Langhorne. I'm your Facilitator. My job is to shuffle you from one stage of life to the next," he explained, as if Covington wasn't merely another ignoble link on an infinitely expanding chain. "Now, I'm sorry, but with all the excitement surrounding your graduation, we're running a bit behind and schedules must be kept."

"Yes," interjected the taxi driver, "we really should get a move on. The meter's running."

Covington glanced over to the driver and winced at the sight of his fetid smile. "I'll explain everything on the way," the driver said, leading him toward the ever-idling taxi.

"Where are we going?"

"Don't worry," the driver assured him. "You'll fit right in. I understand you're the sort of guy who likes to get his revenge."

"Damn right."

"Excellent. There's no rule against that where I come from. In fact, it's just the sort of thing we like to encourage."

As Covington climbed inside the back seat of the cab, his

face contorted into an anguished frown. "What's that fucking smell?" he asked, gagging on the stench.

The driver's grin was fogged over by a brown mist of breath. "I don't smell anything," he said, slamming the door tight.

Flynn and Langhorne considered each other a moment after the taxi drove off.

"Oh, don't look at me like that," Langhorne said, dropping his cigarette and snuffing it under his shoe. "I meant what I said. Despite the havoc it's creating with my schedule, it's why I brought you here once you separated from Limbo. So you might fully understand how much our time together meant to me."

Flynn, a familiar comfort with his old compatriot slowly returning, nodded. "I understand perfectly."

"How'd you like to hang out for a bit? I can bring the dancing girls back and you can enjoy a nice steak, what do you say?"

Flynn shook his head. "I'm afraid there are still things that need to be done."

"Yes," Langhorne said, shrugging with weary resignation. "I suppose there are."

The two men shared a knowing grin and a spark of light flashed above, yanking Flynn skyward.

The taxi once again arrived like a phantom into the living room of the house in Topanga. The driver and Covington got out to greet Langhorne and Flynn, who had just arrived themselves. The bullet still hovered halfway between Thacker's gun and Andy's chest, the redheaded thug remained unconscious on the porch, and the goatee's vacated body was still lying on the bottom landing of the staircase.

The goatee, however, was just then waking up, seated at the

tiny desk of his third-grade class at Saint Bartholomew Primary School, in Gilstead Road, London, taught by the quite lovely Ms. Shultz. She was the only woman the goatee had ever loved with a pure heart. He was no doubt wondering why he was sitting there all alone, wearing blue knickers and a matching vest, with a copy of his favorite book, *Where the Red Fern Grows,* resting on the desk before him. Looking out the classroom window, he must have figured the starkly handsome man behind the wheel of the idling taxi could supply him with the answer.

Covington, however, was not at all concerned with the whereabouts of his henchman's soul as he crouched over his own lifeless undergraduate body. He stared down at his abandoned face like a chick wondering if it were possible to climb back into its shell. "Bloody hell," he whispered.

"Will somebody please explain to me what's going on here?" came Donny's whiny voice from the front seat of the taxicab.

The driver leaned forward from the hood of the cab and brought a finger to his lips, "Shhh—"

With the chaotic circumstances surrounding all of them, Langhorne had not only needed another driver to pick up the goatee, he had not had the opportunity to fully orientate Donny, who now sat sulking in the front seat of the foul-smelling taxi, wearing nothing but a cloth diaper after having woken up in the pine crib his grandfather built for him thirty-seven years before. His really had been a very unhappy life.

"You know," Langhorne said to Flynn, "it was your behavior with Donny that almost tripped you up. The debate over his final dispensation got quite heated."

He was right about that. Once the specifics of the final strategy employed by Flynn were dissected, it was all allowed to pass because a) the other players involved were utterly at fault for affecting so many undue spikes in Undergraduate Probability Indexes, including their intent to see Andy Barnes's and Erin Bannon's pushed to one hundred; and b) because Flynn had not *personally* killed anyone. This last wrinkle concerning Donny's graduation with the mastiffs required the most energy to iron out. The sticking point in Flynn's defense was that he did, in fact, tie Donny to the tree with the lasso.

Ultimately, the decision was made that, because Donny had been personally accountable for Flynn's own graduation, it would be allowed. Hell's representative promptly filed a grievance claiming that Flynn's action with respect to the lasso was, quote, "motivated by revenge, rather than expedience," and that, "the whole 'eye for an eye' argument is a little too Old Testament for these modern times, and should, therefore, entitle Hell to one-tenth of his eternity." The grievance, however, was summarily ignored. Perhaps the subject would be taken up again in the future, it was decided. Or the past. Since to the graduate, they are, of course, one and the same.

"Despite the ruling in your favor," Langhorne said, taking one last shot at Flynn, "it's not too late to come with me and do whatever you want for all eternity."

"I don't think so," Flynn answered, no longer bedeviled by the possibility. He looked to the taxi driver leaning on the hood of his car. "I can only imagine what an eternity of wholly selfish behavior does to a soul."

The taxi driver laughed, spewing his moldy caramel breath from the depths of his rotted core.

Langhorne shook his head, sighing in defeat. "Redemption really is a bitch."

"Yeah," Flynn said, looking toward his brother, frozen in place. "But for him, it'll make one hell of a ghost story."

"Undergrads," Langhorne said, shaking his head. "Makes you feel sorry for them, doesn't it?"

Flynn managed a knowing smile as he stole a look at the mute form of Thacker, eyes caught in a blink, the miserable drop of blood suspended in time and space on its way to the floor. At one time, Flynn had thought of him as more of a brother than Andy. It seemed a lifetime ago. He shook his head at the thought and accepted that he was seeing Thacker for the last time. Thacker was too far gone to ever be considered a *Pale*. Flynn was sure though, that his old friend's eternal sentence was both fair and just.

Flynn took his position on the floor where Thacker's shot had felled him and turned to Covington. "Langhorne and the driver explained the consequences of all this to you?" he asked.

Covington nodded.

"*Please* don't try to change his mind, Flynn," Langhorne called out. "My schedule is getting very disorganized."

Flynn kept his eyes on Covington. "All right, big man," he said. "Free Will. Capital F, capital W. The choice is yours."

Covington stood up from over his abandoned undergraduate body and stepped to the hovering bullet. His eyes glistened like sun reflecting off an iceberg as he settled his gaze upon Thacker. "I told you I'd kill you, ya bastard." He took hold of the bullet between his thumb and forefinger and *turned it around.*

The taxi driver couldn't help but swoon a little. "I just love a happy ending."

Flynn nodded. "I knew he wouldn't let you down."

With Billy Covington's act of free will—that most crucial of all nature's laws—the case of Flynn Barnes was closed, the dispensation of all involved souls was finalized, and Thomas Thacker was allowed to graduate in place of Andy Barnes.

Two gusts of warm wind blew violently into the room from opposite directions, meeting each other head-on, exploding with such force that the walls shook, and the windows rattled. The bullet suddenly shot forward, striking Thacker squarely in the chest, sending him flying backward against the wall.

Andy flinched, a chimera of pain jolting his body from the expectation of imminent death. He felt his chest for bullet holes, unable to comprehend how Thacker had missed. Only then did he see Thacker slowly slide to the floor, his eyes bulging with shock. "I don't understand," Thacker moaned, as the gun fell limply from his hand, landing on the floor next to his sprawled legs. They were the last words he would utter as an undergrad. A fitting epitaph for *all* undergrads, thought Flynn.

A cacophony of shouts and pounding feet sounded out as flashing blue and red lights danced off the walls through the windows. The front door burst open and a phalanx of police stormed inside, guns at the ready, shouting over each other. Andy spun toward the unexpected invasion and raised his hands. "Don't shoot!" he yelled. "Don't shoot!"

The officers took quick stock of the situation as they spread throughout the house. One officer approached Andy and pushed him to the floor. Andy's chin hit the hard wood and yet another wave of pain shot through his skull. "Don't move!" the officer ordered, bringing his hands together at the base of his back. Andy was too exhausted to speak, too battered to even protest his innocence amid the mayhem. Sooner or later, they would connect the dots for themselves and realize he was a victim, not a perpetrator. "Where's Andy Barnes?" the officer said. Andy, surprised the officer knew his name, managed to softly choke out the words, "That's me."

With voices from all corners of the house announcing that

the residence was all clear and the three mastiffs had been secured for animal control, the officer with Andy quickly released his hold and placed a consoling palm on the beaten man's back. "I'm sorry about that, Mr. Barnes. You're going to be okay." The officer spoke into his walkie-talkie, "We are code four on Andy Barnes, priority incident four-eight-five-seven. Request emergency medical for a two-forty-two."

Andy pushed himself to his knees. "Erin," he said.

"She's fine," the officer said. "We have her."

At that moment, the proof of the officer's assurance bolted into the room. Erin made her way through the throng of officers and folded her body into Andy's arms. "I thought I'd be too late," she cried, pulling back to see the swollen face of her only love, her hands caressing his pallid, bruised features.

"I'm okay," he promised her. "I was just scared they hurt you." She kissed him softly and they cried together. "I love you so much," he whispered close to her ear.

"I love you," Erin said, burying her nose into his neck with a deep breath, as if to take in his very essence.

Watching all of this, the taxi driver moaned. "Well *that* sure puts a damper on things." He pulled on Covington's arm, dragging him toward the waiting cab. "Let's go. I'm losing fares hanging around here with you."

Covington, pleased as hell with the sight of Thacker's bloodied body huddled on the floor like a pile of soiled laundry, climbed into the back seat of the cab. In order to position himself in the car, however, he needed to climb over a thickly muscled man wearing a tank top stretched tightly over his massive, tattooed chest. Once Covington was settled, he realized he was squeezed between two of the largest people he had ever encountered. The one to his left offered a gummy pink smile that seemed to revel in showing off a mouthful of missing teeth. The one to his right didn't bother to smile at all, content as he was with grinding his broad elbow into Covington's ribs. "You're gonna love Hell, mate," he said with a Liverpudlian Scouse accent so thick it was nearly impossible for Covington to understand him. "There's always a football game on and nobody stops you from pounding all those Manchester United wankers!"

Covington twisted sideways in his seat. "Screw you," he spit back at him. "I'm from Manchester."

The two enormous hooligans from Liverpool shared a glance, then turned their considerable aggression onto their new traveling companion, pounding him with spirited, violent abandon. Covington's nose, jaw, and left cheek were shattered before the taxi disappeared through the wall like a shadow, Donny crying in the front seat, and the driver laughing the entire way.

"Excuse me, ma'am," a uniformed officer said, stepping up to Erin and Andy. He was holding tightly to Covington's delirious, redheaded cohort. "We found this guy unconscious on the porch. Is he one of the men who kidnapped you?" Erin nodded that he was, and the cop tightened a pair of cuffs on the thug's already swollen wrists.

During the course of the next fifteen years the redheaded thug would spend in prison, he told the story of his capture many times. In time, he came to discover that he enjoyed the *telling* of it much more than he had enjoyed the *living* of it. When he was finally paroled, with five years of his sentence taken off for good behavior, he had long decided never again to tell the story, ashamed of the way he'd been as a younger man. Eventually, though, the story came back to him, and he decided to share it though a popular series of children's books, the hero of which would be a cowboy named *Topanga Flynn* that had once been an outlaw. The redheaded thug turned author would never marry and never have kids to care for, so he donated most of the riches he gathered from the much-loved series of books featuring the do-good hero to a program helping troubled children stay out of harm's way. And when the redheaded author finally graduated at the age of ninety-two, he awoke to find he was still an old man sitting at the drafting table he used to draw and write his stories. It was a fact that the moment he passed on, he was as happy as he had ever been. And there was no taxicab waiting for him outside his window. Redemption is indeed a powerful thing.

For now, the thug offered up no protest as the cop led him away. He left without incident, grumbling something incoherent about the mysterious cowboy.

"Have you found him?" Erin called after the retreating officer. "The man who saved me?"

"Not yet," the cop said. "We can't seem to locate him or his horse."

"No," Andy said, confused, turning to look at the floor behind him. "He's right—"

The body was gone. Andy's mouth hung loose as he struggled to find a logical explanation.

"Andy?" said Erin.

"He was shot..."

"Who?" Erin asked. "Are you talking about the cowboy?"

"Yes. He said he—"

"He said he knew you," said Erin.

Andy turned back to her. "That's right. He told me he was here as payment for everything he took from me, but I didn't recognize him. He talked as though he were..."

The rest of the explanation trailed away—because there was no explanation. What could he say without sounding insane? His mind was still in a haze. It was impossible to piece it all together now, but perhaps he'd eventually come to understand what happened. Yes, he figured, the truth would come to him eventually. For now, he was content to lean into the arms of the woman he loved and just be held.

Flynn and Langhorne stood to the side watching the proceedings.

"No hard feelings, I hope," Langhorne said to him with an outstretched hand.

"Where do I go now?" Flynn asked, reaching for Langhorne's grip. But it was not a handshake being offered. It was *The Happy Graduate Rule Book.* "Beats the hell out of me," smiled Langhorne. "Why don't you check in there and find out."

Flynn took the book and used his thumb to flip a few of the pages, but, of course, he couldn't read them without the glasses. When he looked up, Langhorne was gone. It was fitting, Flynn supposed, that there was no goodbye. "Nothing personal," he imagined Langhorne saying. "I'm just running a bit late and need to go orientate a young woman from Idaho who insisted she just *had* to see the running of the bulls once before she died."

With a swirl of activity around him, Flynn looked at Andy and Erin huddled together, holding each other up against the mystery and violence of the world.

A flash of white light sparked somewhere above, and Flynn smiled.

CHAPTER TWENTY-THREE

THACKER'S EYES FLUTTERED as he awoke. For reasons he could not immediately ascertain, he could not move his arms or legs. Heavy-metal music blared from two large speakers on opposite ends of the dimly lit room, the powerful drumbeats reverberating in his chest. At first, he found it difficult to discern the shapes before him, but as his eyes adjusted, everything became clear. The walls were covered with thick fabric, a deep black, possibly purple, he couldn't quite decide which. He could see though that there were all manner of glistening whips and studded paddles hung from the ceiling on shiny silver hooks.

Thacker's heart raced as he glanced up to his wrists and down to his ankles to discover the reason for his immobility. Someone had tied them with leather straps to the giant bed on which he was lying. His legs chafed under the cuffs of the tight latex shorts squeezing his thighs. The ruddy skin on his exposed ass stung with the familiar heat of a fresh spanking.

From somewhere on the other side of the door came the squeal of tires braking to a sudden stop. A moment later the door creaked opened and into the room stepped a tall, lanky man in a perfectly tailored blood-red suit who seemed to be in his mid-fifties. The man was handsome in an aging schoolboy sort of way and moved in a manner that appeared both meek and assertive at the same time.

"You know," said Langhorne, leaning over Thacker. "Your Happy Place has a lot of similarities to where we're going."

Thacker's eyes bulged and he screamed, but his anguished cries were muffled by the bright orange rubber ball stuck in his mouth.

CHAPTER TWENTY-FOUR

Andy lowered his knee to the edge of Flynn's grave, but the grass was still dewy from the morning chill, so he immediately stood again, wiping at the dampened pant leg of his tuxedo. "I don't think Erin would like it too much if I showed up with grass stains on my knees," he said, offering a chagrined smile to the headstone. "At least the cuts and bruises have faded. So, what do you think?" he asked, looking down at his silk tie and narrow lapels. "Probably not your style, I figure." He plunged his hands deep into his pockets, looking uncomfortable. "It's a rental."

It was still awkward for Andy, talking to his brother. He tried to convince himself that, while their conversations had remained strained and decidedly one-sided, he at least felt Flynn's presence stronger than ever. In his heart, he knew it was a bit of an act. He still wanted to believe everything he had seen and felt that night in Topanga, when his life was saved by the mysterious cowboy—that somehow, Flynn had been there as some sort of guardian angel. But as the weeks passed it had become more and more of an effort.

It wasn't really his fault. After all, undergrads have a hard time discerning between what is real and true and that which is merely wished for.

"I'm still not completely sure what actually happened," Andy said, ignoring the part of him that felt foolish for holding on to the hope that his brother could hear him. "Erin's folks think I might have lost my mind for believing it was you who came back to save us. *Emotionally confused*, is what Jane called it, though Jimmy thought the whole thing sounded pretty cool. I don't know, maybe it was the beating I took. Might have knocked me silly. Erin's not so sure either, but as you can see, she still wants to marry me."

Since that night, Andy had thought much about Flynn and had slowly, and somewhat sadly, come to accept that regret and longing played a large role in his tenuous belief that his brother had returned from the dead. He decided to stop telling the story all together, as it had rapidly become nothing more than a dinner party ghost story that rang less and less plausible with each telling, even to himself. Too many questions were left unanswered, and ultimately the recounting did nothing but amuse some and annoy others. Andy himself fell someplace in between. Now, the best he could do was hope that the love in his heart was also in his brother's, wherever he was.

"I do wish you could be at the wedding, Flynn, standing next to me and Dad." He removed his hand from his pocket and placed it on top of the gravestone. "Who knows, maybe you will be, right?"

The wind blew up the gentle slope of the hill from the meandering road below. Andy looked around, hoping to find some evidence of Flynn's presence. But he was alone.

The organ reverberated off the stained-glass windows of the church. Cameras flashed as guests on both sides of the aisle stood to smile, cry, and watch Erin walk past on her father's arm. But Erin saw none of it. Her attention was solely on Andy standing at the altar, waiting for her so they could begin their lives anew as husband and wife.

With a tender peck on her cheek, Hoyt handed off his only daughter to the man she would always love more than any other. He shook Andy's hand and nodded at his son, Jimmy, who smiled, braces gleaming, and then looked at Harry Barnes, who stood next to Andy as best man, his ill-fitting tuxedo bulging at the waist. With a quick thumbs up to old Harry, Hoyt moved to the front pew and sat with his teary-eyed wife.

Andy squeezed Erin's hand with the promise of an unending number of tomorrows and they turned as one to face the minister. The elderly minister smiled down on them and then looked beyond them to the assembled. A shuffling of feet filled the great hall as the congregation sat.

The minister stood as straight as his frail bones would allow. His soft, kind eyes glistened with wisdom as he spoke with a powerful voice that belied his delicate frame. "We are gathered today to bless the joining of two people in holy matrimony. And we are all honored to be counted amongst their friends and family. For theirs is a love that imbues all of us with its simple yet profound request..."

The minister's eyes widened with a grand appreciation and immeasurable insight into the truth behind his carefully chosen words. It's said that the eyes of a person are the window to their soul, and so it was that if Andy and his father had looked closely enough into the eyes of the wizened minister, they would have realized their secret wish had come true after all—their lost brother and son was with them still.

Flynn, the stole of his robe draping delicately, let his arms drop to his sides and allowed his words to fall as purely and gently as mist. "And that simple request," he went on, "is that we take care of each other and accept the responsibility that comes with calling one another a family. That we don't take for granted the time we spend with each other on this earth. Because if we tend to the love we have for each other, and nurture it to its fullest potential, it will stay with us for all eternity."

The reception was held beneath a massive white tent in Hoyt and Jane's manicured backyard in Brentwood. The warm, summer evening provided the celebration a sheen of contented romance. A parquet dance floor was spread under a trellis of red roses, though the string quartet had yet to give way to the band. Laughter rose up from the linen-covered tables as a small army of waiters and waitresses served drinks and hors d'oeuvres.

Jimmy made his way through the happy crowd, feeling a bit melancholy, as he would at any gathering that included single young ladies. Looking back at the dance floor full of couples swaying to the music, he approached the bar and absently ordered a screwdriver.

"Coming right up," said the bartender, her voice light and airy.

The voice caught Jimmy's attention and he smiled nervously, as if her words had tickled his skin. "Thank you."

"My pleasure," the bartender said. Her bashful smile revealed a mouth full of braces.

As a matter of course upon seeing such a vision, Jimmy began to perspire profusely. Thoughts of unimaginable intent filled his mind as she prepared his drink. Not knowing how he would be able to pull off the impossible task before him, Jimmy fought the impulse to turn on his heel and walk away. If he did, he knew from experience he would spend the rest of the evening sitting by himself, staring from afar at the beautiful blonde girl with the delicate fingers, as she poured yet another drink he was too uncomfortable to order for himself. If he left her then, he would never return. So, he did the unthinkable. He asked for her name.

"Prudence," she said. "But everyone calls me Pru."

"Hi, Pru," said Jimmy.

Having not planned beyond that singular moment, a terrible silence crept in and almost wiped away whatever hope he clung to. But then a miracle happened. He thought of another question. "How long have you worked here?"

Pru smiled again, this time a little wider, showing more of her braces. "You're funny."

"Yeah," he mumbled, swallowing a healthy gulp of vodka and orange juice.

"And cute," she said, offering him a napkin to wipe the sweat from his forehead.

Prudence was certainly not the first young lady Jimmy had instantly fallen in love with, but she would be the last. And they would forever remember the blessed occasion of their first encounter.

Harry sat at a linen-covered table by himself, ignoring the food in front of him with his customary detachment. There had been a question posed earlier, or more exactly an offer, moments before the ceremony, and he was still wrestling with how to respond.

"How 'bout some company?" Andy said, stepping up.

Harry smiled and nodded. Despite every effort, the two men remained in their habitual uncomfortable silence for a few moments, before Harry said, "It's a beautiful reception. I'm enjoying the music."

Andy glanced at the string quartet playing beyond the dance floor. "We can thank Erin and Jane for that. I suggested a DJ."

"This is better."

"Let's see if you feel the same way when the band takes over after dinner," Andy joked.

Harry shrugged. "I'm sure they'll be fine, too."

Andy nodded. "Yeah."

Another awkward few ticks of the clock went by before Andy returned to the question he'd posed before the ceremony. "Have you thought any more about my offer?"

Harry cleared his throat. "I don't want to be an intrusion."

Andy was prepared, however, and had rehearsed what he would say when his father turned him down. "I don't want to lose you, Dad," he said. He didn't try for a casual tone, or God forbid a maudlin one, but rather stated what he felt in a manner that was both direct and unaffectedly sincere. "We're family, and we have to start taking care of each other again. Besides, the guest room has a fifty-inch flat-screen TV. It's like having court-side seats for every Lakers game. Just think about all those Laker Girls in their little purple-and-gold outfits dancing for you in high definition."

Harry's expression didn't change. Andy sighed but remained undefeated. He pressed on, "The truth is, I want you there to watch your grandchildren playing in the backyard."

Harry's throat ached, but his expression remained as stoic

as ever. He stared at his son a long moment. "I'd like that, too," he said, finally.

Andy accepted this was the best his old man could do, and he appreciated the uncomplicated simplicity of it. "How 'bout I get you a beer?" he offered.

Harry cleared his throat. "Make it a Coke."

With a pat on his old man's shoulder, Andy left his father and headed to the bar, where Jimmy and his future wife stood discussing the finer points of good dental hygiene.

"Andy?" called a voice behind him. Andy stopped and turned to see the minister, holding a small wrapped gift. "It's time I said my goodbyes," the minister said.

"Come on, Reverend," said Andy. "There's no rule that says you can't stay awhile."

Flynn let out a tiny laugh. "Actually, there is." He handed the gift box to Andy. "But I wanted to make sure you got this before I left."

"You didn't have to get us anything," Andy said, shaking the minister's hand. The shake went on a bit longer than customary, and for a brief moment, Andy felt a twinge of awkwardness. He didn't know the reverend that well, after all; in fact, the minister who was supposed to marry them had been called out of town, and his replacement had been chosen at the last minute.

"You take care of yourself, Andy," Flynn said, still clutching tightly to his brother's hand.

"Sure," said Andy. "You too."

Flynn leaned close, giving him a tight hug. Andy, surprised by the intimacy, lightly patted the effusive minister on the back. "Thanks for everything."

"No," said Flynn. "Thank you."

And that was that. Flynn headed off, leaving his somewhat befuddled brother behind. As he walked down the driveway, he glanced back to see Erin move to sit with Harry. She said something and the old man laughed, which brought a smile to Flynn.

His step quickened as he approached the ivory limousine idling patiently in the driveway. Next to the limo, holding the door open for him, was a tall, exotic woman with skin like fine brown sand blown smooth by a tropical breeze. Her auburn hair fell on her tanned shoulders and her green eyes shimmered with a tantalizing lust for life. She gave him a little grin as he stepped up.

"You ready?" she said.

Flynn studied her out of the corner of his eye. "You mind if I see your smile first?" he asked.

Her butterscotch lips parted, revealing a dazzling burst of white teeth.

"Just making sure," Flynn said.

She caressed his cheek with her soft palm. "You're adorable. We're gonna have a lot of fun together."

Andy stared after him, wondering what in the world a minister was doing with a stretch limo and woman like that. He absently opened the lid to the tiny box in his hand and looked inside, his eyes immediately shooting back up.

Flynn turned and gave a final wave.

"Don't worry," cooed his impossibly radiant driver. "You'll see him again."

"I know," said Flynn. He gave her a playful grin. With that, he climbed inside the limousine and the driver closed the door.

Andy remained stunned, rooted to the ground. Erin and Harry stepped up to him. "What's this, honey?" Erin asked, looking at the opened box in his hand. She hesitated a moment when she saw the gift, then reached down to retrieve the offering.

Inside the limousine, Flynn looked through the tinted window at his family standing together, staring in his direction. He knew they could no longer see him. All three of them, Andy, Erin, and Harry, rooted together, mouths hanging loose with wonder. In fact, the only movement at all came from the gently swaying black mask dangling from Erin's finger.

"Okay," Flynn sighed. "I'm ready to go now."

"So am I," announced the old man opposite him, smiling.

Flynn glanced over, surprised to discover he was sharing the ride. "Who are you?" he asked.

But the old man didn't answer. He merely stared for a long while as if he knew the infinite secrets to questions Flynn had yet learned to ask. Flynn's mind went blank, and then a single thought came to him, filling his senses with the infinite possibilities of the Universe. "God?" he asked, without even realizing the word had been formed. His voice seemed to come out on a soft breath of air.

The beautiful driver smiled in the rearview mirror, and the old man pulled at the bright wool shawl covering his knobby knees. "You really need to stop thinking like an undergraduate, Flynn," the old man said. His voice was tinged with a South American accent. "My name is Tupacuti-Apo-Mayta," he explained. "I wanted to thank you for getting my masks back."

As the limo's engine shifted into gear, the old man leaned forward and offered Flynn an ice-cold bottle of Budweiser. Heading with gentle ease into his eternal purpose, Flynn popped open his beer, settled back in his seat, and laughed.

ACKNOWLEDGMENTS

My continued thanks and appreciation to Jennifer Silva Redmond and Mary Vensel White for their talent and 20/20 vision of their editorial eyes. Thanks, too, to Nick May and Katherine Flitch for their invaluable expertise.

ABOUT THE AUTHOR

Photo By Chad Savage

Clay Savage is a writer and voice-over actor whose voice has been heard on hundreds of television shows and movies. He lives with his family in Santa Monica, California.

Visit Clay at Theclaysavage.com

www.ingramcontent.com/pod-product-compliance
Lightning Source LLC
Chambersburg PA
CBHW061606190726
48288CB00007B/2203